East Meets Old West

Ki happened to be looking across the street at the Powder Horn Saloon as Custis Long stepped inside through the batwings. Ki started across the street, intending to say hello, until he saw several roughly dressed men emerge from an alley.

A couple of them reached for their guns. Longarm stood, about to be caught in a cross fire between two groups of gunmen. Ki took hold of the batwings, shoved them aside, then used them to support himself as he powered up off the floor and lashed out with both sandal-clad feet, kicking so high that he caught two of the gunmen in the back of the head.

The hard cases flew forward, the guns they had just drawn clattering to the floor. Ki let out a *"Haaiii!"* as he landed between the two remaining gunmen. He whipped a sidehand blow at each man's throat. Ki launched a spinning kick that slammed first one man to the floor, then the other.

That was when guns began to roar.

TABOR EVANS

LONGARM

AND THE LONE STAR TRACKDOWN

JOVE BOOKS, NEW YORK

THE BERKLEY PUBLISHING GROUP
Published by the Penguin Group
Penguin Group (USA) Inc.
375 Hudson Street, New York, New York 10014, USA

Penguin Group (Canada), 90 Eglinton Avenue East, Suite 700, Toronto, Ontario M4P 2Y3, Canada
(a division of Pearson Penguin Canada Inc.)
Penguin Books Ltd., 80 Strand, London WC2R 0RL, England
Penguin Group Ireland, 25 St. Stephen's Green, Dublin 2, Ireland (a division of Penguin Books Ltd.)
Penguin Group (Australia), 250 Camberwell Road, Camberwell, Victoria 3124, Australia
(a division of Pearson Australia Group Pty. Ltd.)
Penguin Books India Pvt. Ltd., 11 Community Centre, Panchsheel Park, New Delhi—110 017, India
Penguin Group (NZ), 67 Apollo Drive, Rosedale, North Shore 0632, New Zealand
(a division of Pearson New Zealand Ltd.)
Penguin Books (South Africa) (Pty.) Ltd., 24 Sturdee Avenue, Rosebank, Johannesburg 2196,
South Africa

Penguin Books Ltd., Registered Offices: 80 Strand, London WC2R 0RL, England

This is a work of fiction. Names, characters, places, and incidents either are the product of the author's imagination or are used fictitiously, and any resemblance to actual persons, living or dead, business establishments, events, or locales is entirely coincidental.

LONGARM AND THE LONE STAR TRACKDOWN

A Jove Book / published by arrangement with the author

PRINTING HISTORY
Jove edition / October 2009

Copyright © 2009 by Penguin Group (USA) Inc.
Cover illustration by Miro Sinovcic.

ISBN: 978-0-515-14725-4

JOVE®
Jove Books are published by The Berkley Publishing Group,
a division of Penguin Group (USA) Inc.,
375 Hudson Street, New York, New York 10014.
JOVE® is a registered trademark of Penguin Group (USA) Inc.
The "J" design is a trademark of Penguin Group (USA) Inc.

PRINTED IN THE UNITED STATES OF AMERICA

10 9 8 7 6 5 4 3 2 1

Chapter 1

From under the tipped-down brim of his Stetson, Longarm watched the pretty blonde across the aisle eyeing him. She thought he was asleep, so she felt free to sweep her gaze from his long legs up his muscular torso to his broad shoulders. The pink tip of her tongue slid out of her mouth and ran along her full, naturally red bottom lip.

To tell the truth, under other circumstances, the gently swaying motion of the Gulf, Western Texas & Pacific railroad car might have caused him to doze off. Longarm wasn't likely to fall asleep. Not after chasing Cyrus Pollack for hundreds of miles. Not with the end of that long chase finally looming.

Because once the train reached Indianola in another half hour or so, Pollack wouldn't have anywhere left to run.

Unless, of course, Pollack managed to board one of the ships docked at the busy little port town and sail away across the Gulf of Mexico for parts unknown. Longarm couldn't allow that to happen.

Two weeks earlier, in the Denver Federal Building office

of his boss, Chief Marshal Billy Vail had given Longarm the job of finding and arresting Cyrus Pollack.

"He's a bad one, Custis," Vail had said to the big deputy marshal. "He embezzled ninety thousand dollars from the Indian agency he was administering down in the Nations, then murdered the BIA agent who showed up to investigate. He's tied in with a whiskey-smuggling ring, too, so he's got plenty of no-good friends in Indian Territory."

Longarm had cocked his ankle on his knee, leaned back in the red leather chair in front of Vail's desk, and shifted the three-for-a-nickel cheroot to the other side of his mouth.

"Anybody with ninety grand is gonna have lots of friends," he'd said as he snapped a lucifer to life on his thumbnail. He set fire to the gasper, puffed on it for a second, and blew a perfect smoke ring toward the banjo clock on the wall.

"That's right," Vail agreed. "And if they think it might help them get their hands on some of that loot, they won't hesitate to give Pollack a hand. Even if it means gunning down a lawman."

Sure enough, Longarm had had to dodge several attempts on his life while he was searching for Pollack in Indian Territory. He'd left a few ventilated badmen in his wake. A couple of times, he'd almost had Pollack in his sights, but the embezzler and murderer was a lucky son of a gun and had slipped away each time, finally escaping across the Red River into Texas.

Seeing as Longarm worked for Uncle Sam, state boundaries didn't mean anything to him, so he just crossed the Red River and continued pursuing his quarry. In Fort Worth, and then in Waco and La Grange, he had come close to capturing Pollack. But his frustration had grown as Pollack again gave him the slip. Pollack had boarded the train in Victoria.

So had Longarm.

The next stop was Indianola, where Powder Horn Bayou flowed into the gulf. Along with Galveston and Corpus Christi, it was one of the busiest ports on the Texas coast. Tall-masted ships from all over the world tied up at its docks to take on and unload cargo. In the days before the Civil War, almost three decades earlier, Indianola was where the camels brought over from Arabia for the army's ill-fated experiment with the humpbacked beasts had landed. That must have been a sight to see, thought Longarm, those funny-looking critters parading down the street with cowboys, sailors, and townsmen gawking at them.

Longarm had been to Indianola before, as he had been to most places west of the Mississippi—and some points east—but not since a big hurricane had almost washed away the settlement several years earlier. The resilient Texans had rebuilt, and while Indianola had not yet regained the prominence it had had before the storm, it was still a bustling town and busy port. If Pollack succeeded in boarding a departing ship, he would be on his way to Mexico or Cuba or even Europe. Longarm sure as hell didn't want to have to chase him to some foreign country. But he would if he had to.

He had thought about trying to arrest Pollack here on the train, but he'd decided that it would be better to wait until they got to Indianola. Less chance of innocents getting caught in the cross fire if bullets started to fly. Also, the local law would have a lockup Longarm could borrow.

So with all that on his mind, Longarm was wide awake despite his casual pose. In fact, he had tipped his flat-crowned, snuff brown Stetson over his eyes specifically so that he could study the other occupants of the car without appearing to do so. He didn't see how Pollack could have any confederates on this train, but Longarm hadn't survived as long as he had in a dangerous profession by taking anything lightly.

None of the passengers struck him as a likely threat, though. Businessmen, salesmen, women with kids, a couple of rugged old-timers who were probably cattlemen . . . the usual folks you found on a frontier train.

And then there was the blonde.

Hair the color of corn silk curled around her strikingly pretty face. Deep blue eyes peered out under carefully plucked brows. A traveling outfit almost the same shade as her eyes hugged a body that managed to have ample curves despite its slenderness. Although she seemed to be traveling alone, the ring on the third finger of her left hand indicated that she was married.

That fact, along with the preoccupation he felt about catching Cyrus Pollack, meant that Longarm didn't take as much interest in her as he might have otherwise. He had a healthy appetite for women, but he tended not to indulge it with married gals.

So she could sit there, lick her lips, and give him those brazen looks all she wanted to, he told himself as he pretended to doze. It wasn't going to do her any good.

Pollack was in the car just ahead of the one where Longarm rode. Longarm had seen him get aboard, and had waited until the last minute to swing up onto the train, to make sure Pollack wasn't trying to give him the slip again. He didn't think that the fugitive had spotted him, but he couldn't be certain about that. Pollack hadn't gotten off the train, though, and there were no stops between Victoria and Indianola. The train was going too fast to risk jumping off, too.

"Excuse me, sir?"

Dad-gum it. She was determined. She'd reached over and put a hand on his knee as she spoke to him. If he didn't want to be rude, Longarm had no choice but to thumb his hat back to its normal position and look at her.

"Something I can do for you, ma'am?"

"Would you mind stepping back to the rear platform with me? I'd really like to get a breath of fresh air, and I'm not comfortable going out there by myself."

It *was* a mite stuffy in here, Longarm supposed. But his determination didn't waver.

"No offense, ma'am, but you don't need anyone to accompany you for that. You'll be perfectly safe back there."

"I'm not so sure about that." She lowered her voice and nodded toward the front of the car. "Do you see that man up there? The one in the brown checked suit and derby hat?"

Longarm had seen the gent earlier when he looked over all the passengers, chalking him up as a drummer of some sort. The outfit and the sample case shoved under the man's seat were pretty sure indicators of his profession.

"He's been on the train with me since Houston. And to be honest, there's a boldness to his manner that disturbs me. He looks at me in a way that's improper for anyone to look at a married woman except her husband."

As if to prove the blonde's point, the drummer picked that moment to turn partway around in his seat and gaze back at her. He swung quickly—and guiltily—toward the front of the car when he saw the blonde talking to Longarm.

"I see what you mean," Longarm said with a nod.

"I tried to go out onto the platform earlier, and he followed me. I was rather frightened of what he might try to do, so I hurried back into the car. You seem like such a stalwart gentleman that I'm sure he wouldn't bother me if you were with me."

"Well . . ." Longarm felt his resolve wavering. The woman just wanted some protection, and as a matter of fact, he felt like he could use a cheroot about now. "Do you mind if I smoke while we're out there?"

A smile lit up her face. "Not at all! My husband smokes a pipe, and I love the smell of it."

"These stogies of mine ain't quite that aromatic, I'm afraid, but maybe they won't bother you too much."

"I'm sure they won't." She got to her feet. "I'm Charlotte Harris, by the way."

"Custis Long." He didn't add the "deputy U.S. marshal" part. Sometimes he used an alias when he was working undercover, but that wasn't the case here.

"I'm very pleased to meet you, Mr. Long."

She didn't offer to shake hands, so he gave his hat brim a tug instead. "It's an honor, Mrs. Harris."

They made their way to the rear of the car. Longarm held the door open for Charlotte Harris, then paused to look at the drummer, who had turned around again. Longarm couldn't resist giving the man a grin. The drummer scowled in disappointment.

Longarm followed Charlotte through the vestibule onto the platform. The air was fresher out here, although tinged with the smell of the smoke coming from the diamond stack of the big locomotive at the front of the train. The next car in line was a freight car, so its blank end wall meant that no people would be passing through this way. With the door to the vestibule closed, Longarm and Charlotte were alone.

She rested her hands on the iron railing around the platform and gazed out at the passing landscape. There wasn't much to see as far as Longarm was concerned.

He was sliding a cheroot from his vest pocket when Charlotte turned toward him and said, "Would you think it was terribly forward of me if I asked you to kiss me, Mr. Long?"

Longarm frowned at her in surprise. "I, uh, thought you said you were married. And you've got a ring on your finger."

"This?" She laughed as she held up her hand and displayed the ring. "Merely a precaution. I've found that when a single woman is traveling alone, she's much less likely to be accosted by strange men if she gives the appearance of being married." She slipped the ring off and dropped it in her bag

"Well, then . . ." A grin spread across Longarm's rugged face. "As a gentleman, I do like to oblige a lady."

"The hell with all this propriety." Charlotte put her arms around Longarm's neck, pressed her body against his, and found his mouth with hungry red lips.

Chapter 2

It was a good kiss, hot, sweet, and thoroughly arousing. Longarm probably imagined it—almost certainly *did* imagine it, considering all the layers of clothing between them—but he would have sworn he felt Charlotte's nipples growing hard and taut as she molded her breasts against his chest.

He damned sure felt a hardening of his own, down at the base of his groin.

Charlotte Harris felt it, too, judging by the way her soft belly surged against his crotch. She pulled her mouth away from his and panted, "Oh, my God, Mr. Long!"

"Custis," Longarm managed to say. "Call me Custis."

"Custis, I want you so much. There's still twenty minutes or so until the train arrives in Indianola, isn't there?"

Longarm didn't know to the minute the train's schedule, nor was he about to pull his watch out and check the time. "About that," he said.

"Long enough," Charlotte said as her fingers fumbled at the buttons of his trousers. Unexpectedly, she giggled. "At least, I hope it's long enough. I'd hate to be disappointed."

Longarm figured there was more than one way a fella could take that, but it didn't really matter. The important thing at the moment was that she had succeeded in getting a soft little hand inside his fly and wrapped it around his throbbing shaft.

Longarm closed his eyes for a second in pure pleasure as she stroked him. But then he opened them again as she tugged and maneuvered and extricated his manhood from the tight confines of his underwear and trousers. It was a mite disconcerting to realize that he was standing on an open platform on the rear of a railroad car, with the train clicking along at a good thirty or forty miles an hour, with his hard dick waving in the breeze.

Not for long, though, because Charlotte turned to lean over the railing, reached behind her to pull up her skirt and petticoat, and said, "Stick that big thing in me, Custis."

She didn't have any drawers on under the traveling outfit. He could see the round, pale globes of her ass. From this angle, he couldn't make out the opening between her legs, but he knew it was there. It seemed to be attracting the head of his shaft like a magnet.

He glanced around at the open, empty fields through which the train was rolling. Nobody was out there to see them. Longarm wished there was some way to lock that door into the vestibule, but they'd just have to trust to luck that no one would interrupt them.

He moved up behind Charlotte, and slid his cock between her legs. He felt a wet heat against it and drove forward, penetrating the fleshy folds of her sex and burying himself inside her.

Charlotte gasped and hunched her hips back at him, obviously trying to engulf every bit of his manhood that she possibly could. Longarm reached around her and clamped his hands on the railing. He flexed his hips so that he and Charlotte both experienced the delicious sensation of his pole thrusting back and forth inside her.

"That's so . . . so good!" she said, her voice choked with passion. "Give it to me, Custis! Give it to me *hard*!"

"Like I said," Longarm ground out between clenched teeth, "I always like to oblige a lady!"

The swaying motion of the train added to the arousing sensations that cascaded through him as he pounded into her.

Excitement so overwhelming couldn't be maintained for long. He felt his climax building inside him, and after a few more moments, when Charlotte cried out and began to spasm around him, he stopped trying to hold back. He let go instead, flooding her with his gushing climax. She shuddered and jerked against him.

With his heart still hammering in his chest, Longarm glanced up in time to see that the train was rolling past some cattle pens and a loading chute. The pens contained a few cattle, but the train didn't slow and Longarm knew they weren't going to be loaded on.

However, a couple of young punchers, probably no more than fifteen or sixteen years old, sat on the top rail of the pen. Judging by the slack-jawed stares the youngsters were giving him and Charlotte, the boys had gotten an eyeful. They'd have a good story for the bunkhouse tonight, except for the fact that the other hands probably wouldn't believe them. With his somewhat less erect member still inside Charlotte, Longarm grinned at the young cowpokes, lifted a hand, and ticked a finger against his hat brim in an informal salute. One of the boys lost his balance and went over backward, arms windmilling frantically as he fell into a pile of cow poop. His yell was lost in the train's whistle.

That shrill blast meant they were approaching Indianola.

Longarm disengaged from Charlotte and tucked his manhood back in his trousers. She leaned on the railing, still a little breathless from the climax that had rippled through her. With an effort, she was able to say, "That . . . that was splendid."

"It was mighty fine," Longarm agreed.

"Are you going to Indianola on business?"

"You could say that," he replied, thinking about Cyrus Pollack—the murdering skunk. It would be both business *and* a pleasure to arrest him.

"In that case, I suppose we won't see each other again." Charlotte turned to face him with her skirts back in their proper place. She came up on her toes and brushed a tender kiss across his cheek. "But I shall always remember you fondly."

"Wait a minute," Longarm said with a frown. "I might have a little spare time while I'm here—"

She shook her head. "I wouldn't dream of bothering you."

"It wouldn't be any bother."

He was about to ask her how he could get in touch with her when she said, "I really must go," and opened the door into the vestibule. Longarm's eyes narrowed as he watched her go on through into the car.

He stayed on the platform and smoked that cheroot he had started to take out earlier, before things got all hot and heavy between him and Charlotte. He leaned out to watch the train's approach to Indianola. Even though the settlement was still a mile away, Longarm's keen eyes could make out the tall masts of ships docked at the wharves where Powder Horn Bayou curved inland from the gulf.

When Longarm returned to his seat, Charlotte was sitting across the aisle again, all prim and proper. She had taken the wedding ring from her bag and slipped it on again.

By the time the train came to a halt, Charlotte hadn't so much as glanced in Longarm's direction again. He didn't try to talk to her. If this was the way she wanted things, then so be it. As the passengers began to disembark, she went toward the front of the car, and he went to the back.

He swung down onto the depot platform without the aid of any portable steps, and went along to the baggage car to claim his warbag, his Winchester, and his McClellan saddle. As he did, he kept an eye on the other passenger car and saw Cyrus Pollack step down from the train. Pollack didn't have any baggage because he had boarded the train in such a hurry.

Longarm pressed a coin into the hand of a porter and nodded toward his gear. "See that my things are taken into the station and have somebody watch over 'em," he muttered. Then he started after Pollack, hanging back far enough so the fugitive wouldn't catch sight of him in the crowd.

Even though his attention was on the man he was after, Longarm was still able to notice Charlotte Harris as he strode past her. She was greeting a stocky man in town clothes. He had a mustache and slicked-down hair, and he took Charlotte in his arms in a rather stiff embrace and gave her a peck on the cheek. Then she knelt and hugged the two children who had come to the station with the man. A boy and a girl, they were both blond like Charlotte and maybe five or six years old. "Mama!" the girl cried as she flung her arms around Charlotte's neck.

Longarm had already figured out that Charlotte really was married. She glanced at him as he walked past, but that was all. She gave no indication that she had ever met him, let alone that less than half an hour earlier, he'd had his cock buried way up inside her. She had to still be wet from his climax. But you'd never know it now, safe as she was back in the bosom of her family.

It took all kinds, thought Longarm. Then he put the whole incident out of his mind. He had an outlaw to catch.

Wagons and mule teams lined Main Street. Pedestrians thronged the sidewalks. From the looks of the town, you'd never know that a powerful hurricane had almost wiped it off the face of the earth. The thought of that made Longarm glance toward the gulf. The water was blue and peaceful today, with gentle breakers rolling in smoothly.

Longarm had thought that Pollack might head directly for the docks, in hopes that he could get a ticket on a ship about to sail. Longarm figured Pollack wouldn't care very much what the destination was, just as long as it was away from the States.

Instead, Pollack turned in at the Powder Horn Saloon, obviously named after the bayou, which was shaped sort of like a powder horn. Longarm frowned. He didn't want to start a shoot-out in a crowded saloon, but this chase had gone on long enough. When Pollack saw that Longarm had the drop on him, maybe he'd surrender and come along peaceablelike.

As he headed for the saloon, Longarm moved his coat back so that he'd have better access to the Colt Model T holstered in a cross-draw rig on his left hip. He pushed the batwings aside and stepped into the establishment. Instantly, he spotted Pollack standing at the far end of the bar, talking to a hulking man in range clothes. Several other men stood nearby, all of them hard-faced and roughly dressed. Longarm had never seen any of them before, at least not that he recalled, but he knew gun-wolves when he saw them.

The sound of footsteps on the plank walk just outside the saloon's entrance made him glance over his shoulder. More hard cases shouldered into the saloon. Longarm realized that he had walked into a trap.

Cyrus Pollack turned toward him, smirked, and said, "Let's see you get out of this, you damn lawdog."

Chapter 3

The tall, dark-eyed man walking down Indianola's Main Street moved with an easy grace. He seemed to flow through the crowd like water seeking the path of least resistance. He was dressed mostly in black, from the Stetson to the leather vest over a collarless tan shirt to the whipcord trousers. But instead of boots, he wore sandals on bare feet, and he didn't carry a gun like many of the men in this frontier settlement.

Not that he was unarmed. The vest concealed a short, curved *tanto* knife tucked behind his belt, and several razor-sharp *shuriken*—throwing stars—rode in special pockets in the vest. His greatest weapon, though, was his superb fighting skill, honed by years of practice with some of the best teachers to be found anywhere in the world.

The dark hair and mustache, the slightly slanted eyes, and the golden tone of his skin were legacies from his Japanese mother. His height and muscular build came from the American sea captain who was his father. A product of two worlds, he was the rare individual who could be at home in either.

But for many years, Texas had been his true home, specifically the vast Circle Star Ranch owned by Jessica Starbuck. His name was Ki, and he was Jessie's friend, companion, and bodyguard. Jessie's father Alex Starbuck had brought Ki to America from Japan more than two decades earlier, when his daughter was only a beautiful, golden-haired child. Ki was several years older than her, and in the time they had been together, he had watched Jessie grow into an even more beautiful woman as the years passed.

The two of them made a formidable team, and together they had faced many dangers over the years, including a long war with the criminal Cartel responsible for the foul murder of Jessie's parents. Eventually, they had succeeded in smashing the Cartel with the help of a deputy U.S. marshal named Custis Long, but in recent years, like an evil phoenix, a new Cartel had begun to rise from the ashes of the old. That troubled Ki, and never more so than now, when circumstances had forced him and Jessie to be apart.

That was why he was glad their separation was almost over. Jessie was due to arrive in Indianola later today on the *Harry Fulton*, one of the ships that belonged to the Starbuck Line.

Ki planned to wait for the ship at the dock. Indianola offered the same sort of pleasures and diversions as any other frontier town, but he wasn't interested in them at the moment.

That didn't mean he was unaware of his surroundings. His keen eyes constantly roved over the street, alert for any sort of threat. Years of living on the edge of danger had ingrained that habit in him.

For that reason, he happened to be looking across the street at the Powder Horn Saloon when the tall man in the brown tweed suit stepped through the batwings and disappeared into the saloon's shadowy interior. Although Ki caught only a glimpse of the man's face, and that in profile, there was no mistaking the deeply tanned, hawklike features of Custis Long.

Ki wasn't particularly surprised to see Longarm. He knew that as a deputy marshal, the big lawman's job took him all over the West. Ki started across the street, intending to say hello and inform Longarm that Jessie would soon be arriving in Indianola, too. He knew that she would be glad for the chance to spend some time with Longarm again. The two of them shared a lot of history.

While Ki was still crossing the street, though, he saw several roughly dressed men emerge from the alley beside the saloon and move quickly toward its entrance. A couple of them reached for their guns, slid the weapons up and down in their holsters to loosen them.

Ki didn't like the look of that at all. He didn't care for the way the men crowded into the saloon behind Longarm either.

He stepped up onto the boardwalk in time to hear a man say in a smug voice laced with hatred, "Let's see you get out of this, you damned lawdog."

In that moment, Ki no longer had any doubt. Longarm had been caught in a trap. As Ki stepped up to the batwings, he saw some of the saloon's customers scurrying for cover, moving so fast that they overturned chairs in their haste. Longarm stood there about a dozen feet inside the saloon, about to be caught in a cross fire between two groups of gunmen.

With Ki, to think was to act. He took hold of the batwings, shoved them aside, then used them to support himself as he powered up off the floor and lashed out with both sandal-clad feet, kicking so high that he caught two of the gunmen in the back of the head.

The hard cases flew forward, the guns they had just drawn clattering to the floor. Ki let out a *"Haaiii!"* as he landed between the two remaining gunmen in this bunch. He whipped a sidehand blow at each man's throat. They staggered back, struggling to draw air through crushed windpipes. Ki launched a spinning kick that slammed one man to the floor, then the other.

That was when guns began to roar.

Longarm barely had time to decide that he was going to put a bullet right in the middle of that smirk on Cyrus Pollack's face, no matter what else happened, before he heard the batwings slapped open behind him. Then men crashed to the floor, and he heard a familiar *"Haaiii!"*

Ki.

Longarm had no idea what his old friend was doing here in Indianola, but right now he would take all the good luck he could get. He didn't turn around, trusting that Ki would handle the gunnies behind him. He slapped leather instead, his hand flashing across his body to the holstered .44.

Faster than the eye could follow, the gun was in Longarm's hand. Flame spurted from the muzzle as he triggered the first shot. The smirk had already disappeared from Pollack's face as the fugitive clawed under his coat for a gun. A look of shock and horror replaced it as Pollack's head jerked under the impact of Longarm's slug. The bullet bored through Pollack's brain and burst out the back of his skull in a grisly spray of blood and bone fragments.

Pollack slumped into the big man he'd been talking to when Longarm came into the saloon. That hombre cursed and shoved the boneless corpse aside with a shoulder as he filled both hands. The guns were still angled toward the floor, though, as Longarm fired again and planted a slug in the man's chest. His trigger fingers jerked in an involuntary reflex and both guns roared. The bullets chewed into the planks at the big gunman's feet.

Longarm was already shifting his aim as the gunman sagged. Three hard cases remained, and they all had their guns out. Longarm triggered twice in the blink of an eye and sent two of them spinning off their feet.

But that left the third and final man, and Longarm knew he wasn't going to get that son of a bitch in time. He braced his body for the shattering impact of a bullet.

That impact didn't come. Instead of firing, the last of the killers dropped his gun and staggered against the bar, pawing at his blood-spouting throat as he did so. Longarm saw the razor-edged *shuriken* lodged in the man's throat. He hadn't seen Ki make the throw, but it had been perfect as usual. The dying gunman stumbled over Pollack's body and pitched to the floor.

Longarm didn't lower his gun. He wheeled around to make sure none of the other men still posed a threat. He saw immediately that they didn't. A couple of them flopped around like fish out of water, evidently suffocating, and the other two were either out cold or dead. Ki stood over them, his face impassive. He still gripped a *shuriken* in his left hand. Seeing that he wasn't going to need it, he slipped it back into a pocket on his vest.

Then he smiled and nodded to Longarm. "Marshal Long," he said. "It's good to see you again."

"The feeling's mighty mutual," Longarm said, "especially considerin' that those boys had me whipsawed. Is Jessie here in Indianola?"

Ki had to wait to answer because one of the choking

men let out a rattling moan and then slumped in death. The
other one expired a second later.

"Jessie's on board a ship that's due to arrive later today,"
Ki said as silence descended once more on the saloon.

The bartender peeked fearfully over the bar, and several
of the customers and saloon girls who had dived for cover
looked out from behind overturned tables.

Longarm said, "Don't worry, folks, the shooting's over."
He started reloading the four chambers he had emptied
during the brief but intense fight.

"Were you after all of these men?" Ki asked.

"Nope, just one of 'em." Still holding the Colt, Longarm
walked over and nudged Pollack's shoulder with the toe of
his boot. "This varmint right here."

From behind the bar, the bartender asked, "Are . . . are
you a lawman, mister?"

"I sure am," Longarm said. "Deputy U.S. marshal. Anybody know this big galoot?" He used the barrel of the gun
to point at the man Pollack had been talking to.

One of the gaudily painted saloon girls peered over a
table and said, "Yeah, that's Jasper Milroy. He's supposed
to have killed a dozen men."

Longarm grunted. "Well, he won't kill any more."

"One of these men is still alive," Ki said. He was hunkered on his heels next to the gunmen who had planned on
ventilating Longarm from behind. "I'm afraid the other
one's neck is broken."

Ki rolled the man onto his back and slapped his face to
bring him around. The man groaned as his eyes opened.

His eyes opened even wider as Ki slipped the *tanto* knife
from his belt and held it to the man's throat, pressing so that
the blade's keen edge penetrated skin and drew blood.

Ki said in a hard voice. "Why did you try to ambush Marshal Long?"

"I . . . I don't know nothin' about it!" the man stammered. "I didn't know he was a lawman! Milroy got a telegram from an old pard of his, said the fella was willin' to p-pay to get rid of some hombre doggin' his trail. That's all I know! I swear!" The man looked past Ki at Longarm and added, "Please, mister, don't let this crazy Chinaman cut me!"

"Oh, now that was a mistake, old son," Longarm told him with a smile. "Ki here is part Japanese, not Chinese. Them two bunches don't always get along so good."

The hired gunman started to sob. He must have thought that Ki was about to slice his throat wide open.

Before anybody could do anything else, a man burst through the batwings, leveled a shotgun, and ordered, "Nobody move!"

Chapter 4

The bartender called, "Don't shoot, Hank! That tall drink of water there's a federal lawman."

The newcomer blinked beady eyes at Longarm. He was a short, wiry man with a mustache so bushy, it seemed like it ought to weigh just as much as the rest of him. "Is that right?" he demanded. "You work for Uncle Sam?"

"That's right," Longarm said. He had already spotted a deputy's badge on the man's vest. "If you promise not to get an itchy trigger finger, I'll reach inside my coat and get my badge and bona fides for you to look at."

The local star packer lowered the Greener's barrels a little and nodded. "That's a good idea. Let's see 'em."

Longarm fished out the leather wallet that contained his credentials. The deputy took it and studied the badge and identification card for several seconds.

The deputy finally handed back the wallet and said, "I reckon you're a lawman, all right. Who's the Chink?"

Ki rolled his eyes but didn't say anything.

"He's a friend of mine," Longarm explained. "He gave

me a hand when a fugitive I've been pursuing tried to kill me, along with these hired guns here."

"Jasper Milroy's bunch, eh? Yeah, they're bad 'uns. I don't mind a bit seein' 'em leakin' blood all over the floor."

"It's not *your* floor," the bartender pointed out. "That's gonna be hell to get cleaned up."

The deputy finally lowered his shotgun all the way to the floor and gave Longarm a friendly nod. "Nice to meet you, Marshal Long. I'm Deputy Sheriff Hank Anderson."

Longarm asked, "Where's the sheriff?"

"Out of town," Anderson said. "He left me to look after things. I'll start by gettin' the undertaker down here to haul off these carcasses." He sniffed and waved the shotgun at the one hired killer who had survived the fight. The gunnie flinched, as if he thought the Greener was about to go off and blow his head off his shoulders. "Want me to lock this one up?"

"I'd appreciate that, Hank. I'll send a wire to my boss and ask what he wants done about this. The fella did try to assault a federal law officer after all."

Anderson snorted. "That was a piss-poor decision."

He hustled off to fetch the undertaker. Longarm turned to Ki and asked, "How about sitting down and having a drink?"

"I really need to get to the dock to meet that ship," Ki replied.

The bartender had stood up and was wiping the hardwood with a rag now. He asked, "What ship is that, mister?"

Ki turned to the man. "The *Harry Fulton*. It's due today."

The bartender shook his head. "Not anymore. I hear all the gossip from the docks, and accordin' to what I was told, the *Harry Fulton* is runnin' a day or more behind schedule.

It had to skirt around some bad weather out in the gulf between Cuba and New Orleans, so it didn't leave New Orleans until a day after it was supposed to."

Ki frowned. "You're sure?"

"That's what the harbormaster told me," the bartender replied with a shrug. "He got a wire from New Orleans."

"That sounds pretty certain," Longarm said. "Now you've got time to have that drink with me."

They stayed in the Powder Horn, taking a table in the corner once the black-suited, top hat-wearing undertaker and his helpers had dragged the corpses out of the saloon. An elderly swamper started trying to mop up the spilled blood.

Longarm asked for a bottle of Maryland rye. The bartender sent one of the girls over with it on a tray, along with a couple of glasses. She leaned forward as she set the tray on the table, her low-cut, spangled gown giving both Longarm and Ki a fine view of the enticing valley between her creamy breasts. She was a redhead, with a scattering of pale freckles across her chest, and Ki thought that her fresh-faced attractiveness was an indication that she hadn't been working in the saloon for long.

She had been there long enough to have a bold invitation in her eyes as she smiled at Ki, though.

Longarm poured the drinks and then held up his glass. "To old friends," he said.

"Old friends," Ki agreed, clinking his glass against the lawman's. Both men threw back the whiskey.

"Thanks again for giving me a hand with those varmints," Longarm said as he set his empty glass on the table. "I'm mighty lucky you came along when you did."

Ki shrugged. "If I hadn't come along, I'm sure you would have handled them by yourself, Marshal."

Longarm shook his head. "I ain't so sure about that. Odds of nine to one?"

"You've had odds that bad against you before, and you're still here."

Longarm shrugged in acknowledgment of that point. "All the same, I appreciate it."

Ki nodded. "Are you staying in Indianola? I know that Jessie would like to see you."

Longarm grinned. "Reckon I'd better wire Billy Vail and tell him that I'm gonna be held up here for a day or two. Want to allow plenty of time for a proper reunion."

Ki knew good and well that previous "reunions" involving Longarm and Jessie had been anything but proper. A great passion had always existed between the two of them. Ki regarded Jessie as his sister, but he had long since learned that any brotherly protectiveness he showed toward her would not be welcome, especially when it came to her private affairs.

The passion between Longarm and Jessie had cooled a bit in recent years, since circumstances had kept them apart most of the time. But to tell the truth, Ki harbored the hope that one of these days, when Longarm and Jessie both realized that it was time for them to settle down, they would decide to spend the rest of their lives together.

Of course, they both had to survive long enough to get to that point, which, considering their adventurous lives, might be unlikely . . .

Longarm refilled the glasses and said, "I reckon it was business that took Jessie to Cuba?"

Ki nodded. "Yes, on one of the Starbuck sugar cane plantations. Then she planned to stop in at New Orleans to check on some other holdings on her way back."

"How come you didn't go with her?"

The bluntness of the question didn't surprise Ki. Longarm wasn't a man to mince words.

"I was laid up at the time," Ki explained. "Broken leg. I let myself get between an angry bull and a corral fence."

Longarm winced. "That ain't a good place to be."

"Yes, so I found out. I asked Jessie to postpone the trip until my leg healed so that I could go with her," Ki continued.

"I'll bet *that* went over real well."

Ki smiled. "Jessie said that the business wouldn't wait and that she was perfectly capable of taking care of herself."

"She is, you know," Longarm said. "At least, most of the time."

"No doubt. So she left me on the Circle Star to recuperate and sailed for Cuba. I would have followed her when my leg was well enough, but she gave me strict orders not to do so."

Longarm nodded. "Yep. That's Jessie, all right."

The redheaded saloon girl came back over to the table. "Can I get you gentlemen anything else?" she asked.

"I reckon I'm fine," Longarm said. He looked at Ki. "How about you?"

"I require nothing, thank you," he told the girl.

"Really?" she said. "Everybody needs something." She smiled at him. "If you need anything, mister, you just ask for Luisa. That's me."

"Thank you. I will."

Her hips had a definite sway to them as she went back to the bar. Longarm grinned and said, "You got that gal all hot and bothered, Ki."

"You think so? Perhaps it is you to whom she is attracted."

"Naw. She's got her eye on you. And since you've got to stay in Indianola an extra night . . . Well, think about it, that's all I'm sayin'."

"Perhaps I will," Ki said as he nodded slowly. The girl called Luisa *was* rather attractive.

"So," Longarm said, "that leg of yours is all healed up?"

"As good as new," Ki said.

"That's good, in case you have to do any . . . ridin'."

Chapter 5

"Oh, my God!" Luisa cried as she clutched at him that night. "Ride me, Ki! *Ride me!*"

He felt like they were already galloping as he poised between her wide-spread thighs and plunged his stiff manhood in and out of her wet, heated depths.

She raised her legs high over his hips and spread them wide to open herself to him. His buttocks bobbed up and down swiftly as his iron-hard shaft pistoned into her.

They were in her small room on the second floor of the Powder Horn Saloon. A lamp on the tiny table next to the bed provided dim illumination. Before bringing him up here, Luisa had told him that she wasn't a whore and she didn't expect him to pay her. She was doing this because she wanted to.

Ki reveled in the sensations that stormed through him. Luisa's hips bucked to meet his thrusts, allowing him to delve deeper and deeper inside her. She cried out softly, the cords in her neck standing out as she tipped her head back. Ki pulled back, plunged into her again and then again, and Luisa began to shudder as she tipped over the edge into her climax.

Ki allowed himself to succumb to his own release, which felt wonderful. He emptied himself into her willing vessel. She let out a long, satisfied sigh as she felt herself being flooded with his heated juices.

Then they both began the slow, delicious slide down the far side of the peak they had just scaled. With his member still inside her, Ki tightened his arms around her and rolled onto his back, taking her with him. She sprawled on top of him and drew her knees up to give her enough leverage so she could work her hips back and forth. Even though he had already come, his shaft was still hard enough to slide back and forth tantalizingly within her drenched folds.

"My goodness," she breathed as she smiled down at him. "That was just . . . just wonderful, Ki!"

His own pulse and respiration were somewhat faster than normal, although he was able to maintain good control over them even in circumstances such as these. He said, "It was highly stimulating indeed."

She stared at him, frowning slightly. "Is that a highfalutin' way of saying it was a good fuck?"

"Yes," Ki agreed. "A very good fuck."

"I'm glad." She leaned down and nuzzled her lips against his neck. "I wanted it to be good for you."

Ki stroked her back and her hips. When he softened enough so that he slipped out of her, she made a little noise of disappointment. She wasn't disappointed for long, though, because he turned so that they lay on their sides and slid a hand between her legs. With expert precision, his fingers stroked along the sensitive opening until he found the tiny bud of flesh at the top of it.

"Oh, my!" Luisa said again as Ki's thumb circled that nubbin. Slowly at first, then faster and faster, beating like the wings of a hummingbird. Her hands clawed at his chest as she began to pant again. "You can't . . . not again . . . not so soon . . .!"

"Perhaps I cannot," Ki said with a smile, "but you certainly can."

She proved that by jerking and spasming under his touch as he swiftly brought her to another climax.

When she caught her breath enough to be able to talk again, she said, "I wish you could stay in Indianola forever, Ki."

"My life is elsewhere."

"I know," she said sadly. "But a girl can wish." She reached down and grasped his manhood, which was already growing hard again. "Right now I wish you'd put this in me again!"

As he mounted the redhead again, he spared a fleeting thought for Jessie, somewhere out there on the gulf. He hoped that wherever she was, her voyage was going well.

"Son of a *bitch*!" Jessie exclaimed as the ship bucked and heaved and rolled, throwing her across the cabin. She grabbed the table to keep from falling. The floor tilted under her, so she felt like she was climbing a mountain as she pulled herself along the table toward a chair that was also bolted down. Just as she reached the chair, the ship rolled the other way, and she grunted in pain as she was pitched into the chair. "Damn it!"

She knew it was unladylike to cuss so much. If her father could have heard her, he would have been disappointed. Or maybe not. Alex Starbuck had been enough of a realist to know that sometimes a few curses were the only way to vent the frustration a person was feeling.

Jessie was mighty frustrated at the moment . . . in more ways than one.

Ever since leaving Cuba, the *Harry Fulton* had been playing a game of tag with a storm. The ship's captain, a wild Irishman named Seamus O'Malley, worried that it might turn into a hurricane. O'Malley didn't fear many things, but a hurricane was one of them. He had circled widely in an attempt to avoid the disturbance.

For the most part, O'Malley had been successful. They had gotten in front of the storm. However, it was still behind them, the clouds lurking like blue gray monsters on the horizon. And then today, the storm had picked up speed, growing larger and stronger. The *Harry Fulton* was still well ahead of it, but tonight some of the minor squalls thrown out in front of the main storm had caught up to the ship.

Jessie didn't know what was going to happen, and that uncertainty gnawed at her nerves because she couldn't control anything in this situation. She was in the hands of the captain and the crew, and they were all at the mercy of nature.

And Jessie knew how unforgiving nature could be at times.

Her frustration also stemmed from the fact that she was supposed to have dinner tonight with Andre Dumond, a French expatriate cotton trader who had come aboard in New Orleans, bound for Vera Cruz. He and Jessie had dined together several times, and in the natural course of events, after one of those dinners in her cabin, they had wound up in her bunk, making enthusiastic, passionate love. Jessie had hoped for a repeat of that tonight.

That was looking more and more unlikely, though. She didn't see how anyone could make love with the ship rolling and pitching like this, and supper was out of the question. She didn't think her stomach would be able to stand any food.

Anyway, Andre hadn't shown up. He was probably holed up in his cabin, sick as a dog, praying that they wouldn't all wind up at the bottom of the sea before the night was over.

So she was surprised when, over the howling of the wind and the roar of the waves, she heard someone rapping on her door. She started to get up, then clutched the table and stayed in the chair as the deck heaved again. "Come in!" she called.

The door swung open to admit Andre Dumond. He was a tall, lean man with a shock of black hair and a pleasantly ugly face. The once-broken nose showed that he hadn't spent all his life making deals for shipments of cotton. He had been more adventurous than that, sometime in the past. He grinned as he stepped into the cabin, clutching the door-jamb to steady himself, and said, "Quite the refreshing breeze, eh, Jessie?"

"Oh, shut up," she said. "I hope you didn't show up expecting dinner."

"Not *dinner*, no." The smile on his face showed that he might still have the other part of the planned festivities in mind, though.

Jessie couldn't help but laugh. "You really are a Frenchman, aren't you?"

"Mais oui, mademoiselle."

"Well, come on in," she told him. "And shut the door."

As the primary stockholder in the Starbuck Shipping Line and therefore the de facto owner of the *Harry Fulton*, Jessie had been given the finest passenger cabin on the ship. The furniture was built of thick, heavy wood polished to a high gleam. The cushions were thick and comfortable. The brass fittings around the cabin and the trim around the port-hole shone brightly in the light from several hanging oil lamps that swayed back and forth with the motion of the ship.

Jessie tried to get up, but once more the ship's violent pitching made her stumble. When she clutched at the table, the cloth slid and she wasn't able to steady herself. She was about to tumble off her feet when Andre leaped forward agilely and caught her. His arms went around her waist and tightened.

He laughed. "You see, Jessie, not even a hurricane can keep me away from you."

"This isn't a hurricane," she said. "It's just a little squall. It'll probably blow over in a little— *Oh!*"

The ship tilted so far, Jessie was sure it was going to roll over and be smashed to kindling by the waves. In that terrifying moment, she wished she could see Ki again, to make sure he knew how much she really loved and respected him, and she thought about Custis Long, too, the one man in her life other than Ki and her father she had really, truly trusted.

As the floor threatened to trade places with the ceiling, Jessie and Andre found themselves falling. Luckily, they landed on the bunk's soft mattress. Tangling in the sheets, they rolled up against the bulkhead.

Jessie was dizzy and disoriented, but after a moment, she realized that the ship had somehow righted itself again. Right now, in fact, the room had returned to normal, except for the fact that she and Andre were sprawled on the bunk with their arms around each other.

"It seems that the gods of the deep have plans for us, *ma cherie*," Andre said. "We should not tempt fate by disappointing them."

"You Frenchmen talk too much," Jessie told him. "Shut up and kiss me before this damn boat sinks."

Chapter 6

The air in Indianola had a hot, sultry edge to it the next morning that put Longarm's teeth on edge as he walked from the hotel where he'd spent the night toward the county courthouse at the far end of Main Street from the wharves and Powder Horn Bayou. There was no breeze, which was almost unheard of here along the coast, where salt-laden winds blew almost constantly from the sea.

Deputy Hank Anderson had told Longarm that the sheriff's office and jail were located in the courthouse. He wanted to check on his prisoner, who had seemed to be all right other than having a headache from being kicked in the head by Ki. After that, he would stop by the Western Union office and see if there had been a reply to the telegram he had sent to Billy Vail.

Taking out a cheroot, he lit it as he entered the courthouse and began looking for the sheriff's office. He found it down a hallway and went in. Deputy Anderson was sitting behind a desk, his chair leaned back and his booted feet propped on the scarred top of the desk.

"You better be careful," Longarm warned. "That soup strainer of yours probably weighs so much it might unbalance you."

Anderson sniffed in disdain. "You're just jealous 'cause your mustache ain't half as magnificent as mine." He stroked the hirsute growth proudly.

Longarm grabbed a ladder-back chair, turned it around, and straddled it. "How's the prisoner?" he asked around the cheroot clenched between his teeth.

"Singin' like a bird. Turns out he knowed more about Pollack than he was lettin' on yesterday, and he's eager to spill it now 'cause we found out he's wanted for killin's in Arkansas and Indian Territory. He's mighty a-feared o' the hangman's rope and hopes that talkin' might help him." Anderson shook his head. "It won't. He's gonna swing, no matter."

"So tell me what he said about Pollack," Longarm went on, prodding the garrulous deputy.

Anderson sat up, the front legs of his chair thumping to the floor. "Pollack was plannin' to catch a ship bound for Vera Cruz. I reckon he figured that if he could get into Mexico, the federal authorities couldn't touch him. But he knew you were a stubborn bastard so he wanted to make sure you was dead first. He sent a wire to Jasper Milroy, who'd been mixed up with him in some sort o' whiskey-smugglin' ring in Indian Territory."

Longarm nodded. "I know about the whiskey smuggling. Never ran across any mention of Milroy, though."

Anderson's mustache bristled as if he didn't care for being interrupted. "Milroy was a cold-blooded killer, and Pollack knew it. In his wire, he told Milroy to round up some other hard cases who wouldn't mind gunnin' down a federal star packer and meet him at the Powder Horn Saloon. That's the meetin' you walked in on." He sniffed again. "Mighty careless of you, Marshal, if you ask me."

Longarm told himself not to let the little deputy ruffle his feathers. He said, "I didn't have any way of knowing that Pollack was meeting a gang of gun-wolves here in Indianola. I thought he was just running, trying to get out of Texas any way he could, as fast as he could."

"Well, he won't be gettin' out. Buryin's this afternoon. You gonna be there?"

"I doubt it. My business with Cyrus Pollack is done with."

He had said as much to Billy Vail in his telegram. Longarm would have preferred to arrest Pollack, take him back for trial, and see him hanged properlike after being found guilty. But in the end, Pollack wound up in Hell either way, so it didn't matter all that much.

Anderson jerked a thumb over his shoulder in the direction of the cell block door. "What do you want me to do with that fella? Who's gonna pay for keepin' him locked up here?"

"The Justice Department will foot the bill, I reckon. I'll let you know what my boss says as soon as I hear back from him."

"You do that. The sheriff'll chew my ass good if I take in a prisoner and the county winds up havin' to pay for him."

Longarm stood up and extended his hand across the desk. "I'll be in touch," he promised.

Anderson got to his feet and shook hands. "You do that," he said.

It would serve the pompous little varmint right if he just left the prisoner there and never came back for him, Longarm thought as he left the courthouse. Of course, he wouldn't do that. He wasn't above bending a rule or two on occasion, but Billy Vail would never let him hear the end of it if he just abandoned a prisoner.

Vail hadn't replied yet to Longarm's telegram, the big lawman found when he stopped at the Western Union office right next door to the train station. As Longarm stepped out, a gust of wind swept in from the gulf. The waves were starting to pick up. That was an improvement over the sultry stillness that had hung over the town earlier, Longarm thought.

He wondered where Ki was this morning. Ki had a room at the hotel, too, but he hadn't answered when Longarm knocked on the door, thinking that they could have breakfast together. Ki's absence didn't really come as a surprise to him. More than likely, Ki had spent the night with that redheaded Luisa gal from the saloon.

So Ki was probably pretty worn out, Longarm mused with a chuckle. Luisa looked like she was pretty limber, and Longarm was willing to bet that she threw her body and soul into her romping. Ki was a lucky son of a gun.

Longarm had spent the night alone, which didn't particularly bother him. His encounter with Charlotte Harris on the train still had a bad taste lingering in his mouth.

He knew what would take care of that and completely wash away any bad memories of Charlotte—the fresh, clean beauty of Jessie Starbuck.

Longarm strolled toward the docks. Maybe somebody would be able to tell him when the *Harry Fulton* was due to arrive.

By morning, the squall had moved on, but there was still a strong wind carrying the ship westward, toward the Texas coast. And low black clouds still lurked behind it, like a horde of menacing beasts stalking their prey.

Wearing a green dress, Jessie stood at the railing, her long, copper blond hair loose around her shoulders and whipping in the gusts. From behind her, a voice said, "Ah, there's something wild and beautiful about ye, lass, standin' there like that. Like a sea nymph lookin' longingly toward her home."

Jessie turned with a smile. Captain Seamus O'Malley stood there with a grin on his rugged face, his cap pushed back on his thatch of rusty hair.

"Good morning, Captain," Jessie said.

"Did ye sleep well last night, despite the storm?"

"Tolerably well," Jessie replied with a shrug.

As a matter of fact, once the squall had settled down, she had slept very well indeed. That was probably because she'd been satiated by the expert lovemaking of Andre Dumond.

Even now, a fluttering went through her lower belly at the memory of the sensations he had aroused inside her. Andre lived up to the reputation of his countrymen when it came to having a talented tongue, that was for sure.

Seamus O'Malley's voice brought her out of that tantalizing reverie. "I expect you're anxious to get back to your ranch," the captain said.

"Yes, I am," she agreed. "I've been away for too long."

"Well, I expect we'll reach Indianola around midday. You'll be back on the Circle Star in another day or two."

"You should come visit us there, Captain," Jessie suggested.

"Ah, it's likin' that I would be, I'm thinkin'," O'Malley replied. "I've never seen anything of Texas except the coast from Galveston to Brownsville."

"There's a lot more to the state than that. You can find almost anything there, from deserts to mountains to forests. And cities like San Antonio, too." Jessie turned to cast a glance back at the dark clouds behind the ship. "Do you think we'll reach land ahead of that storm?"

"Oh, aye, I've no doubt about that. It appears to have slowed down again." O'Malley shook his head. "Although I've learned over me years at sea that ye can never be sure what a storm will do. I think we've got this one beat, though."

"I hope so. I've had enough of being thrown around like we were last night."

"I'll do me best to get ye home with smooth sailin' from here on out," O'Malley promised.

The captain made good on his word. By mid-morning, the Texas coastline was visible in the distance as a low green line on the horizon. It grew steadily as the ship approached.

Andre Dumond joined Jessie on deck. With a crooked grin, he said, "I must admit, I am quite glad to see land again."

"I know the feeling," Jessie admitted. "I hate being helpless."

"I suspect it is a rare occasion indeed when the famous Jessica Starbuck finds herself helpless."

She frowned at him. "Famous? What do you mean by that? I'm not famous."

"Please, *cherie*, no false modesty. It is not becoming to you. Everyone involved in business knows the name Starbuck. You rule what amounts to an empire, Jessie. And of all the American tycoons and magnates, you are the only one who manages to be a beautiful woman as well. Your name is legendary."

Jessie shook her head. "I don't think of it that way at all. I'm just someone trying to do the best she can. And there are a lot of people whose livelihoods depend on the success of the Starbuck holdings."

"Beautiful, rich, and generous. You are the perfect woman, *ma cherie.*"

"Are you making fun of me, Andre?" she asked sharply.

He held up a hand as if to swear an oath. "This I would never do. You are the most impressive woman I have ever met."

"Well . . . flattery isn't necessary." She smiled again. "But I'll take it. I *am* a woman, after all."

"Very much a woman," Andre said as he slipped an arm around her waist. "I hope that I shall be able to spend some time with you on shore, while the ship is docked at Indianola."

"We'll see." Jessie leaned her head against his shoulder.

That would all depend on what she found waiting for her, she supposed.

Chapter 7

Ki reached up to hold his black Stetson on his head as a strong gust of wind threatened to pluck it off and carry it away. Thick gray clouds had moved in as the morning went on.

Ki's steps took him toward the pair of long wharves that extended several hundred feet into the gulf near the mouth of Powder Horn Bayou.

As Ki approached the waterfront, he saw that Longarm was already there, talking to an old-timer who wore a sailor's cap. The big lawman grinned and lifted a hand in greeting.

"Howdy, Ki. How're you feeling this morning?"

"Fine," Ki replied. "Why would I feel otherwise?"

Amusement twinkled in Longarm's eyes as he took a cheroot from his vest pocket and put it in his mouth. "Thought maybe you'd be a mite tired, that's all."

"I'm fine," Ki said.

It was true, however, that a lesser man might have been weary this morning, after the night that Luisa had put him

through. The redheaded saloon girl was seemingly inex-
haustible.

But Longarm didn't need to know that, so Ki changed
the subject by asking, "Have you heard anything about when
Jessie's ship will arrive?"

"I was just asking Cap'n Andy about that," Longarm
said as he inclined his head toward the old salt.

The man said, "With the seas runnin' the way they are,
and the wind up like 'tis, that ship should be makin' good
time. I 'spect 'twill be here by midday."

Ki frowned as he peered out over the gulf. The sky was a
bluish gray. "It appears that we're in for a blow."

"I was just down to th' Signal Office a while ago,"
Cap'n Andy said. "Mr. Reed, the observer in charge o' the
office, said he ain't had no messages from Galveston. The
storm warnin' flags ain't up there."

"Cap'n Andy tells me he used to sail on the gulf," Longarm said.

The old-timer nodded. "Man an' boy, I spent nigh on to
forty years on those waters. Finally got too old to take it
anymore. Saddest day o' my life."

"What's your opinion?" Ki said. "Will there be a
storm?"

"Folks around here are sort of hopin' there will be. It's
been mighty dry in these parts. We could use some rain."

Ki suppressed the urge to sigh in exasperation. Getting a
straight answer out of this old salt appeared to be as easy as
pulling teeth. "So you *do* think there will be a storm?"

"Might be," Cap'n Andy said. "Might not be."

Longarm grinned at Ki.

"My personal feelin'," Cap'n Andy went on, "is that
there will be a storm. A big blow at that."

Longarm's grin disappeared, to be replaced by a frown

of concern. "You reckon it'll be as bad as the one that came through here a few years back? That one almost wiped out the town, didn't it?"

Cap'n Andy nodded. "The whole settlement near washed away. So what did folks do? They went and rebuilt it in the same place. They tried to relocate a couple o' miles inland, up the bayou, but they couldn't get the railroad to go along with it. Reckon it would've cost more to move the tracks than the GWT&P wanted to spend."

"Foolishness," Ki muttered.

"There're some that say this is the safest place in the world now," Cap'n Andy said. "They claim there's no way a hurricane can hit the same place twice." His bony shoulders rose and fell in a shrug. "Me, I wouldn't know about that."

He took an old, blackened pipe from his pocket and put the stem in his mouth, clenching it between the stubs of his teeth. Then he went on. "You fellas wouldn't happen to have the price of a drink to spare, would you?"

"Here you go, old-timer," Longarm said as he dug in his pocket. He brought out a coin and flipped it to Cap'n Andy, who caught it with surprising deftness. The old man grinned, bit the coin to check its authenticity, then strolled off whistling toward a waterfront tavern with the name RED MIKE'S scrawled on a board nailed over the door.

"Where did you meet that old man?" Ki asked Longarm.

"He was hangin' around the docks here," Longarm replied. "I figured him for a beggar right off, but he's a friendly old cuss, so I don't begrudge helping him out."

"Do you think he was right about the storm?"

"*Quién sabe?* A few years ago, I met a fella down south of here, at Rockport, who was interested in forecasting the weather. He claimed that with enough scientific gadgets to take measurements of the temperature and the wind speed and the air pressure, things like that, you could predict it. Could be he was right. I like to watch the way the animals are behaving myself." Longarm nodded toward a nearby corral, where half a dozen horses were milling around skittishly. "From the looks of that, something's got those horses upset. Might be a storm."

Ki frowned. "I believe that Jessie and I will set out for the Circle Star as soon as possible after her ship arrives."

"That won't leave much time for me and her to say howdy," Longarm complained.

"I'm sorry, Marshal, but Jessie's safety is more important than your . . . howdies."

A fresh gust of wind reinforced that feeling by making the flags tied on poles along the wharf pop loudly as they whipped back and forth.

"I reckon you're gonna wait right here for the *Harry Fulton* to show up?" Longarm asked.

Ki nodded. "I believe I will."

Longarm put his cheroot back in his mouth and nodded. "Then I believe I'll wait with you."

Jessie stood at the forward railing with Andre Dumond, watching the shore draw closer. Captain O'Malley was up on the bridge with the helmsman, and the other officers and crew of the *Harry Fulton* were busy with their tasks. The wind blew briskly, billowing the sails and sending the ship skimming over the increasingly choppy waters.

"I have traveled a great deal at sea and always enjoyed it," Andre said, "but I do not mind admitting that today I will be glad to feel the solid ground under my feet again."

Jessie agreed. "I've had enough of the ocean for a while."

She wondered if Ki would be there to meet her. She was

going to be very surprised if she didn't see him waiting on the wharf. The only thing that would keep him away, she knew, was if his injured leg hadn't healed properly. She couldn't bring herself to believe that would happen.

Captain O'Malley had a telescope extended and held to his eye so that he could peer through it. When he lowered the spyglass, he called to Jessie, "The warnin' flags aren't up at the Signal Office. Maybe the blow won't be too bad."

"We'll be safely ashore before the storm gets here, won't we?" Andre asked her.

The sky was overcast now, but the darkest clouds were still far to the rear. Jessie smiled and said, "We'll be ashore in less than half an hour. That storm is still hours away, if it even comes through here. Squalls can change direction pretty capriciously, even big ones like that."

O'Malley called a slight course correction to the helmsman. The ship responded as the man turned the big wheel mounted on the bridge. The sails caught the wind even better now. Within minutes, Jessie could make out several men moving along the wharf toward the spot where the *Harry Fulton* would dock. She thought she recognized one of them, a tall, lithe figure dressed mostly in black.

But who was the even taller man beside him? Something about him struck Jessie as familiar. He was wearing a flat-crowned hat the color of snuff . . .

"Excuse me, Andre," Jessie said suddenly. Before the Frenchman could ask her what she was doing, she turned and hurried toward the steep, narrow steps that led up to the bridge. She took them with an athletic ease, being careful not to trip on the long hem of her skirt.

Captain O'Malley looked surprised and not all that happy to see her up there. "What can I do for ye, Miss Starbuck?" he asked.

"I'd like to borrow your telescope, Captain," she replied.

"Me spyglass? Well, I suppose 'twould be all right." He had closed the telescope and slipped it into his coat pocket. He took it out now and handed it over to Jessie, who swiftly extended it and raised it to her right eye. She closed the left one and squinted through the glass.

It took Jessie a moment of moving the telescope around before she was able to focus on the wharf. When she did, the figures of the men waiting there sprang into sharp relief. Most of them were dockworkers, waiting to catch the large hawsers thrown from the ship by members of the crew and make them fast to the thick pilings that supported the wharf. Jessie saw Ki standing there as well, his presence coming as no surprise.

But she *was* surprised to see the man standing next to Ki. She instantly recognized the tanned, strong-featured face, the curling longhorn mustache, the Stetson and the brown tweed suit and the high-topped black boots. She would know that muscular, powerful frame and that ruggedly handsome face anywhere.

Longarm.

Chapter 8

Longarm's eyes followed the ship's progress, the white sails bright against the leaden sky behind it. When it was a couple of hundred yards away, he could make out a green-clad figure on the bridge, who had shining golden hair.

That had to be Jessie, he told himself. It was going to be damned nice to see her again, even if Ki got his way and they left Indianola once Jessie's bags were unloaded. There would at least be time for a hug and a kiss between old friends.

Longarm saw a reflection from something in Jessie's hands, and realized that she was holding a spyglass. Knowing that she was watching him, he lifted a hand in greeting. On the ship's bridge, Jessie lowered the telescope and lifted an arm above her head to return the wave.

"Looks like she's glad to see us," Longarm commented to Ki.

"One of us anyway."

Longarm laughed. "Hell, old son, don't start thinkin' like that. You mean more to Jessie than I ever will."

"I would not be so sure, Marshal. Don't mistake that uncertainty for jealousy on my part, however. I have never wanted anything for Jessie except her happiness, wherever she might find it."

"We're in agreement on that then."

One of the roughnecks who worked on the dock came along and ordered in a harsh voice, "Move back, you two. Real men got work to do here."

Longarm saw Ki stiffen, and knew that he didn't appreciate the veiled insult. "Let it go," Longarm advised in a low voice. "We don't want Jessie to come home to a brawl, do we?"

"I doubt if she would mind all that much."

Longarm chuckled again. "Yeah, you're probably right about that, come to think of it. She's started a few ruckuses of her own in her time."

For now, however, Longarm and Ki were content to get out of the way and allow the burly workers to catch the hawsers and make them fast as the *Harry Fulton* drew up next to the wharf. The ship's captain had brought the vessel in with consummate skill, so that its hull barely kissed the fenders.

Longarm watched Jessie hurry down from the bridge. By the time the ship's crew had the gangplank in place between the deck and wharf, she was waiting to cross it. "Ki!" she called. "Custis!"

Longarm nudged Ki in the side with an elbow. "See? What'd I tell you?"

Ki ignored him. His normal reserve had slipped a little. He wore a big grin on his face as Jessie crossed the gangplank and threw herself into his arms. The man folded her into his embrace and hugged her tightly.

Longarm saw a tall, sort of gawky-looking fella leaning on the ship's railing nearby, watching the reunion between

Jessie and Ki. The man frowned like he didn't care for what he was seeing.

After a moment, she stepped back from Ki. She turned to Longarm. "Custis! It's wonderful to see you again."

She put her arms around his neck and tilted her head back to receive the kiss he gave her. Their mouths met with a fierce intensity. Longarm thought she tasted just as hot and sweet as ever. He slid his arms around her trim waist and held her against him, enjoying the way her body molded to his without being too brazen about it.

After a moment, Ki cleared his throat and asked, "Is this gentleman coming off the ship acquainted with you, Jessie?"

She broke the kiss with Longarm—drat the luck, he thought—and turned, still smiling. "Yes, he is," she said. She stepped forward to take the man's hand as he reached the end of the gangplank. He was the gent Longarm had spotted at the railing earlier. "Andre, this is Ki," Jessie said. "I told you about him."

"But of course," the man called Andre murmured.

Jessie used her free hand to indicate Longarm. "And this is a dear old friend of mine, Deputy United States Marshal Custis Long. Boys, meet M'sieu Andre Dumond."

"Howdy," Longarm said with a nod, while Ki spoke to Dumond in French. Ki was the sort of hombre who could always surprise you with the things he knew.

Both of them shook hands with Dumond, while Jessie explained, "Andre is a cotton trader from New Orleans. He's on his way to Mexico on business."

"It is a pleasure to meet you two gentlemen," Dumond said, even though from what Longarm had seen earlier, he hadn't been too pleased with Jessie's greeting. Longarm knew Jessie pretty well, and figured there had been a little shipboard romance between her and Dumond. That was over now, though. Jessie was headed back to the Circle Star, and Dumond was going on to Mexico. In all likelihood, their paths would never cross again.

"What are you doing here, Custis?" Jessie asked, still holding Dumond's hand. "Don't tell me you were on a case, I'll bet. Chasing a fugitive."

Longarm nodded. "That's right."

"And you caught him?"

"With Ki's help. The buryin's this afternoon," he added. "If the storm holds off."

"The captain tells me it will be several hours before the storm gets here," Jessie said. "I want you to meet him, too." She let go of Dumond's hand at last and turned to call to the man who had come down from the bridge and now stood on deck near the gangplank, watching to make sure that the ship was moored properly. "Captain O'Malley!"

The captain, a big, redheaded Irishman who looked tough enough to have cleaned out all the waterfront dives between here and Havana, came onto the wharf at Jessie's summons. He shook hands with Longarm and Ki as Jessie introduced him.

"How long do you plan to be in port, Captain?" Ki asked.

O'Malley cast a wary eye toward the skies. "We'll not be sailin' until the morrow at least. I won't take the ship back out in weather like that."

"Perhaps we can all have dinner tonight," Jessie suggested.

"I thought we'd load up the wagon and head for the Circle Star immediately," Ki said.

Jessie frowned. "There's no need to rush off like that, is there?"

"Surely you recall that Indianola was nearly destroyed by a hurricane several years ago. I'm not sure it's a good idea to stay here tonight."

"But this isn't a hurricane," Jessie protested. "It's just a storm. A squall. Isn't that right, Captain?"

O'Malley shrugged broad shoulders. "All I can tell ye is that the hurricane flags aren't up at the Signal Office. That means there haven't been any warnin' signals from the observation posts on up the coast betwixt here and Galveston."

Jessie turned to Ki. "You see, it's perfectly safe."

Longarm wasn't sure he would go so far as to say that, but from what he had seen of the buildings in Indianola, they were built to be extra sturdy. He supposed that was because of the lessons learned by the citizens from the previous hurricane.

Ki looked like he wanted to argue with Jessie, but after a moment he nodded. "As you wish," he said. "I'll get a room for you at the hotel."

She nodded, then turned to O'Malley and Dumond. "I'll expect to see both of you in the hotel dining room at seven."

"I shall be there," Dumond promised, while O'Malley grinned crookedly and said, "Can't very well turn down an invite from the owner of the whole blamed shippin' line, now can I?"

"It's not a command performance," Jessie said with a slight tartness to her tone.

"Oh, no, ma'am, I didn't mean anything like that," O'Malley assured her. "I'll be there, and it's thankin' you for your kindness that I am." He jerked a thumb over his shoulder. "Right now, though, I got to see to it that the cargo comin' off here gets unloaded properlike."

"And I should return to my cabin," Dumond said. "But I will see you later, mademoiselle." He took Jessie's hand and held it for a second before releasing it and turning to go back up the gangplank.

"Thought for a second that French fella was gonna kiss the back of your hand," Longarm said when Dumond was gone.

"Would that have bothered you, Custis?"

"Bothered me? Nope." Longarm felt his ears growing unaccountably warm. "It's none of my business what that Frenchman kisses."

"Good," Jessie said with a sparkle in her eyes and a grin on her full red lips. She linked arms with Longarm and Ki, one of them on either side of her, and started along the wharf toward Indianola.

Chapter 9

The Gulf Hotel was the finest hostelry in Indianola, with comfortably appointed rooms, curtains on the windows, woven rugs on the floor, and big, soft beds. Longarm knew that for a fact because he had slept in one of them the night before.

And also because he occupied one of them now, stretched out flat on his back, buck naked, with Jessie Starbuck straddling his hips and riding his cock.

"It's been . . . *uh!* . . . too long since we did this, Custis," she said as she rested her hands on his broad chest. Her hips pumped hard as she sheathed and unsheathed his thick shaft inside her.

"Amen to that," Longarm managed to say. He raised his hands and cupped her high, firm breasts in his palms, rotating them in sensuous circles. After he had done that for a few moments, he shifted his grip so that he could strum her erect nipples with his thumbs. Jessie closed her eyes and sighed with pleasure as those brown buds of pebbled flesh hardened even more under Longarm's arousing touch.

Longarm, Jessie, and Ki had eaten lunch together in the

hotel dining room. Outside, the wind continued to blow harder, and the clouds had thickened and grown darker. The talk among the other guests and the locals in the dining room was mostly of the coming storm. People were excited about the possibility of the drought breaking, but no one seemed particularly frightened. After all, in the past the Signal Office had put out the warning flags every time there was the least chance of a hurricane, and today no flags were flying.

Following the meal, Jessie had yawned and mentioned that she wanted to lie down for a while. Longarm caught the message in the glance she gave him, and knew that she would welcome his company in her room. Jessie went upstairs, while Longarm stepped out onto the hotel porch with Ki and smoked a cheroot as they chatted and watched the comings and goings on the busy street.

Then Longarm had made his excuses and told Ki he was going up to his own room for a while. He had a feeling that Ki knew perfectly well where he was really going. There were no real secrets between Jessie and Ki, but they always played this game anyway, pretending that the half-Japanese, half-American friend was unaware of what was actually going on.

Longarm put those thoughts out of his mind as he knocked on the door of Jessie's room and heard her call softly, "Come in."

She had pulled the curtains so that the gray light stealing in around their edges only dimly lit the room. Jessie stood next to the four-poster bed, wearing some sort of gauzy wrap that did nothing to conceal the fact she was naked underneath it. She smiled a welcome as Longarm closed the door behind him.

"What if it hadn't been me knocking on your door?" he had asked with a smile of his own.

"Don't you think I know your knock by now, Custis?" As she spoke, she had shrugged her shoulders so that the wrap slid off them and fell to the floor, puddling around her feet. She stood there before him, as gloriously naked as a goddess, her honey-toned skin smooth and sleek and lovely, the thick waves of her hair tumbling around her shoulders. The triangle of fine-spun hair at the juncture of her thighs was a shade darker than that on her head, with more of the copper tint than the gold.

Longarm had moved toward her, unable to resist the lure of her beauty any longer. There was something incredibly arousing about holding a naked woman when he was still fully clothed, especially when that woman was Jessica Starbuck. She raised her face to his for the hungry kiss that he brought down on her mouth. Their lips parted with the ease of remembered passion, and their tongues met and swirled around in a heated dance.

After that, Jessie helped him with his boots, turning her back to him and bending over, which provided quite an arousing view. Then she unbuttoned his trousers and pushed them down along with his long underwear, kneeling in front of him as she did so. Jessie opened her mouth to take him inside for a few moments as she reached between his legs to cup the heavy sac that hung there.

It had been so long since they'd been together, Longarm had worried that he would explode right then and there in the hot, wet cavern of her mouth. So he'd taken hold of her shoulders and raised her up, gently guiding her back onto the bed. As her thighs splayed open in invitation, he moved between them and touched her, finding that she was already slick and ready for him. He paused long enough to heighten her arousal even more with his fingers and tongue. Then Jessie had urged him onto his back and swung a leg over him. She caught hold of his long, thick shaft and guided it to her entrance. He was so hard and she was so wet that he went inside her with no effort at all. She sat back so that his entire length was buried within her, and stayed like that for long moments, luxuriating in the sensation of fullness, until her hips began to pump instinctively.

Now Longarm struggled to maintain control as the slick, buttery walls of her sex clasped and unclasped on his cock. Jessie bit her bottom lip and tossed her head back and forth as she rode him. He saw a flush spreading across her chest as she shuddered. Her culmination had her in its inexorable grip.

Knowing that, Longarm gave in to his own urges and allowed his climax to boil up from deep inside him. He gripped Jessie's thighs to steady her as his hips bucked up from the bed and he thrust as far into her as he could go. His juices exploded from him in a series of shuddering, white-hot bursts, filling her to overflowing. Jessie cried out in passion.

As the last of Longarm's seed drained from him, he felt a great lassitude sweep through him. That delicious languor caught Jessie as well, judging from the way every muscle in her body seemed to go limp at the same time, so that she sagged forward to rest on his chest. Longarm felt the strong, steady beat of her heart through her sleek, tawny skin. His own heart was galloping along pretty good just then, too.

He put his arms around her as she pillowed her head on his shoulder. He stroked her back, ran a hand down to the swelling curves of her rump. His boldly exploring touch between her cheeks made the velvety walls that still enclosed his member clench around it.

"Don't you do it, Custis Long," she whispered a warning. "Don't you make me go off again. It might kill me."

"Well, I wouldn't want that," Longarm said with a chuckle.

His amusement vanished as a particularly strong gust of wind rattled the windowpane. Jessie opened her eyes and tilted her head in that direction, too.

"I sure hope everybody who says this storm ain't gonna amount to much is right," Longarm said.

"I trust Captain O'Malley's judgment . . . but even he admitted that it's almost impossible to predict the sea."

"There's still time for you and Ki to load up the wagon and head inland."

Jessie shook her head. "What good would that do? Then we might be caught out in the open when the storm hits, rather than being in a good sturdy building."

That was true, thought Longarm. Here in Indianola, there would be the danger of flooding if the storm brought in some huge waves, but there were also the winds to consider. If this was a hurricane, the winds would be just as fierce for miles inland, toppling trees, spawning tornadoes, and sending debris flying through the air with the speed and force of deadly missiles. Jessie was right—even if she and Ki had left Indianola as soon as the ship arrived, it was doubtful they could have gotten far enough inland to be completely safe.

"Reckon we'll just have to hope for the best," Longarm said. "I'm glad we got to spend a little time together, no matter what happens from here on out."

"So am I." Jessie rolled off him to lie beside him, propped up on one elbow. "Custis, I was thinking . . . what are the chances Billy Vail would allow you enough time to come back to the Circle Star with Ki and me?"

"I reckon it would depend on what other jobs Billy's got lined up for me."

"Surely being a lawman can wait awhile. There'll always be plenty of outlaws for you to chase."

Longarm tucked his hands behind his head. "I ain't so sure about that. The West is changin'. It's gettin' more and more civilized all the time. Most of the Indians are on reservations, the railroads go just about everywhere, and I hear that they're puttin' in more and more of those telephone gadgets, so people can talk to folks far away without even being there. Civilization's gonna put all the owlhoots out of business sooner or later."

Jessie let out an unladylike snort of disbelief. "Do you really believe that, Custis?"

"Well . . ." He rasped a thumbnail along his jawline as he pondered her question. "Come to think of it, that don't seem likely, does it? Human nature bein' what it is, I mean."

Jessie sat up. "No, it doesn't seem likely at all. Some people are always going to be greedy and angry and filled with hate. And some of them will act on those feelings. That's why the world is always going to need men like you, Custis. Men who stand up for what's right, even when it's difficult and even dangerous to do so. The world will always need heroes."

It was Longarm's turn to snort. "Don't go pinnin' no hero sign on me, Jessie. I'm just a fella who tries to do his job the best he can."

"That's a hero in my book," Jessie whispered as she leaned closer to him. "And you didn't answer my question about coming back to the Circle Star with me."

"We'll just have to wait and see what Billy says whenever he gets around to answerin' my telegram."

"All right. I suppose that's the best I can do for now." She rested a hand on his chest for a second, then slid it down over his belly toward his groin. "Speaking of things standing up for what's right . . ."

Chapter 10

By nightfall, the wind was blowing so hard that most people had retreated indoors. The optimism that had been common in the town earlier in the day had faded and been replaced by growing worries.

In the dining room of the Gulf Hotel, Longarm, Jessie, Ki, Captain Seamus O'Malley, and Andre Dumond sat at a large, round table having dinner. Longarm saw how the Irishman's gaze flicked toward the windows again and again, and he knew O'Malley must be worried about the ship. The *Harry Fulton* was tied up securely, but that wouldn't matter if the storm washed away the entire wharf.

The diners at the other tables were nervous, too, and one by one they emptied out, until Longarm and his companions were the only ones still eating. What had been meant to be a festive occasion had turned into a somber gathering instead.

O'Malley finally threw down his napkin and said, "I'd best be gettin' back to the ship."

"You can't be planning to spend the night on board, Captain," Jessie protested. "Stay here instead."

"A captain's place is on his ship," O'Malley insisted with a stubborn frown. "Anyway, I left a couple o' men on night watch, and I want to tell them to get ashore."

"But you're going to stay . . . alone."

O'Malley shrugged.

Longarm saw the angry gleam in Jessie's eyes, so he had a pretty good idea what was coming. Jessie leveled her gaze across the table at O'Malley and said, "Captain, I hate to pull rank, but I *am* the owner of that ship and you work for me. I'm ordering you to come back ashore once you've relieved those crew members of their duty."

O'Malley stiffened. "Leave the ship to its fate, is that what you're sayin', ma'am?"

"It is. Your lives are more important."

"Then ye might as well go ahead and relieve me of command, because ye've given me an order I cannot carry out."

"But you know there's nothing you can do. Whatever the storm does, you can't stop it."

"I can go with me ship, wherever the storm takes it."

"Go down with the ship, you mean?" Jessie demanded. When O'Malley didn't answer her, she turned to Longarm and Ki and asked, "Can't the two of you talk some sense into him?"

"A man does what he must," Ki replied.

"I'm glad to see that somebody understands," O'Malley said.

Jessie looked at Longarm again. "Custis?"

Longarm shrugged. "Sorry, Jessie. I ain't in the habit of tellin' a fella how he ought to live his life." He looked at O'Malley. "I'll say this much, though. It'd take a damn fool to think he ought to stay on a boat on a night like this."

O'Malley's big hands clenched into fists. "A damn fool,

is it?" he said. "I'm gonna be a mite busy for a while, Marshal. Why don't you and I continue this discussion at a later date?"

Longarm shrugged again. "Whatever you want, Captain. When I was a boy back in West-by-God-Virginia, though, my ma raised me to speak my mind. That's all I done here."

"Aye, and sometimes a man must stand behind his opinions."

"No argument there."

Andre Dumond suddenly spoke up. "Please, gentlemen, there's no need for such veiled threats and posturing. We're all just on edge because of the storm. We should relax." He reached for his glass. "Have some more wine."

"Not me." O'Malley shoved his chair away from the table and stood up. "I'll be seein' you." He put his cap on, gave Jessie a curt nod, and stalked out of the dining room, pausing at the entrance just long enough to glance back and say, "'Tis grateful I am for the fine meal, ma'am." Then he was gone, out into the stormy night.

"Well, *hell*," Jessie said. "Why wouldn't he listen to reason?"

"According to his beliefs," Ki said, "he was being very reasonable."

"Just not very practical," Longarm added.

"You're a fine one to talk," Jessie snapped. "I'll bet if there was some outlaw out there you were supposed to catch tonight, you'd be going after him."

Longarm chuckled. "More than likely," he admitted.

The proprietor of the hotel came into the dining room. "Folks, I'm going to have to ask you to leave," he said. "We're going to be boarding up the windows, and the people who work here want to get to their homes."

"I don't blame 'em a bit," Longarm said as he put his

napkin on the table. "What about the windows in our rooms?"

"They'll be boarded up, too," the hotel owner promised. "Just as soon as we can get to them."

Longarm listened to the howling wind for a second, then said, "Might ought to hurry."

The man nodded grimly and left the room. The sound of hammers could already be heard outside.

Longarm, Jessie, Ki, and Dumond stood up. Longarm said, "I think I'll run up the street to the Powder Horn and pick up a bottle. It's liable to be a long night, and some good Maryland rye might come in handy before morning."

Dumond reached out and snagged the wine bottle that sat on the table still half-full. "I believe I will take this with me," he said. "With your permission, of course, Jessie."

She waved a hand. "Of course."

Dumond suggested, "I would be glad to bring it to your room and share it . . ."

His voice trailed away as Jessie shook her head. "Thank you, Andre, but that's not necessary."

"I . . . see." Dumond glanced at Longarm, and the big lawman saw the anger and jealousy in the Frenchman's eyes.

Dumond forced a smile and a Gallic shrug and bade them all good night. That left just Longarm, Jessie, and Ki in the dining room. Longarm said to Ki, "See that Jessie gets to her room all right, would you?"

"Of course," Ki said.

"I don't need an escort," Jessie said. "I'm fine, Custis."

"I know that." Something windblown clattered across the roof of the hotel, causing Longarm to glance upward. "I just don't reckon it's a good idea for anybody to be alone tonight if they don't have to."

Jessie grimaced and shrugged her acceptance. She and Ki headed for the stairs while Longarm went through the lobby and stepped out onto the boardwalk in front of the hotel.

He caught some motion from the corner of his eye, and turned his head to see Deputy Hank Anderson hurrying along the street toward him. "There you are, Marshal!" Anderson hailed him, raising his voice so Longarm could hear him over the wind. "I was just comin' to look for you."

"Is there a problem, Hank?" Longarm asked, half-shouting himself.

"It's that prisoner o' yours. He's raisin' a commotion, yellin' about how we're all gonna die in this storm and sayin' I got to let him go so he won't drown or blow away."

Longarm shook his head. "I've seen that jail of yours. It's the sturdiest building in town. He'll be safer there than anywhere else."

"That's what I tried to tell him. Anyway, I explained to him that if he drowns or blows away, all it means is that he won't have to hang. That didn't seem to comfort him, though."

"What do you want me to do?" Longarm asked.

"Unless you can make this storm turn and go somewheres else, I don't reckon there's anything you *can* do. I just wanted to let you know that if that hombre keeps bellerin', I'm liable to tie and gag him. He's gettin' on my nerves."

"Have at it," Longarm said. "I'm not gonna complain. You'd best be careful that he don't jump you and try to escape."

"He won't do that. I got a couple o' jailers who'll help me. They came in tonight because they figured the jail was the safest place in town, too. You're welcome to join us."

Longarm thought about Jessie and shook his head. "Thanks, but I'll pass. I've got friends here in the hotel I need to look after."

"Suit yourself." Anderson snorted. "Damn hurricane."

"You think that's what it is?"

"Isaac Reed down at the signal office says it ain't. He's got a wire hooked direct to Galveston, and he says no warnin's have come over it. But I was here back in '75, and I don't like the looks o' this. No, sir."

"Well, good luck, Deputy," Longarm said as he held out his hand.

Anderson shook it. "You, too, Marshal."

The two lawmen parted company. Anderson headed back toward the jail while Longarm went the other way, bound for the Powder Horn Saloon.

When he got there, he found several men nailing planks at angles across the front windows. Longarm recognized one of them as the bartender, who might be the owner, too, as far as he knew. The man turned to Longarm and yelled over the roaring wind, "Sorry, we're closed!"

"Thought I'd get a bottle of Maryland rye!" Longarm shouted back.

The bartender shook his head. "Sorry! All the stock's boxed up in the storage room until after this storm's over!"

Longarm sighed. If Hank Anderson hadn't stopped him, he might have gotten here in time to snag that bottle. He didn't blame the saloon man for trying to save his business, though. He just nodded and said, "Good luck then!"

"Good luck to you, too, Marshal!" The bartender glanced up at the angry heavens. "Reckon we're all gonna need it!"

Longarm didn't doubt that. He turned and walked quickly back toward the hotel. He had to lean hard to one side just to stay upright as the gale pounded against him.

If this wasn't a hurricane, it was the next thing to it, he thought. He had seen how low-lying the whole settlement was, barely above the level of the water. The waves wouldn't have to rise very high at all before they washed ashore and flooded everything in their path. A bad feeling filled him. Now that he had been outside and seen how ominous things were looking, he realized that it would have been a good idea if everybody in Indianola had gotten the hell out of town while it was still possible to do so. Now they were all trapped, at the mercy of whatever the storm was going to do.

He hoped Seamus O'Malley had changed his mind about spending the night on the ship. He liked the big, rugged Irishman, and he was fairly certain that if O'Malley tried to stay on board the *Harry Fulton* tonight, no one would ever see him again.

Of course, Longarm thought as he neared the hotel, that might be true of all of them . . .

With that gloomy foreboding occupying his mind, he didn't notice the other danger until it was too late. In the darkness of the alley beside the hotel, Colt flame suddenly bloomed in the thick shadows, and even over the racket of the wind, Longarm heard shots slam out.

Chapter 11

"I really don't need a keeper, you know," Jessie said as she and Ki went up the stairs to the hotel's second floor.

"Indulge me," Ki said. "Your father brought me to this country to be your bodyguard as well as your companion after all."

"That was when the Cartel represented such a danger," Jessie pointed out. "There's not much anybody can do about a storm like this."

"The Cartel still exists . . . or rather, it has been reborn. But it is still a threat."

"To be dealt with at another time." They reached the second-floor landing and turned down the corridor toward their rooms. "Right now, I'm more worried about that wind—"

As if to justify the concern Jessie was expressing, the window at the far end of the hallway suddenly shattered, crashing inward in a spray of glass. Jessie cried out involuntarily and flinched back. Ki stepped in front of her, instinctively moving to protect her, to get between her and danger.

A long, jagged piece of a thick plank rested in the

window frame, surrounded by shards of glass. It probably weighed quite a bit, but obviously the wind had picked it up and carried it through the air like it was no more than a bit of straw. That wind now whistled down the hallway from the broken window.

Several doors popped open, and startled guests peered out to see what had happened. The lamps blew out in the gusts, however, dropping a black pall over the corridor. Jessie reached out in the darkness to clutch her companion's arm. "Ki?"

"I'm here," he told her. "Let's get you to your room."

"That window—"

"There's nothing we can do about it. It should have been boarded up earlier. Then it might not have been broken."

The citizens of Indianola had severely underestimated the strength of the storm that was now coming in, Jessie thought. The attitude that because a hurricane had hit the settlement once, it couldn't happen again, was proving to be dangerously optimistic.

But they might be able to ride it out here on the second floor of the hotel, Jessie thought. She wished Longarm was with them, instead of wandering around town looking for a bottle of whiskey.

She and Ki had to work their way along the corridor by feel. They reached the door to her room, which was number seven. Jessie's fingers traced the brass numeral tacked onto the door, so she knew they were in the right place. She dug in her bag for the key, found it, and thrust it into the lock. As she turned the knob, Ki said, "Let me go first and light the lamp."

He stepped through the opening door in front of her. Flame flared up from the match in his hand as he struck it with his thumbnail.

Jessie gasped in surprise as that harsh, sudden glare revealed five men crowded into her room. In the glimpse she
had of them, she saw that they all wore long black dusters
and had broad-brimmed black hats pulled low over their
faces. "Get the Chinaman!" one man growled as several of
them rushed at Ki.

Attacking Ki head-on was usually a mistake. He dropped
the match, and as it spiraled toward the floor, still burning,
its light cast grotesque, twisting shadows. Ki leaped high
and kicked one of his assailants in the chest, spun and drove
an elbow into another's jaw.

"Get the woman!" the man giving the orders yelled.

"Jessie, go!" Ki said as he landed agilely, bent at the
waist, and lashed out with another kick that landed in a
man's belly. As the attacker doubled over, Ki kicked him
again, this time in the head.

Jessie didn't want to desert Ki, even though she knew
that five-to-one odds were hardly insurmountable for him.
But she also knew that if she stayed and tried to help him,
he would be distracted by worry about her, and such dis-
tractions could prove fatal. She turned to run back along the
hall toward the stairs. Maybe she could find Longarm, she
thought, and he would be able to help Ki.

She had taken only a few steps before she crashed into
something almost as hard and unyielding as a brick wall.
She cried out in pain and shock. Ki must have heard her,
because he shouted, "Jessie! What—"

The way his voice cut off so abruptly frightened her. She
wondered fleetingly if he had been hit or stabbed or injured
in some other way. She didn't have time to ponder the question, though, because strong arms closed around her in a
brutal grip. She started to scream, but a hand clapped over
her mouth, silencing her.

"Help the others," a voice rasped. The wind now howled through the corridor because windows broken elsewhere in the hotel by flying debris created a draft, and it distorted the voice. Jessie thought it was familiar anyway. She struggled as hard as she could, twisting and writhing in an attempt to break the hold on her, but her captor was too strong. She thought he was wearing one of the long dusters, too.

Violent crashing and thudding from the direction of her room told her that Ki was still alive and still putting up a fight. The reinforcements that had come up the hall behind them might be too much for him, though. As Jessie jerked around, she caught a glimpse of men fighting in the hallway. It was too dark for her to make out any details, but she had no doubt that Ki was in the middle of that struggling knot.

The man who had hold of her started dragging her toward the stairs. "Don't fight," he grated in her ear. "You will just make things worse for yourself."

Don't fight, *hell*! Alex Starbuck hadn't raised his daughter to give in meekly whenever danger threatened. Jessie drove an elbow back into the man's belly. The blow didn't seem to do any good, so she reached behind her as best she could, fighting to get her hand on his face. When she did, she clawed at it with her fingernails.

"*Merde*!" he exclaimed. The French obscenity sent a shock through her. Now she knew why his voice had been familiar, even muffled by the wind the way it was.

The man with one hand clamped brutally over her mouth and the other arm around her, pressing painfully into her breasts as he dragged her along the hallway, was Andre.

Ki had fought many battles in darkness, or near darkness. When one could not *see* one's enemies, one had to *feel* them. Instinct told him where they were, where he needed to strike. He had the advantage, too, of being alone. Anyone he struck was bound to be an enemy.

But he was even more outnumbered now than he had been when the battle began. More men had rushed up the hall behind him and Jessie. He had heard her cry out, knew she was in danger, and started to call to her when something—probably a gun butt—slammed against his head and sent him staggering against the wall. He caught himself and used the wall to launch himself off. As he flew across the corridor, his feet flashed out in powerful kicks and his stiffened hands slashed like knives at his enemies.

Men grunted in pain and fell away from him, but there were always others to replace them. Fists crashed against him. Someone kicked the back of his knee, and that leg folded beneath him. It had to be blind luck; no one could have aimed that blow in this stygian gloom.

Someone grabbed his hair. "He's down!" the man shouted. "The Chinaman's dow—"

The triumphant yell ended in a gurgle of agony as Ki's stiffened hand shot forward like a sword into the man's crotch. His other hand bunched in the front of the man's duster, but before Ki could haul himself to his feet, more blows showered down on him. Gun butts and barrels pummeled him. Gunsights tore his flesh, leaving blood-dripping cuts on his face. He was shoved back and forth, kicked, punched, lambasted until consciousness threatened to flee from him. He struggled not to pass out.

A heavy weight landed on his back, driving him forward. He sprawled on the corridor floor. A man yelled, "Stomp him! Stomp him!" Then, "Ow! Shit! Not me, you dumb sons o' bitches! The Chinaman!"

The weight left Ki's back, but he was no longer able to rise. Booted feet slammed into him again and again, rocking him back and forth. Although his spirit was as indomitable as ever, his body was too battered and bruised to respond to the commands of his heart and his brain. He knew that the men were going to stomp and kick him to death, and there was nothing he could do to stop them.

Suddenly, a huge roar rose all around them, and Ki had the bizarre thought that a freight train was coming along the hotel corridor. A man screamed, and then rending crashes filled the air. The kicking stopped. Ki rolled onto his back and forced his eyes open. He hadn't been aware until this instant that they were closed.

The sight that met them was like something he had never before witnessed. The roof of the hotel had lifted right off the walls, and now it was breaking up into massive chunks as it was whirled around and around by madly spinning winds. A tornado was right on top of the hotel, Ki realized.

The men who had been trying to kill him were fleeing for their lives now. Thin and faint, as if they came from miles away, Ki heard terrified screams. To his amazement, the vortex suddenly plucked one of the men running down the hall into the air. He shrieked and flailed his arms and legs, but there was nothing he could do. He disappeared into the tornado's hungry maw as if he had never been there.

The floor shuddered underneath Ki. He hoped now that the kidnappers had gotten Jessie out of the building, because he feared that the hotel was about to collapse. Of course, being caught outside in this terrible storm wouldn't be any safer. They were all doomed, and a part of Ki wanted to close his eyes and make peace with his ancestors, for surely they would soon be welcoming him into the shining realm they now inhabited.

But he was too stubborn to simply give up like that. He rolled onto his side and forced himself onto his hands and knees. With one hand against the wall, he struggled to climb to his feet. The building swayed crazily, sickeningly, in the terrific winds. It felt as if it were shifting on its very foundations.

The roaring faded. The tornado had moved on to wreak death and destruction elsewhere in Indianola. But the hurricane winds remained, howling like mad banshees. As if a giant bucket had been upended, drenching rain suddenly slammed down from the sky. With no roof above his head to protect him anymore, Ki was soaked to the skin in seconds.

That was a minor inconvenience compared to everything else that was going on. A voice in his head shouted a warning to him. He had to get out before the building collapsed. He feared there was no sanctuary to be found in Indianola on this fateful night, but if he stayed here, he was doomed.

He found the stairs, started down them. Too late. With a series of shattering cracks, the walls themselves gave way. The stairs fell out from under Ki's feet, and he plummeted after them. He caught a glimpse of churning water below him, and realized that giant waves borne by the hurricane had come ashore. The hotel was floating now, even as it fell apart around him.

Then Ki plunged into the cold water, felt a terrific impact against his head, and knew nothing more.

Chapter 12

Longarm felt as much as heard the wind-rip of a bullet's passage beside his ear as he threw himself to the side. His hand flashed across his body to the Colt in the cross-draw rig as he fell. Muzzle flashes continued to blossom in the alley. He felt a slug pluck at his coat as he landed on his knees at the edge of the boardwalk.

The revolver in his hand bucked twice as he triggered a couple of shots toward the alley. He rolled under the board-walk's railing and dropped to the street. That gave him a little cover, but not much. Not enough to allow him to stay there. Instead, he snapped another shot at the bushwhackers hidden in the alley, and powered up into a run toward a nearby trough where teamsters watered their mules.

Longarm's hat flew off his head. He didn't know if the wind had taken it, or if a bullet had knocked it off. Either way, it was gone, carried away by the screaming wind.

He launched himself into a dive that landed him flat on his stomach on the street with the water trough between him and the alley mouth. Shots still roared out like thunder. He heard slugs thudding into the thick wood of the trough.

Longarm raised himself high enough to fire twice more at the men trying to kill him. That emptied his Colt, since he normally carried just five rounds in the cylinder so the hammer could rest on an empty chamber. He rolled onto his side so he could pull more cartridges out of his pocket, then rolled the other way, opened the cylinder and dumped the empties, and started thumbing in the fresh cartridges.

While he was doing that, the guns of the ambushers fell silent. Not a good sign, thought Longarm. They probably figured he was reloading, and might be taking advantage of the lull to spread out and catch him in a cross fire.

He knew that was true when a shot suddenly came from a different direction and chewed splinters from the water trough only inches from his head. He snapped the Colt's cylinder closed and rolled farther into the street, catching a glimpse as he did so of two men charging toward him. The wind caught the long black dusters they wore and billowed the coats behind them, so that they flapped like the wings of birds of prey. The men fired, their guns spouting flame.

Longarm's Colt blasted. One of the men went backward as the slug drove into his chest. The other one veered to the side and kept firing.

Unfortunately for the second bushwhacker, he didn't have eyes in the back of his head. He didn't see the piece of debris that came sailing up the street behind him, carried by the demonic winds. It was a window shutter, or maybe part of a door, Longarm couldn't tell which. But it slammed into the back of the bushwhacker's head and shoulders with the force of a runaway train, flattening him in the street. The man didn't move again.

He wasn't the last of the ambushers, though. Bullets plowed into the street from the opposite direction, just as Longarm expected. He twisted around, trying to get a shot off, but his gun flew out of his hand as a slug burned across his forearm. It wasn't a serious wound, but it was enough to disarm him.

The two remaining gunmen stopped shooting. They approached him cautiously, keeping him covered as he lay in the street, which was now empty except for Longarm and the bushwhackers. Everyone else had retreated inside from the storm.

With their black dusters flapping, the men reminded Longarm more than ever of buzzards closing in on what they thought was a helpless victim. They didn't see his hand stealing into one of his vest pockets to close around the two-barreled, .44-caliber derringer he carried there. The chain attached to the butt of the little weapon looped across to his other vest pocket, where it was attached to his Ingersoll watch. The derringer served as a deadly watch fob that had saved his bacon more than once.

"Don't move, Marshal," one of the gunmen called over the wind.

So they knew who he was. That came as no surprise to Longarm. He didn't think anybody would be foolish enough to carry out a simple robbery attempt during a hurricane, which was what this storm was building to in a hurry.

With a grim look on his face, Longarm glared up at them and asked, "Did Dumond hire you?"

His first thought when the shooting started was that Andre Dumond himself was in that alley, firing at him. He suspected the Frenchman wanted to eliminate him as competition for Jessie's affections. But when it became obvious there was more than one bushwhacker, Longarm's theory had changed. However, he still thought Dumond might be behind the attempt on his life.

But instead of confirming that idea, the gunman laughed

harshly and said, "Dumond? You don't have a clue what's goin' on here, do you, Long?" The man raised his gun. "The Empress says burn in Hell."

Longarm didn't let the shock he felt at those words slow him down. His arm flashed up and the derringer in his fist went off with a small but wicked crack that was all but lost in the havoc of the storm. The gunman's head jerked back as the .44-caliber slug angled up under his chin and into the base of his brain. He spasmed and staggered backward.

Instantly, Longarm switched his aim toward the remaining man and fired again. The bushwhacker moved just as Longarm pressed the derringer's trigger, so instead of the bullet tearing into his throat, it nicked the top of his right shoulder. That was enough to make him cry out in pain and drop his gun, though. He went diving after it, reaching for the weapon with his other hand.

Longarm tackled the man before he could get hold of the gun. They rolled in the street, wrestling desperately with each other. Longarm got a hand around the man's throat and hung on for dear life. When they stopped rolling, he was on top. He drove a knee into the man's groin and clamped down even harder on his throat. The man threw punches at Longarm's head, but they became increasingly feeble as the big lawman closed his other hand around the man's throat.

Longarm knew that if he could keep up that pressure for another minute, the hombre would pass out. Then Longarm could haul him into the hotel and try to get to the bottom of this mess. The other man's mention of the Empress had given him a pretty good idea of what was going on. Longarm needed to warn Jessie as soon as possible.

That was going to be difficult, however, because when a rumbling roar prompted him to look up, he saw a wall of water at least four feet tall barreling down the street toward him.

Cold horror filled Longarm to the very center of his being. The storm surge had arrived in Indianola and was washing into the town even now. Longarm let go of the man he'd been struggling with and lurched to his feet. Instinct cried out for him to run, but there was nowhere to go, no place to hide. The settlement was flat and right on the gulf. There was no high ground.

Choking, still unaware of what was coming, the remaining bushwhacker rolled onto his side and tried to catch his breath. Longarm reached down to grab hold of him and haul him upright, but even as he tried to do that, the wall of water slammed into them, knocking them apart. Longarm caught a glimpse of the man's terrified, screaming face. Then he was gone.

Longarm tried to stay upright as the surging water swept him along the street. He saw one of the posts that supported an awning over the boardwalk and lunged toward it. He managed to hook one arm around it. The pull of the water was incredible, but he hung on until he got the other arm around the post. The strong current still swirled around him, but he wrapped both legs around the post as well and started climbing. He had the crazy idea in the back of his mind that if he could get on top of the building, he might have a better chance to survive.

Another horrifying roar made him look up. The night had gone almost pitch-black, but he was able to make out the whirling funnel that dipped down from the clouds and struck the hotel. The wave had carried Longarm a good fifty yards down the street before he was able to grab the post, so he had a good view as the hotel's roof flew upward into the tornado's cylinder and started to break apart.

"Jessie!" Longarm shouted, knowing it wouldn't do any good. Wherever she was, she couldn't hear him now. But he couldn't hold in the horrified yell.

The water kept pounding him as it continued to rise. Longarm felt the post tilt crazily. The water was tearing it loose, he realized, but he maintained his grip on it. There was nothing else to hold on to. He heard a racket and looked up, saw the planks that formed the awning over the boardwalk being peeled off and flung away by the wind. Torrents of rain suddenly slapped him in the face as the downpour arrived to make things even worse. Feeling like he was drowning, Longarm lowered his head and hunched his shoulders to keep the rain from sluicing down his nose and mouth.

Well, he was going to die, he thought as the post tilted even more. There wasn't much doubt about it now. And there was a good chance no one would ever find his body. If that turned out to be the case, at least Billy Vail would have a pretty good idea what had happened to him. He was glad he had sent that telegram to Billy. The chief marshal knew he was in Indianola, and when Billy read about the hurricane and Longarm failed to report in, Billy would figure he'd been lost in the storm.

Longarm had always known the odds were against him dying a peaceful death in bed, surrounded by his family, but he had figured he would cross the divide with outlaw lead in him, after a fierce gunfight in which he had given as good as he got.

Drowning was a piss-poor way for a fighting man to go.

That thought roused the stubborn defiance of fate that was part of Longarm's nature. He tightened his grip on the post and started climbing again. Even though the wind had stripped away the awning, some of the support boards remained. He got hold of one of them and hauled himself up onto it. Just as he did, the post he'd been climbing gave way, tearing loose to go sailing off through the flood. The board Longarm was on sagged underneath him. Ignoring the pain from the splinters that dug into his hands, he scrambled up it to the edge of the building's roof and hurdled over it.

He didn't know what building this was, but he spread-eagled himself on its roof to offer as little wind resistance as possible, and slowly worked his way toward its peak. He was completely soaked by now, and a chill had begun to work its way through his bones. Something caught his eye, and as he turned his head to look, he saw that one of the buildings down the street was burning. That didn't seem like it should be possible in a torrential rain like this, but he saw the flames shooting up with his own eyes.

Longarm kept climbing until he was at the roof's highest point. If the floodwaters didn't get too deep—if the winds didn't pick him up and carry him away—if another tornado didn't come along—he thought he stood a bare chance of surviving. As he lay there trying to catch his breath, fear for the safety of Jessie and Ki gnawed at him like rabid weasels. They were trapped somewhere in the storm, and there wasn't a damned thing he could do to help them.

He couldn't even help himself, he realized as he felt the building move under him. It lifted and turned, and he knew the floodwaters had picked it up off its foundation. The building began to spin, slowly at first and then faster and faster, and all Longarm could do was cling to it as it was carried off into the maelstrom.

Chapter 13

"Andre!" Jessie yelled at her captor as he wrestled her down the hotel stairs. He had taken his other hand from her mouth so he could use it to help control her. "Andre, what are you doing? Let me go!"

"I told you to stop fighting, *ma cherie!*" he said in her ear. "It will do you no good. You are coming with us."

"Who are you? Why are you doing this?"

"You will find out soon enough, if we live through this terrible storm!"

As they reached the bottom of the stairs, the walls of the hotel began to shake. A huge roar filled the air. Jessie had experienced tornadoes before, and she knew that they often appeared at the same time as hurricanes, an offshoot of those devastating tropical disturbances. From the sound of it, this one was right on top of the hotel.

And Ki was still up there, still fighting with the men who had accompanied Andre.

Clearly, Dumond was no cotton trader as he had claimed to be. Jessie wondered if he had booked passage on the

Harry Fulton knowing that she would be on the ship. He might have been supposed to kidnap her as soon as they reached Indianola, only to have his plans frustrated temporarily by the presence of Ki and Longarm. If that was the case, then the timing of this storm had played right into his hands.

Assuming, as he had said, that they lived through it.

Dumond shoved her across the deserted lobby toward the rear door of the hotel. All the other guests were hiding somewhere, probably praying for all they were worth.

Dumond forced her along a short hallway and then outside, where the wind tore at her dress and flung her hair around her head. Two or three of the duster-clad gunmen followed them. In all this chaos, she couldn't tell exactly how many allies Dumond still had with him.

A couple of men were waiting behind the hotel with horses. The rearing and plunging animals were clearly frightened out of their minds by the storm, and the men holding their reins had to fight to keep the maddened horses from stampeding.

Jessie felt Dumond lift her. She kicked at him, but couldn't stop him from throwing her across the back of one of the horses. He vaulted into the saddle behind her and jerked her upright in front of him. Once again, he clamped an arm across her torso while he grabbed the reins with his other hand. A few feet away, the other men struggled to mount up as well.

"My God, Dumond!" one of them yelled. "The water!"

Jessie twisted her head around, but couldn't see anything at first because the wind had pushed her hair in front of her face. She tossed her head to clear her vision, and almost wished she hadn't as she saw waves rolling through the

streets of Indianola, swirling around the buildings. The
hurricane-tossed gulf threatened to swallow up the whole
town.

Dumond jammed his boot heels into his horse's flanks
and sent the animal leaping forward. The other men followed.

Water splashed around the horses' hocks. Dumond led
the way, hauling hard on the reins as he turned onto Main
Street. The horse stumbled, and for a second Jessie thought
it was about to go down. If they fell into that current, it
would sweep them away and probably drown them, she
knew. Even though she hated being a prisoner, and was still
baffled about why Dumond and the others had kidnapped
her, she was grateful when the horse regained its footing
and plunged ahead.

She thought her mind was playing tricks on her when
she seemed to hear someone shout her name, somewhere
behind them. She tried to twist her head and look, but
jammed up hard against Dumond's chest as she was, she
couldn't see anything behind them. As dark as the night
was, she probably wouldn't have been able to anyway.

Rain lashed at them now. Dumond grunted in her ear
as the downpour pounded at him. Because of the wind,
the rain was coming down almost horizontally, and since
the riders were heading inland, Dumond's body shielded
Jessie to a certain extent.

She stopped fighting. Exhaustion had her in its grip,
along with a numbing fear at being caught out in such a
dreadful storm. She still didn't know from one second to
the next if she was going to survive, or if she did, what was
going to happen to her then.

Something massive tumbled past them—a tree that the
wind had uprooted and flung through the air like a child's

toy. More debris followed it. Boards, whole pieces of shattered walls, a steamer trunk . . . all that and much, much more, all of it deadly for anyone unlucky enough to be caught in its path.

That was what happened to one of Dumond's confederates. His horse had drawn even with the one carrying Jessie and Dumond. Jessie heard a rattle and then a scream, and when she glanced over, she saw a sheet of tin go sailing past. The man's arm was gone, sheared off neatly at the shoulder by the sharp edge of the tin. Blood spouted from the hideous wound where the arm had been; then the man passed out and toppled from the saddle, landing with a splash in the water that still lapped around the horses' hooves.

Now that the huge wave was inland, it had begun to spread out and lose some of its depth and force, but it still covered the land for as far around as the eye could see in the thick gloom. The wind still howled, and all those who were fleeing from the storm could do was keep moving and hope that they could stay ahead of the worst of it. That didn't really seem possible to Jessie, but Dumond seemed determined to escape—and take her with him. His grip on her never weakened. He held her as if his very life depended on it.

That thought was the last coherent one she had for a while. Stunned and overwhelmed, her mind refused to continue working, and her head sagged forward as she sank into a stupor.

Longarm had ridden many a bucking bronco during his years as a young cowboy, before he ever pinned on a lawman's badge. In the time since then, he had found himself on some pretty salty cayuses, too, the sort that liked to buck and sunfish and do their damnedest to bend a man's spine and rattle his teeth out of his head.

But he had never experienced quite as wild a ride as the one he took that night, on top of a building caught up in a hurricane-fueled flood. The roof shuddered and tilted and spun, dropped like the earth had fallen out from under it, rose again as if it were going to fly right up into the storm-tossed heavens. Longarm dug his fingers under the wooden shingles as best he could, and clung to them. He knew that if he ever lost his grip, he was doomed.

Several times, the roof smashed against some unseen obstacle and almost jolted him loose. Gradually, he came to realize that the roof no longer had a building underneath it. The tempest had pried it loose, and now it bobbed and floated like a giant raft.

The movement stopped abruptly with a crash and a lurch. The roof had jammed against something sturdy enough to hold it against the battering ram of the current. Longarm lifted his head, blinked water out of his eyes, and saw that the chunk of roof to which he clung was wedged between a pair of thick-trunked live oaks that had probably been growing there for decades. He thought he recalled seeing a couple of trees like that near the train station. Completely disoriented as he was, he had no idea if the storm had carried him in that direction.

As he lay there, something plopped down on the back of his neck. He felt it writhing against his skin and he let out an instinctive yell of revulsion as he realized it was a snake. Risking letting go with one hand, he reached up, grabbed the snake, and jerked it off him. He flung it as far away from him as he could. It fell in the water and disappeared.

Longarm remembered hearing about other hurricanes where hordes of snakes had appeared, driven up from their dens by the flooding, picked up and tossed hither and yon by the wind and waves. That could happen with other varmints, too. It would be just his luck, he thought, if an alligator came flying through the air and landed right on this piece of roof with him.

In that case, he and the gator would just have to share, because he wasn't going anywhere. The roof was above the level of the water—not by much, mind you, but enough. And the flood would go down after a while, once the storm surge had spent its force. That left flying debris and rising water from the torrential rain as the main dangers. Longarm crawled over next to one of the tree trunks and got behind it, using it to partially shield him from the wind. If the water came up too high, he would climb the tree, he decided.

Since he had done all he could to keep himself safe for the moment, he rested his head against the rough wood of the shingles. Sleep was out of the question, but at least he could catch his breath. The rain still pounded him, but the limbs of the tree above him broke some of its force.

He didn't actually doze off, although he slipped into a state of numb blankness. He didn't think, didn't hope, didn't do anything except lie there and exist. So he wasn't sure how much time had passed when he suddenly realized that the rain had stopped. As he raised his head, the howl of the wind began to fade. Within minutes, it was gone. A gentle breeze brushed his face, but that was all. When Longarm raised his head even more and peered at the sky above him, he was shocked to see pinpoints of light against the ebony backdrop. He was looking at the stars.

He was in the eye of the storm.

Chapter 14

Longarm struggled to his feet and clung to the tree trunk to steady himself, since the roof was wedged between the trees at an angle and it slanted underneath him. He looked around, trying to figure out where he was.

The moon peeped out from behind the thinning clouds and helped him orient himself. He thought he was near the train station, but it was difficult to be sure because everywhere he looked, he saw mostly just water. The gulf had swallowed Indianola.

He spotted a few wrecked buildings here and there, some with missing roofs, some with walls that had collapsed, and all of them crooked, as if giant fists had pounded them out of their normal shape. Far to his left, he made out a large building jutting up from the water, and realized after a moment that it was the courthouse. He could even see the distinctive cupola on its roof. The sturdy stone structure appeared to have come through the hurricane better than any other place in the settlement.

But the storm wasn't over, Longarm reminded himself.

This was just a lull. After a while, the wind would begin to blow again, and the rain would come back, and once more nature would pound what had been the busiest port between Galveston and Corpus Christi.

Longarm wondered how deep the water was. Could he wade or swim to the other end of town and get inside the courthouse somehow? He knew that if he were caught in the water when the hurricane returned, he wouldn't stand a chance. Not only that, but the water was probably teeming with snakes as well. At least here on the roof, he could see them if they started crawling toward him.

He shifted his weight, bouncing up and down on his feet. He wanted to see just how secure the roof's position was. It seemed to be wedged pretty tightly between the trees, but could he count on that?

The roof didn't budge when he bounced on it. He would be better off staying here and trying to ride out the rest of the storm, he decided. The wind had stripped the live oaks of leaves and broken off some of the branches, but the gnarled trunks seemed sturdy enough. He would just have to take the chance.

He looked toward where the hotel had been, and thought he saw one wall of it still sticking up out of the water. The rest of the building was gone. Grief throbbed through him. Jessie and Ki had been in there. He hoped they had escaped death somehow, but he knew the odds were against it.

For a moment, he debated whether or not he ought to try to make it to the hotel so that he could look for his friends, but the same arguments that had decided him against making a try for the courthouse weighed against the possibility. Too many snakes, too much of a chance of being caught out in the open when the storm came roaring back.

As it was going to do soon, Longarm realized as a stronger gust of wind blew against his face. Rain began to patter down around him. The respite was over.

He took off his belt and used it to lash himself to one of the trees. If the piece of roof came loose and washed away, he wouldn't go with it. His fate now rested on a gnarled old oak tree.

He recalled hearing that the back side of a hurricane wasn't as bad as the side that came ashore first, but the misery he endured over the next couple of hours was plenty bad enough. Wind and rain pounded him, snakes slithered past him, debris flew through the air and crashed into the tree that sheltered him.

As the sky finally began to lighten with the approach of a gray dawn, he saw bodies floating past in the water. Men, women, and children alike, so many of them that after a while Longarm was so sickened by the sight, he had to close his eyes and shut out the agonized faces that were already starting to bloat.

After a while, the sound of splashing made him open his eyes again. As he did so, a man's voice yelled, "Hello! Hello on the roof! Are you alive?"

Longarm waved an arm to show that he still lived. He peered through the gloom and saw a long, thick beam that had probably been a floor or ceiling joist from a house drifting toward the roof. A man, a woman, and two kids clung desperately to it. The man and the woman tried to hang on with one hand and paddle with the other so they could steer the beam, but they weren't having much success. The beam went where the current wanted to take it.

Fortunately for them, that was toward the roof. The wind had died down a little and the rain wasn't as hard. Longarm dared to hope that the worst was over. He unfastened himself from the tree and crawled over the roof toward the spot where the beam would pass the closest. He carried his belt in his hand. When he reached the edge of the roof, he wrapped one end of it around his wrist and called to the man, "I'll throw you my belt as you pass by! Grab it!"

The man nodded that he understood. They would probably get only one chance. Longarm hoped the beam would hit the roof and get stuck against it long enough for the family to scramble to safety—well, relative safety anyway. But as the beam drifted closer, he saw that it was going to slide by without stopping.

That meant the man *had* to catch the belt if he and his family were going to have any hope of survival. Longarm tried to time the toss perfectly. He threw the other end of the belt out, saw the man lunge for it—

And miss.

Longarm's breath hissed between his teeth in disappointment. The man wasn't going to give up, though. He let go of the beam and dived after the belt, getting hold of it this time. As his head came out of the water, his wife grabbed his leg and hung on tight. She still had her other arm looped around the beam, so it was halted for the moment, as long as everyone could hang on.

"Send the children!" the man shouted at his wife. "They can hang on to us and pull themselves to the roof!"

She nodded and started talking to the kids, who appeared to be seven or eight years old. They were too terrified at first to let go of the beam, but their mother finally persuaded them to try. Clinging to the parents as if they were a living rope ladder, the youngsters worked their way one by one to the roof, where Longarm was waiting with an outstretched hand to grab them and pull them onto the shingles.

"Crawl over there to that tree and hang on to the trunk!" he told them. "Don't move from that spot until your folks get there!"

The shivering children, a boy and a girl, did as he told them. Longarm sat with his feet braced against the roof and both hands gripping the belt as he shouted to the woman, "Let go of the beam and hang on to your husband, ma'am! I'll pull you both in!"

"I . . . I don't know if I'm strong enough!" she called back. "Now that the children are safe . . ."

Longarm knew what she was about to say. She was going to give up and let go of her husband, let the water wash her away with the beam. He yelled, "Don't you do it, ma'am! Those youngsters of yours still need you! Doggone it, let go of the beam and hang on to your husband!"

"Do like he says, Martha!" the man pleaded. "Don't leave us!"

"All right," she said, her voice growing weaker. "I'll try."

With that, she released her hold on the beam. Longarm hauled back on the belt, pushing with his feet against the roof as well. The man reached out with his free hand as soon as he was close enough and got hold of the edge of the roof. He let go of the belt and used that hand to grab his wife's arm. Straining against the current, he hauled her close enough for Longarm to lean forward and take hold of her other arm. He lifted her onto the roof as the man climbed out of the water on his own.

"Come on!" Longarm urged. "Let's get over there by the tree! It's safer there!"

As the couple started crawling away from the edge, Longarm paused to look down at the water washing around the roof. He realized with a shock that it was flowing the other way now, back out to sea. The surge had reversed itself. He wasn't well-educated enough about hurricanes to know if that was a common occurrence as the big storms wound down. All he knew as he watched more buildings collapse and be washed away was that the water was still doing a hell of a lot of damage.

Eventually, though, the level of it would go down, and that was exactly what happened as Longarm and the family he had rescued huddled on top of the piece of roof that had been their salvation. As the sky continued to lighten, the wind decreased and the rain tapered off to a drizzle. Although water still covered the ground for as far around as Longarm could see, he could tell now that it was only a few feet deep. The level continued to drop slowly.

Longarm said, "I reckon we can start thinking about gettin' off this roof. Doesn't look like it's more'n an eight-foot drop from the lowest part of the roof. I'll slide down and you can hand the young'uns to me. I'd better carry 'em, though. Could be snakes in the water."

"Snakes!" the little girl cried in fear.

"Don't worry, honey," Longarm told her with a smile. "I won't let 'em bite you."

The woman shook her head. "Where are we going to go?" she asked in a dull voice. "Our home is gone. The storm took it."

"There's bound to be someplace," Longarm said. "You can't stay here on this roof."

The woman looked at him with eyes that were empty of hope. "It's as good a place as any."

Her husband put his arms around her shoulders and pulled her against him as she began to sob. He looked at Longarm and said, "Don't worry about us, mister. We'll figure out something in a little while. For right now, I reckon we'd be just as well off sitting here and resting some."

Longarm shrugged. What they did was their decision. "All right," he said. "Just be careful when you do climb down. Like I said, there are liable to be more snakes around than usual."

And bodies, too, he thought grimly. He was already spotting them, sprawled here and there in awkward attitudes of death, left behind by the retreating water.

He slid along the slanting roof to its lowest point, hung off it, and then dropped to the ground. His boots hit the water and slid in the slimy muck underneath. He waved his arms in the air to catch his balance. Then he looked up at the four people he was leaving behind and waved farewell to them. As he started slogging toward what had been Main Street, he realized that he didn't know their names, except for Martha's, and they didn't know his.

In circumstances such as these, such things didn't really matter, he supposed.

Jessie and Ki were uppermost in his mind now. He wanted to get to the hotel—the place where the hotel had been anyway—and start searching for them. He didn't hold out much hope of finding either of them alive, but it went against his nature to give up without any proof.

He hadn't reached the hotel yet when he heard a voice calling, "Hey! Hey, somebody! Anybody! Help!"

Longarm found a man clinging to a drainpipe attached to the gutters of a house that had been washed off its foundation and appeared to be on the verge of collapse. The man was about eight feet off the ground. Longarm called up to him, "Why didn't you just jump down?"

"These old bones o' mine are too brittle! They'll snap like kindlin' wood!"

Longarm frowned as he realized the elderly tones were familiar. "Cap'n Andy? Is that you?"

"Yeah!" The old salt twisted his head around to look down at Longarm. "Marshal?"

"That's right." Longarm set his feet as best he could in the muck. "Jump. I'll catch you."

"You'll drop me in that snaky water!"

"No, I won't," Longarm insisted, his frustration and impatience growing. "But if you don't want to jump, just shinny the rest of the way down that pipe."

"I ain't much for shinnyin'," the old man complained.

Longarm muttered a curse. "Just jump then! I got you!"

"Don't you drop me!" Cap'n Andy warned. Then he let go and fell toward Longarm.

The big lawman wrapped his arms around the frail body of the old sailor. He had to take one step back to keep his balance, but that was all. Cap'n Andy didn't weigh much. Longarm set him down on his feet and said, "You're lucky that house didn't wash away completely."

"You're damn right. When the water come up, I just climbed the nearest thing I could find to climb."

"I thought you said you weren't much for shinnyin'."

"A fella can climb better when there's a flood lappin' at his feet."

"I'm goin' on to Main Street to see if I can find some of my friends who were in the hotel," Longarm said. "Why don't you come with me?"

"All right . . . but you ain't gonna find much of the hotel left."

"I know," Longarm said.

In fact, as he and Cap'n Andy trudged through the water and started up Main Street, Longarm saw there wasn't much left of Indianola at all.

They were looking at a scene of complete and utter devastation.

Chapter 15

The water was still receding so that it was only a few inches deep along Main Street. That wasn't nearly enough to hide the destruction. Jumbled piles of debris were everywhere, mostly lumber from the wrecked buildings, but also furniture and other household goods. A large, cast-iron safe stood in the middle of what was now an empty foundation; the building that had contained the safe had been washed away around it.

The fire had been worse than Longarm realized. All up and down the street, charred timbers jutted up from the mud, evidence that those buildings had burned before the hurricane had a chance to knock them down or wash them away. Longarm saw only three buildings that appeared to be relatively undamaged: the courthouse, one of the churches, and a small, windowless hut that had evidently been used for storage of some sort. As Longarm and Cap'n Andy walked up the street, they saw several people emerge from that hut. The citizens had evidently taken refuge there, and judging by the looks on their faces, they were amazed to still be alive this morning.

"It's as bad as it was when that other hurricane hit," Cap'n Andy said in an awed voice. "Worse maybe."

The train station was a pile of rubble. Longarm looked for the tracks, but didn't see them. The storm had wrenched the steel rails loose and carried them away. It had been that powerful.

But in one of those bizarre happenstances of nature, the long wharves that extended out into the gulf appeared to be mostly intact, although they had lost quite a few planks here and there. The ships that had been tied up there were gone, however, either carried off or smashed and sunk. Longarm grimaced as he thought about the *Harry Fulton* and Captain Seamus O'Malley.

A few bodies were lying in the street. Longarm looked at them as he and Cap'n Andy walked by, fearing that he might see the lifeless faces of Jessie and Ki. He didn't recognize any of the corpses, though, and was thankful for that, even as he mourned the lives that had been lost here. As long as he didn't see his friends' bodies with his own eyes, he could cling to the hope that they were still alive.

They reached the lone remaining wall of the hotel. Bits and pieces of a couple of other walls remained, and that was probably all that kept this wall still standing. Heaps of rubble were piled around. Longarm's jaw tightened as he saw arms and legs sticking out from under some of the piles, not moving.

He leaned forward as he heard a groan coming from the debris. "Somebody's alive in there!" he said to Cap'n Andy. "Give me a hand!"

"I ain't much good at—" the old man started to complain in a whining voice.

"Just move some of this lumber, damn it!" Longarm

snapped as he started tossing aside broken boards in the pile where he thought the groan had come from.

With a reluctant sigh, the old-timer began to help him. Longarm heard another groan; then a feeble voice pleaded, "Help me . . . Is anybody there? Help me . . ."

"Hang on, old son!" Longarm called. "We'll have you out of there in a minute."

"Thank God! Oh, thank God!"

A moment later, Longarm uncovered a pair of legs. He could tell that they were broken in several places. No wonder the fella was groaning. He had to be in agony from those crushed legs. Longarm grabbed another board and pitched it aside, then another and another.

"Son of a bitch!" Cap'n Andy suddenly exclaimed as he stumbled back a couple of steps. Longarm had uncovered the broken legs up to the waist—and that was where the body ended in a gory smear. He didn't know where the rest of this poor hombre's body was, but it was obvious the voice he had heard hadn't come from it.

"Where are you, mister?" he called. "Speak up if you can."

"H-here," came the weak reply from a couple of feet away. Longarm resumed his excavation efforts, and motioned for Cap'n Andy to do likewise.

A few boards later, Longarm found an arm that seemed to be attached to a body. He grasped it and asked, "Do you feel that, old son?"

"Yes! Get me out of here!"

"Hang on." Longarm pulled away several more boards and found the man's torso and head. He was battered and scratched, but didn't seem to be badly injured, just trapped under the rubble. As the man sobbed in relief at being rescued, Longarm and Cap'n Andy cleared away the rest of the debris pinning him down, then pulled him free and helped him to his feet. The man was able to stand up, although he was pretty shaky.

"Were you a guest in the hotel?" Longarm asked him.

The man nodded. "Yes. I was in my room on the second floor when the place collapsed."

"You didn't happen to see a really pretty young woman with reddish blond hair and a fella who looked like he was half-Japanese, did you?"

"No, I'm sorry," the man replied with a shake of his head. "I didn't see anybody. I was alone, and then the floor fell out from under me and everything came down on top of me . . ." His voice trailed off. He put his hands over his face and started sobbing again.

"Go find a place to sit down and take it easy for a spell," Longarm advised him.

"Thank you. Thank you . . ."

Longarm and Cap'n Andy moved deeper into the wreckage of the hotel, being careful not to dislodge anything that could cause an avalanche of rubble. "Anybody here?" the big lawman called. "Anybody hear me?"

A muffled shout sounded from another pile of debris. Longarm and Cap'n Andy started digging again, and a few minutes later they pulled out a man with a broken arm whose face was covered with blood from a bad cut on his forehead. They sent him stumbling out of what was left of the hotel and resumed their search.

In the next half hour, they found two more people who were alive—and seven who weren't. The other half of the corpse that went with the broken legs hadn't showed up. Longarm didn't know if it ever would. But most importantly from his point of view, they didn't find Jessie or Ki. A faint flicker of hope still burned within him.

They came to a large chunk of the staircase that had remained intact when it collapsed. It was wedged up against the wall that was still standing. A great deal of mud had washed up and gotten trapped under the stairs. Longarm was walking past it when he heard a faint "Help."

Longarm bent to peer underneath the stairs. He didn't see how anybody could be under there. The space appeared to be completely filled with mud. But that was where the voice had seemed to come from, so he called, "Is somebody there!"

"Yes!" The voice was muffled but unmistakable. "Help me, please!"

"Ki!" Longarm yelled. "Ki, is that you?"

"Marshal Long?"

Longarm felt hope rise within him. If Ki was alive, then maybe Jessie was, too. "Is Jessie with you?"

"No. I'm sorry."

Longarm's heart sunk. He had hoped that Jessie and Ki would be together, as they so often were, and that Jessie would be all right.

For the moment, though, he had to concentrate on getting Ki out of there. "Are you hurt?" he asked as he began pawing at the mud, pulling out dripping handfuls of the sticky stuff and flinging it aside.

"I don't know . . . I don't think so. Not too much."

"Marshal," Cap'n Andy called, "I got somebody else over here askin' for help."

"Then go ahead and try to dig 'em out," Longarm told the old salt. "I'll give you a hand as soon as I can."

He leaned into the opening he was creating in the mud and forced both hands into the slick, gooey mess. He slung the stuff behind him and kept digging. After a few moments he saw a hand emerge from the other direction, and realized that Ki was helping to dig himself out. Working together, they soon had the opening enlarged enough so that Long-arm could grasp Ki's wrists and pull him out into the open air.

Ki slithered through the tunnel, and then slid down into the muck at Longarm's feet. His chest heaved as he dragged air into his lungs. "It was getting a little . . . close in there," he managed to say.

Longarm hunkered on his heels. "How'd you get stuck under the stairs like that?" he asked.

"I'm not sure," Ki replied as he sat up. He had a swollen, blood-crusted lump on his head where something had hit him. "I was on the stairs when they collapsed. I hit my head and lost consciousness when I fell. I must have washed up under that part of the staircase when the town flooded. That was when I came to. I was able to tread water as the water level rose, and luckily it stopped rising before I was com-pletely out of air. There was a little pocket of it under there, at the very top of the space. Then the mud came in and packed tighter and tighter around me . . . I could barely move. It was almost like being buried alive, I suppose. I didn't know how much time had passed, but then I heard someone moving around . . ." Ki paused to grasp the law-man's arm with a mud-stained hand. "Marshal, have you seen Jessie?"

Sadly, Longarm shook his head. "Not yet. I was hopin' she'd be with you. Did the two of you get separated by the storm?"

"Not the storm," Ki replied with a grim shake of his head. "When we got upstairs to her room, men were wait-ing there for us. Waiting to attack me and kidnap Jessie."

Longarm leaned back in surprise. "Kidnap Jessie? Why the hell would anybody want to do that?" An ominous thought occurred to him. "These varmints who jumped you . . . were they wearin' long black dusters?"

Ki nodded. "They were. How did you know that?"

"Because some of 'em bushwhacked me on my way back to the hotel." Memories that had been forced to the back of Longarm's mind by the catastrophic events of the night came flooding back, just as inexorably as the Gulf of Mexico had flooded Indianola. "And I know who they were working for, too. One of 'em bragged about it. Said the Empress wanted me to burn in Hell."

"The Empress," Ki breathed. "You mean . . .?"

"Katerina von Blöde her own self. The Cartel sent those bastards after us, Ki."

"And now they have Jessie."

Longarm looked at the terrible destruction that surrounded them and said, "If she's lucky, they do, because that means she's still alive . . . and we can go get her."

Chapter 16

When Jessie came back to full awareness, the first thing she realized was that she didn't feel the horse swaying underneath her. Nor was Andre Dumond's arm pressed across her chest like an iron bar, so tight that she could barely breathe. Gradually, she came to understand that she was lying down on something soft. It wasn't comfortable, however, because the surface was wet and a chill shivered through her bones.

She forced her eyes open, but couldn't see anything. After a moment, she figured out that was because a curtain of her own water-soaked hair hung in front of her face. She lifted a hand and shoved it back, blinking against the light that stung her eyes.

The light wasn't particularly bright. In fact, the day was rather overcast, she saw as she looked around. The wind still blew, although it was nothing like the howling gale it had been the night before, and occasional drizzles of rain spat down. But after being mostly unconscious for what seemed like a long time, even the gray, gloomy light seemed harsh to Jessie.

Although she couldn't be sure because she didn't know

how long she had been unaware of her surroundings, she had a sense that it was morning, rather than afternoon. The landscape was flat, covered with scrub brush and an occasional clump of trees. They were still in the coastal plain, but probably well inland by now.

She heard sucking sounds and turned her head toward them. She saw a pair of black boots coming toward her. The muddy ground tried to hang on to the boots with every step the man took, and that was what made the sounds.

Mud, Jessie thought. She was lying in the mud. That was why she was wet and cold and miserable.

The boots stopped beside her. The man wearing them hunkered down so that he could look at her. "You are awake, *ma cherie*."

"G-go to h-hell, D-Dumond," Jessie rasped as she shivered.

"You have no cause to be angry with me," Dumond said. "I was only doing the job I was paid to do. In fact, you might well be grateful to me. It is because of me that you escaped from Indianola before the full force of the hurricane struck."

Jessie tasted grit in her mouth. She spat it out and said, "I didn't escape. You hauled me out of there by force. I was kidnapped."

Dumond shrugged. "Call it what you will. You are alive, and I venture to say that a great many who were in Indianola last night cannot say that this morning."

Jessie pushed herself up on an elbow so that she could take a better look around. She saw half a dozen men and horses nearby. The group had stopped in a grove of trees. Jessie lay at the foot of one of the trees, with her back against the trunk. She used it to brace herself as she stood up.

The other men wore black dusters and hats like Dumond. They weren't attempting to cover their faces with masks or anything like that. None of them looked familiar to her, but she knew their type—hard-bitten hired guns who would do anything if the price was right..

She knew Dumond wasn't behind the abduction himself; he'd admitted as much when he said that he had been hired to do a job. Jessie pushed her hair back again with a muddy hand—she was already covered with the stuff, so there was no point in being fastidious now—and said, "You came on that ship just to get to know me and make sure I wouldn't suspect you until it was too late."

"And I got to know you quite well," Dumond said.

Jessie's arms and legs weren't tied. Her hand flashed up and cracked across Dumond's face in a sharp slap that rocked his head to the side. He swayed and almost lost his balance. He put a hand on the ground to keep from sitting down in the mud, but it slipped and he tilted even more.

Jessie swept a leg around in a move that Ki had taught her. It caught Dumond at the knees and knocked his legs out from under him. Already off balance as he was, he sprawled on the ground. Mud splashed up around him as he yelled a curse in French.

Jessie didn't hesitate. She lunged forward at him, lowering a shoulder and driving it into his chest. Caught unprepared, he went over backward. Jessie had already spotted the black butt of a revolver sticking up from a holster at his hip. She made a grab for it now and got her fingers around the grips.

The gun was a .45, heavier than the .38 she usually carried when she was packing iron. Desperation gave her strength, however. She hauled the gun out of its holster and swung it up, raking it across Dumond's face as she did so. He grunted in pain.

Dumond's shout had warned the other men that something was wrong. They started toward Jessie and the Frenchman, but they froze when they found themselves staring down the barrel of Dumond's gun, held steady as a rock in both of Jessie's hands. She continued to cover them as she got to her feet.

"Mon Dieu!" Dumond exclaimed from the ground. "You are afraid of a mere woman? Stop her!"

"That woman's Jessie Starbuck," one of the men said. "She knows how to use a gun, and she's got the drop on us."

"Damn right I do," Jessie snapped as she moved to the side so that she could cover Dumond at the same time as the other men. "Now move away from those horses, all of you."

"Do *not* let her escape," Dumond warned as he climbed to his feet. "You know what will happen to all of us if she does."

"Yeah, Dumond's right about that," another man said. "Our lives won't be worth a plugged nickel if we let her get away."

Jessie saw the worried looks on the unshaven faces and wondered just who they were working for. Whoever it was had to be a holy terror if he could scare a bunch of hardcases like this. She gestured with the gun and said, "I won't tell you again. Get away from the horses."

Dumond sidled away. "No, *cherie*. I cannot allow it. You must come with us."

"You take one more step, Dumond, and I'm going to put a bullet in your knee. You'll never walk right again."

Dumond stopped, but the damage had already been done. There was too big a gap now between him and the other men. Jessie couldn't watch all of them at once. Suddenly, one of the others leaped toward her, reaching for the gun in an attempt to wrench it out of her hand before she could fire.

Unfortunately for him, he underestimated her reaction time. Jessie squeezed the trigger. The gun blasted, and the .45-caliber slug struck his hand, blowing the thumb completely off it. The hard case howled in pain and staggered.

Dumond jumped her at the same time, coming at her from the side. Jessie tried to twist back around and get a shot off at him, but he hit her arm and knocked the gun barrel out of line. She pulled the trigger, but the bullet whined off harmlessly. Dumond crashed into her an instant later.

Jessie slashed at his head with the gun, but all she succeeded in doing was knocking his hat off. He closed his fingers around the wrist of her gun hand and gave it a brutal twist as his lips drew back in a savage snarl. Jessie cried out as the pain caused her fingers to open involuntarily. The gun thudded to the muddy ground at their feet.

Dumond brought up his other hand and slapped her as she had slapped him a few minutes earlier. The blow landed with dizzying force. Jessie would have fallen to her knees if not for Dumond's grip on her wrist. He pulled her close to him and glared into her face. Blood dripped down his cheek from the cut that the gunsight had opened up when she hit him with it.

"Enough!" he said. "I was told to deliver you alive, but nothing was said about what sort of shape you had to be in otherwise!"

"I'm not . . . afraid of you!" she panted as she struggled against his grip. Now that he was set, though, she wasn't strong enough to break it.

"Perhaps you should be," he warned her. "You do not

want me to lose patience with you, Jessie, and I am on the verge of doing just that."

She continued glaring at him, determined not to let him see the despair that threatened to well up inside her. Still holding her tightly, he looked away and asked, "Mullins, how badly are you wounded?"

"That bitch shot my thumb off!" the injured man yelled.

"Well, bind it up so that you don't bleed to death. You can still ride, can't you?"

"Yeah, I reckon," the man admitted. "It's my left hand, so I can still use a gun."

"Good," Dumond said with a thin, dangerous smile, "because otherwise you would be of no further use to me." He glanced at the others. "One of you pick up my gun and make sure the barrel was not fouled when it fell in the mud. The rest of you, see to Mullins's hand and then mount up. We have allowed the horses to rest long enough."

Jessie stopped struggling as he wrestled her over to his horse. Outnumbered, surrounded by ruthless men, she knew that she would have to play along for the time being. When Dumond said, "Will you mount up on your own, or shall I throw you on the horse's back again?" she reached for the saddle horn and put a foot in the stirrup.

Dumond gripped the reins tightly. "Just so you do not get any ideas about bolting," he said.

Jessie didn't dignify that with a response. She swung up onto the horse, settling herself just ahead of the saddle because she knew Dumond would be riding behind her. One of the men handed Dumond's gun back to him first. He pouched the iron, then mounted up.

The other men climbed onto their horses as well, including the wounded Mullins, who now had a dirty rag tied tightly around his left hand. Blood from the stump of his thumb had already put a dark red stain on the cloth. Jessie wouldn't have made a bet on the odds of him not coming down with blood poisoning. She wouldn't lose any sleep over it if he did.

Dumond urged his horse into motion. The riders moved out from under the trees. The rain had stopped completely now, although from the looks of the thick gray clouds in the sky, it might start up again at any moment. Jessie wasn't sure of the direction they were going, but figured that they were headed inland, either west or northwest. The wind was in their faces. By now, the hurricane that had hit Indianola was probably miles from the coast and wasn't even a hurricane anymore, just a storm with some strong winds and drenching rain—and all the destruction that it had left behind.

Jessie thought about what had happened and wondered whether or not Ki had survived, not only the battle with Dumond's men, but also the hurricane itself. She thought about Seamus O'Malley, who had been so determined to stay with his ship. And she thought about Longarm, whom she hadn't seen since he left the hotel in search of a bottle of Maryland rye. Was he still alive, or was his body floating somewhere in muddy, debris-filled water, already beginning to swell?

Dumond must have felt the shudder that went through her at that thought, because he said, "I wish I could tell you not to fear, *cherie*, that everything will be all right. Unfortunately, I cannot. All I can promise you is that if you cooperate, you will be safe . . . for the time being."

"There's one thing I can promise you, Dumond," she said without turning her head to look at him.

"And what might that be?" He sounded amused.

"If anything has happened to my friends because of you," Jessie said, "sooner or later I'm going to kill you."

Chapter 17

Cap'n Andy was still struggling to free the man he had been trying to uncover. Longarm and Ki pitched in, and in a couple of minutes they were hauling out another victim of the hurricane. The man had a broken leg and broken arm, and maybe other injuries. Since he couldn't walk, they made him as comfortable as possible on a door that lay among the rubble. Then Longarm and Ki picked it up and carried it out of what was left of the hotel.

Already, those who had come through the storm relatively unscathed were combing through the rubble all up and down what had been Main Street, looking for other survivors. The water had gone down to the point that, while there were still large puddles in many places, the ground wasn't completely covered anymore. The mud that was left behind was almost as treacherous as the water, though.

Longarm spotted a man carrying a medico's black bag and called to him, "Hey, Doc, got another patient for you!"

"Set him down somewhere," the doctor said as he bent over a woman who was groaning and writhing on the ground. "I'll get to him as soon as I can."

"These people need help," Ki said. "Otherwise, many of these people will not live through the next night."

Longarm knew Ki was right. With a sigh, he said, "I'd like to start tryin' to find out what happened to Jessie, but we can't turn our backs on these folks, Ki. We got to do what we can to help them."

Ki nodded. "Providence allowed us to live through the storm when we might just as easily have died. It would fly in the face of that Providence if we ignored the suffering of everyone else."

Not to mention they didn't have horses, weapons, or any idea what had happened to Jessie, thought Longarm as they set about joining the rescue efforts. For the next few hours, they combed through the rubble, pulling out survivors and those who had lost their lives alike. Somebody came up with a mule-drawn wagon from somewhere, and the corpses were piled in the back and taken to the church, which had made it through the storm without being damaged.

A woman appeared with a pot of coffee and a single tin cup. Longarm didn't know how she had managed to start a fire and boil coffee in this soaked morass, but it was a welcome miracle. She passed the cup around and let the men sip from it. When the coffee was gone, she said, "I'll be back with more," and the men let out a cheer.

Around midday, Longarm and Ki paused to rest and figure out what they were going to do next.

"We've got to figure that those kidnappers carried Jessie off before the storm got them," Longarm said. "They probably had horses waitin' behind the hotel."

Ki nodded. "That seems logical. One thing we can assume if the Empress is behind this is that the operation was well planned. More than a dozen men took part in it, too, counting the ones who ambushed you, Marshal. Unfortunately for them, they were unable to plan on a hurricane striking Indianola on the same night."

Out of habit, Longarm started to reach for a cheroot, then stopped as he realized that even if he still had any in his pocket, they would be soaked and crushed and ruined by now. He grimaced and said, "Maybe not so unfortunate. They didn't succeed in killing either of us, but they got Jessie, just like they wanted."

"We don't know that."

"Damned if we don't." Longarm gestured toward the rubble where the hotel had been. "Do you think she's still in there somewhere, or does it feel to you like she's still alive?"

"You mean we should put our faith in a hunch?"

"Wouldn't be the first time I have," Longarm said. "And my hunches are right most of the time. If they weren't, I wouldn't have lived this long."

Ki thought about it for a moment, then shrugged. "It is as you say, Marshal. Whatever connection there is between Jessie and me, I think I would know if it had been severed. My instinct tells me that the kidnappers were successful in getting her out of town before the worst of the storm hit."

Longarm nodded. "Let's figure out where we can get our hands on some horses and guns." He looked up the street toward the courthouse. "I got an idea about that."

When he and Ki reached the courthouse a few minutes later, they found that a makeshift hospital had been set up there. Injured people lay everywhere, some moaning, some cursing, some just lying there with numbed expressions on their faces. The doctor Longarm had seen earlier was working among them, along with several women who had either been drafted or volunteered to serve as nurses. Longarm and Ki weaved through the ranks of the injured and made their way to the sheriff's office and jail.

Longarm was glad to see Deputy Hank Anderson. The little lawman with the huge, brushy mustache seemed to have come through the hurricane all right. He was behind the desk in the sheriff's office, thumbing shells into a double-barreled shotgun. He set the weapon down, then bounded around the desk and grabbed Longarm's hand, pumping it enthusiastically.

"Damn, it's good to see you, Marshal," Anderson said. "I figured you'd been killed in the hurricane."

"Came too close for comfort a couple of times," Longarm replied with a weary smile. "Looks like the courthouse weathered the storm without too much damage."

Anderson nodded. "We were lucky. Some water got in, but didn't get too high, and the buildin' stood up to the wind just fine. It tore down some fence and a gate outside the jail, but we can replace that." The deputy let out a weary sigh. "We come through a lot better than the rest of the town, that's for sure."

"That prisoner still all right?"

"Yeah. I don't think he even got his feet wet. You plan on leavin' him here?"

Longarm shrugged. "Got no other place to put him, and I can't get a telegram out to my boss to ask him what to do."

Anderson tugged at his mustache and nodded. "Yeah, all the lines are down. I hear the railroad track's torn up, too, so we can't even get trains in and out."

"I've got another problem right now," Longarm said. "A good friend of mine came in on the ship that docked yesterday afternoon. She was kidnapped last night."

"Kidnapped!" Anderson exclaimed. "In the middle of a hurricane?"

Ki said, "We believe she was abducted just as the hurricane struck."

Anderson frowned at him. "Who're you, mister?"

"His name is Ki," Longarm said. "He's a friend of mine, too. He works for Miss Jessica Starbuck, the lady who was snatched."

"Starbuck . . . I know the name, of course. Starbuck ships dock here pretty often, and there's a big ranch out in West Texas that belongs to the family, too, ain't there?"

"There's no family, just Jessie."

"Somebody figure on holdin' her for ransom?"

Longarm didn't want to go into the details of the long-running war between the Cartel and Jessie Starbuck. And at this point, he didn't know why Katerina von Blöde had ordered the kidnapping. So he just said, "Ki and I intend to find out. That's why we need horses and guns."

"You're goin' after the bunch that grabbed the lady?"

"Damn right we are," Longarm said.

Anderson pulled at his chin as he frowned in thought. "I reckon the sheriff's office might be able to spare a couple of pistols and rifles and some ammunition. I don't know where you're gonna find any horses, though. Not to mention, how do you know which way the varmints went?"

That was a problem, all right, and Longarm didn't have an answer to the question. He and Ki were both excellent trackers, but how could you follow a trail in the aftermath of a storm like this one? They would have to question everyone they could find and try to locate someone who had seen the kidnappers fleeing with Jessie. If they could just come up with a place to start . . .

Longarm voiced that hope. Anderson nodded and said, "It's a long shot, but I reckon that's about all you got." He went over to a locked cabinet and took a key from his pocket. As he unlocked the door, he went on. "You can help yourself to guns and cartridges. I need to get outside and let folks see that Indianola still has law and order. Don't want anybody gettin' the idea that it's all right to start lootin'. Not that there's a whole hell of a lot left to loot."

He picked up the shotgun from the desk and left the sheriff's office, telling Longarm to lock the cabinet when he and Ki were finished. Longarm still wore the cross-draw rig, although he had never gotten his revolver back after he dropped it during the fight with the bushwhackers. He selected a Colt .45 that would fit the holster, loaded it from a box of cartridges that was in the cabinet, too, and slid the iron into leather.

"You want a six-gun?" he asked Ki, knowing that the man seldom carried a firearm.

Ki surprised him by extending a hand and saying, "I believe such a weapon might come in handy. If we are facing the Cartel, the odds will be high against us."

"You ain't whistlin' 'Dixie,'" Longarm said. He slapped the butt of an unloaded Colt into the palm of Ki's hand. Ki loaded the weapon and tucked it behind his belt.

Longarm took down a couple of Winchesters and a box of ammunition for them. He and Ki filled their pockets with cartridges for the rifles and the pistols.

As they were finishing with that, Hank Anderson came back into the office with someone trailing behind him. "Got a fella here who's lookin' for you, Marshal," the local lawman said.

Longarm turned, not sure who in Indianola would be looking for him, and was shocked to recognize the man accompanying Anderson as Captain Seamus O'Malley. The big Irishman looked like he'd been through the wringer, with bruises on his face and a bloody cut on his forehead. But he was alive, and that was a lot more than Longarm had expected.

"O'Malley!" he exclaimed. "You didn't go down with the ship."

"Never mind about that," O'Malley snapped. "You and Ki have to help me, Marshal. I have to find Miss Starbuck!"

"We don't know where she is," Ki said. "We were about to go looking for her ourselves. But not here in Indianola. You see, last night—"

"I know, I know," O'Malley interrupted. "I saw those spalpeens in their black dusters gallopin' out of town with her. It looked to me like she was bein' kidnapped!"

Chapter 18

Longarm reached out and gripped O'Malley's arm. "You saw which way they headed when they rode out of town?"

The Irishman nodded. "Aye, that I did. I would have tried to stop them, but just then a piece o' board came whirlin' along and clipped me on me noggin." He gestured toward the cut on his head. "Knocked me silly for a few minutes, it did, and when I came to me senses, they were gone."

Ki looked over at Longarm and said, "It's the best lead we have."

"The *only* lead we have," Longarm said. "Which way were they goin', O'Malley?"

"Northwest, I'd say," the captain answered. "That would take 'em straight inland and get 'em as far away from the water as they could get in the shortest time."

Anderson grunted. "Pretty smart when there's a hurricane comin' in, I'd say."

Longarm couldn't argue with that.

Texas was a mighty big state, he thought, and just because the kidnappers had started northwest with Jessie, that didn't mean they had continued to follow that course. But he and Ki could head in that direction themselves and hope to find someone who had seen those duster-wearing bastards . . .

"We still have the problem of finding horses," Ki pointed out.

"If you fellas are goin' after Miss Starbuck," O'Malley said, "then I'm comin' with ye!"

Longarm wasn't sure that was a good idea. At this point, he didn't know where he and Ki would find horses, let alone a mount for O'Malley.

Before he could bring that up, he heard the sound of some sort of commotion outside the courthouse. People were yelling. Anderson glanced toward the door and muttered, "What the hell's wrong *now*?"

"We'd better go find out," Longarm said.

The four men started out of the courthouse. Longarm felt a little better now that he was armed again. Whatever threats might be facing him, he was better equipped to deal with them with a Colt in his fist.

The thing causing the uproar wasn't a threat, however. The citizens of Indianola were shouting in relief. Newcomers had walked into town carrying boxes of food and medical supplies. People had fallen in to trail the group as it headed toward the courthouse and stopped in front of the building.

One of the strangers stepped forward and said, "Who's in charge here?"

"I reckon that'd be me, if anybody is," Anderson said as he moved forward, too. "Deputy Sheriff Hank Anderson."

"Well, we're from Victoria, and we've come to help you folks any way we can."

A cheer went up from the crowd even before the man

finished his sentence. When the commotion died down some again, the man went on. "The storm was still mighty bad when it got to us, so we knew it had to be really terrible down here. People started getting supplies together right away, and we brought them on the train."

"How close were you able to get?" Longarm asked. "The tracks are gone here."

The man from Victoria grunted. "Yeah, we know. The train had to stop a mile and a half northwest of here. The tracks are torn up that far inland."

To tell the truth, that was better news than Longarm had expected. He had thought that the destruction of the railroad tracks might extend even farther. An idea was beginning to form in his mind, too.

"Was the train gonna wait where you left it?" he asked.

The leader of the relief group nodded. "Yeah, until one of us gets back to let the engineer know what the situation is here. Then he'll probably head back to Victoria to pick up more supplies and bring them down." The man looked around at the devastation. "Looks like you folks can use all the help you can get."

"You never said truer words, friend," Anderson declared. "You bring a sawbones with you?"

One of the men from Victoria stepped forward and said, "I'm a doctor."

Anderson pointed out the local medico. "There's our doc. If you could give him a hand, we'd all sure appreciate it."

The doctor nodded and set down the box of supplies he'd been carrying. He hurried over to assist the local physician with the injured.

Anderson went on. "If you folks want to take that other stuff into the courthouse, we'll start settin' up a way to distribute it. Then, if you want to pitch in, there's still a whole heap o' rubble to be gone through, lookin' for folks who're hurt . . . or dead."

The leader of the relief group nodded and motioned for the others to follow him into the courthouse.

Longarm put a hand on his arm to stop him. "I'm a federal lawman," he said. "Couple of hombres and I need to get to Victoria and borrow some horses. We'll carry the message back to the train so folks will know what happened here in Indianola."

"That's all right with me," the man said with a shrug. "Just make sure the engineer tells people in Victoria how bad it is here and how much these folks need help."

Longarm nodded, then turned to Ki and O'Malley. "Come on," he told them. "I reckon we can maybe follow the railroad right-of-way, even if there ain't any tracks on it anymore. You still want to come with us, O'Malley?"

"Damned right I do," the Irishman said as he clenched his fists.

"Can you handle a gun?"

"Aye. Not as well as ye, to be sure, Marshal, since I don't make me livin' with it, but I can gen'rally hit what I aim at."

"Let's get a rifle and a pistol for you, and then we'll head for the train."

Once O'Malley was armed, Longarm shook hands with Deputy Anderson and said, "Good luck, Hank. I got a feelin' that you're gonna need it."

"You're right about that," Anderson agreed with a glum nod. "Things are gonna be pretty bad here for a while, until folks get back on their feet again. And to tell you the truth, Marshal, I ain't sure Indianola can come back this time.

This is twice now the town's been practically wiped out. Seems like somebody's tryin' to tell us somethin'."

Longarm thought the same thing, but it wouldn't do any good to tell that to Anderson. He just clapped a hand on the deputy's shoulder, squeezed for a second, then turned to leave with Ki and O'Malley.

The roadbed where the railroad tracks had run was slightly elevated, and it hadn't completely washed away during the flood. Starting from the place where the station had been—only part of the foundation was left—the three men were able to follow the roadbed northwestward out of town.

The deep, thick mud made walking difficult. With each step Longarm, Ki, and O'Malley took, their feet came loose from the mud's grip with ugly sucking sounds.

The trek out to the place where the train waited took a little more than an hour. During that time, the men saw upward of five hundred snakes, Longarm estimated. Some snakes he didn't mind, but he had to battle his instincts every time he saw a rattler or a copperhead or a cottonmouth. He wanted to blow those scaly bastards' heads off. However, he couldn't afford to use his bullets that way, so he suppressed the impulse and warned Ki and O'Malley to do likewise.

Snakes weren't the only annoying critters. Clouds of mosquitoes swarmed the men. Longarm and O'Malley waved their arms, trying to make the buzzing little pests go away, but that didn't do much good. Longarm looked over at Ki and saw that although the mosquitoes flew around him, none of them seemed to be lighting on him.

"Don't those varmints bite you?" Longarm asked with a frown.

Ki shook his head. "Insects usually leave me alone. I think it has something to do with my spirit being more at peace than that of most people. Mosquitoes are attracted more to hot-blooded people."

O'Malley slapped at his neck. "That explains why the little buggers are chewin' so much on me then. The Irish are a hot-blooded race."

"How'd you make it through the storm anyway?" Longarm asked. "You must not have gone back out to the ship after all?"

"Ah, but I did," O'Malley replied. "I relieved me men o' their duties, just as I said I was goin' to, and figured to spend the night out there meself. But as the seas got worse, I saw that the ship could not hope to ride out the storm where 'twas . . . so I moved it."

"You moved it?" Ki said.

"Aye. I cast off and sailed around into the bayou."

"By yourself?" Longarm asked.

"I'm not sayin' 'twas easy, mind ye."

Longarm let out a laugh of admiration at the captain's audacity. "What happened to the ship?"

"She ran aground about half a mile up the bayou, and then when the waves came in, they lifted her and pushed her even farther up on shore. The hull's damaged, the masts snapped off in the wind, and the sails are long gone. But the *Harry Fulton* will sail again, by God!"

The clouds thinned and the sun began to peek through them. As Longarm strode along the roadbed, he took his coat off. A muggy heat had settled over the landscape. Longarm looked at the coat, which was torn and filthy, encrusted with dried mud, and then tossed it aside after taking out the wallet that contained his badge and bona fides. He didn't need the garment anymore. He stripped off his vest, too, and discarded it after removing the pocket watch and the derringer connected by the watch chain. He started to roll up the sleeves of his shirt, then decided against it. That would just give the mosquitoes some fresh places to bite him.

A few minutes later, Ki pointed out some smoke rising into the air ahead of them. "The engineer's keepin' up some steam in the locomotive," Longarm guessed. Sure enough, a moment later they came in sight of the train itself, stopped just short of the place where the steel rails ended. The rails had been twisted crazily, Longarm saw.

It was a short train, just a locomotive, a tender, a passenger car, and a caboose. The engineer and the fireman dropped down from the cab as Longarm, Ki, and O'Malley approached. "Are you fellas from Indianola?" the engineer called.

"That's right," Longarm said. "The fellas you brought down here made it there all right with the supplies, and they're tryin' to help clean up now."

"Is there anything left of the town?" the fireman asked.

"Not much. A few buildings made it all right. The rest are either wrecked or flat out gone."

Both of the trainmen let out heartfelt curses. "We knew the storm was bad in Victoria," the engineer said, "but we were hopin' the worst of it missed Indianola."

Longarm shook his head. "Nope, it was a direct hit. The fella in charge of the relief party said to tell you to head back to Victoria and get all the supplies and volunteers down here that you can."

"We sure will. We'll have to back all the way, since there's no way to turn around, but we ought to be able to get more help down here before the day's over."

"You're gonna have three passengers while you're backin' to Victoria, too."

That surprised the trainmen. "You're not goin' back to Indianola?" the fireman asked.

Longarm shook his head. "I'm Deputy U.S. Marshal Custis Long, and I got to ask you boys to take me and my friends to Victoria. We got law business to tend to, and we need some horses. I figure Victoria's the closest place to get 'em."

"You're probably right about that, Marshal," the engineer agreed. "Climb into that passenger car if you want to."

"We're a mite muddy and dirty," Longarm pointed out.

The engineer shook his head. "At a time like this, nobody gives a damn. The car can be cleaned later."

"Much obliged, old son."

The engineer waved the fireman back into the cab. "Come on, Clyde. Let's get some more steam up."

Longarm, Ki, and O'Malley climbed into the passenger car and sank gratefully onto bench seats. Longarm sighed and closed his eyes.

Ki made him open them again by saying, "You know, Marshal, when you were talking to the engineer, you made it sound as if we're on an official assignment for the government, but that isn't the case."

Longarm grunted. "Hell, I know that. Billy Vail don't have a clue what's goin' on down here. Once he hears about that hurricane, he won't know if I'm even still alive."

"And yet you're going after Jessie as if you had been assigned to locate and rescue her."

"Last time I looked, kidnappin' was still against the law, and I'm a lawman. I intend to use all the power of Uncle Sam I have, if that'll help us find her. You ain't complainin' about that, are you?"

"Not at all," Ki said. "In fact, I appreciate your efforts, Marshal. I was just pointing out that they may eventually cause some trouble for you with your superiors."

Longarm shook his head. "I ain't worried about that. If we get Jessie back safe and sound, Billy can do whatever the hell he wants, and so can the Justice Department."

"And if we're not successful?"

"Then it won't matter none to me," Longarm said, "because I'll be dead. I intend to get Jessie away from those varmints . . . or die tryin'."

Chapter 19

The swaying motion of the car and the fact that he hadn't had any real sleep to speak of in more than twenty-four hours caused Longarm to doze off as the train backed toward Victoria. He woke up as they jolted over a trestle just outside town. As Longarm yawned and glanced out the window beside him, he saw that the torrential downpour from the hurricane had caused the Guadalupe River to swell until it was out of its banks.

Ki and Seamus O'Malley were yawning and stretching, too, evidence that they had nodded off as well. O'Malley said, "Are we gettin' close?"

"I reckon we must be," Longarm said. "The train's slowin' down."

He looked out the window again, caught sight of church steeples and other buildings. A few minutes later, the train lurched to a halt next to the platform attached to a big, red brick depot. The platform was crowded, Longarm saw as he and his companions swung down from the car. The citizens of Victoria had turned out in hopes of hearing some good news from Indianola.

They weren't going to get it, thought Longarm. There wasn't anything encouraging to report except for the fact that the storm hadn't killed everyone in Indianola. Any survivors were better than none.

A stocky, middle-aged man with a lawman's star pinned to his vest stepped forward and demanded, "Who are you fellas?"

"Deputy U.S. Marshal Custis Long," Longarm said, introducing himself. He waved a hand toward Ki and O'Malley. "These hombres are working with me. You're the sheriff around here?"

"That's right," the man said with a nod.

"Well, I hate to start asking for favors as soon as I've introduced myself, but we need the loan of some good horses, Sheriff. The government will reimburse whoever provides them for the expense."

He hoped that was true. Billy Vail had to sign off on any expense vouchers he turned in, and sometimes Billy could be a mite persnickety about those things. Not as much so as Henry, though, who would deny every expense if he thought he could get away with it.

"You're working on a case, Marshal?" the sheriff asked.

"That's right. A woman's been kidnapped, and we have to get her back."

"But you came from Indianola?"

Longarm nodded. "That's where the kidnapping took place."

"Now, I'm gettin' all mixed up. There was just a big hurricane at Indianola. All of us were hoping that when the train got back, there would be good news."

"I'm afraid not." Quickly, Longarm sketched in the death and destruction that had befallen Indianola, then said, "The engineer can tell you more about it. What you need to do is gather up some more supplies and send them down there, along with anybody who wants to help."

"We've already got the supplies together, and it won't be a problem getting more volunteers."

"What about those horses?"

The sheriff rubbed his jaw. "I reckon we can go talk to Brister down at the livery stable. He's always got some good mounts."

The sheriff led the way, after passing along the order to start loading more supplies on the train. He introduced Longarm to the soft-spoken liveryman, who was more than happy to help out the law.

"Pick out whatever you want from what's there in the corral, Marshal," Brister said. "I got some decent saddles and tack I can let you have, too."

"We appreciate this," Longarm told him. "I'll try to see to it that you get paid back, if it happens that we can't return these horses."

Brister waved a hand and said, "Just do what you can. I know you wouldn't be asking if it wasn't important."

Within fifteen minutes, Longarm had picked out a horse for himself and one for O'Malley. The ship's captain had very little experience in choosing horseflesh and wasn't hesitant about saying so. Ki settled on a horse for himself, a rangy buckskin that looked like it had plenty of sand. Longarm saddled up a black with a white blaze on its face and one white stocking, then showed O'Malley how to get the saddle on the gray he had picked out for the captain.

"You sure you know how to ride?" Longarm asked O'Malley. "If you can't keep up, we'll have to leave you behind."

"I can keep up, don't ye be worryin' about that," O'Malley insisted. "'Tis true that it's been a while since I did much ridin', but when I was a boy back in Ireland, I was on a horse almost as much as I was on me feet."

"I hope you're right, because I've got a hunch we're gonna be in the saddle a lot."

They stopped at a general store to pick up some supplies before they left Victoria, including hats for all three of them. A man who might need to ride all day could cook his brain without a Stetson to shade it. They picked out new clothing, too. Longarm told the storekeeper to burn the ragged, filthy garments they had been wearing. They got more ammunition as well, along with enough food for several days. Longarm signed markers for all the purchases, and told the store's proprietor to send the markers to Chief Marshal William Vail in Denver.

While they were downtown, Longarm, Ki, and O'Malley saw that the hurricane had done extensive damage here in Victoria, too. A number of buildings had collapsed under the battering of the wind, and many of those still standing had had their roofs blown off. Trees were snapped, even some with thick trunks.

And yet, despite their own problems, the citizens of Victoria were banding together to help out the even more unfortunate inhabitants of Indianola. These folks would do whatever it took to aid their fellow Texans.

Longarm wished he could have done more, but there was one Texan in particular who needed his help right now—Jessie Starbuck. Her safety was really the only thing on his mind as he and Ki and O'Malley rode out of Victoria a short time later.

It was about thirty miles back to Indianola. They made about as good time on horseback as they had on the train, since the train had been forced to back the whole way and

couldn't go as fast as usual. They ate jerky and biscuits in
the saddle as they rode. Longarm hadn't really realized how
ravenous he was until he started putting some food in his
belly.

When he had finished eating, he reached in his pocket
for one of the items Billy Vail was likely to disallow—a
nice, fresh cheroot. Fishing a lucifer from the pocket of the
butternut shirt he now wore, Longarm snapped the match to
life with an iron-hard thumbnail and held the flame to the
end of the tightly packed cylinder of tobacco. The smoke
felt wonderful as he drew it into his lungs.

"You reckon we'll be able to pick up their trail?"
O'Malley asked.

"We just might," Longarm said. "That many horses must
have left quite a few tracks."

"But won't the rain have washed them out?"

Ki said, "Rain doesn't destroy tracks nearly as quickly
as most people believe. It's possible we may pick up some
sign left by the kidnappers."

"We'll ride back to where you spotted 'em," Longarm
said, "and then head in the direction they were going. Maybe
we can find somebody who saw them."

O'Malley shook his head. "Sounds chancy to me."

"It is," Longarm agreed. "But they didn't leave a map
for us to follow, so we'll just have to do the best we can."

It was late afternoon before they reached the vicinity of
Indianola. Longarm saw several columns of smoke rising
from the area where the town had been located. The survivors were burning some of the debris, he thought. That was
the quickest and easiest way to get rid of it.

They might be burning bodies, too, he realized grimly.
With the whole town still awash, burying the dead might
prove difficult. But they couldn't be left around to rot, be-

cause that risked widespread disease, not to mention the smell.

"Are we going all the way into town?" O'Malley asked.

Longarm shook his head. "No need. We know which direction those bastards took Jessie. We'll head that way and see what we can find. It's taken us a long time to get started. I'd like to cut their lead down a little before nightfall."

"You're an optimistic man, Marshal," Ki said.

"I don't believe in givin' up before you get started good, if that's what you mean."

The three riders skirted around what was left of the settlement. As they neared Powder Horn Bayou, Longarm spotted the *Harry Fulton* run aground, just as O'Malley had said. The ship was damaged and bedraggled, but not completely wrecked.

"Was it near here that you spotted those varmints with Jessie?" Longarm asked.

O'Malley nodded. "Aye. About a quarter mile toward town, I'd estimate."

The three men slowed their mounts. Longarm and Ki kept their eyes on the ground, searching for tracks or any other indication that Jessie's kidnappers had passed this way.

Even so, Longarm couldn't help but notice from time to time how O'Malley grimaced and shifted around in the saddle. The sea captain had admitted that it had been a long time since he'd been on horseback. After the ride from Victoria, certain portions of O'Malley's anatomy were probably getting a mite tender about now.

"Need to stop and rest for a while?" Longarm asked.

"No!" O'Malley replied without hesitation. "Don't be worryin' your head about me, Marshal. 'Tis fine I am."

"There is no shame in a physical limitation," Ki said.

"I told ye both, I'm fine," O'Malley said between clenched teeth.

Longarm shrugged. "It's your balls and backside, Cap'n."

A few minutes later, Ki reined in sharply and pointed to the ground. "Several horses came along here since yesterday."

Longarm brought his horse to a stop, too, and leaned forward in the saddle to study the tracks Ki had spotted. He swung down and hunkered on his heels to get an even better look at them.

"You're right," he said. "Since the sun came out this afternoon, it's baked the mud a little, but you can tell the tracks were made recently. I count six horses."

"I agree," Ki said. "And one of them is carrying double."

"Got to be them."

O'Malley said, "How can ye tell so much about who made the tracks? I can barely see 'em."

"You can look at the sky and the water and know many things, true?" Ki said.

"Aye, but that's my business. More than business really. More like a callin'."

"Well, trackin' owlhoots is my business," Longarm said. "And Ki's done a heap of it, too. You can trust us on this, Captain."

"I do," O'Malley said. "Do we follow yon tracks then?"

"We do." Longarm glanced at the sky. "We've got maybe an hour of daylight left. Let's put it to good use."

Chapter 20

Andre Dumond kept his men moving at a fast pace the rest of the day, pushing their horses as hard as they dared and stopping to rest the animals only when they had to. Jessie knew that wasn't smart when someone was facing a long trip. Even the strongest horses would be able to withstand only a few days of such hardship.

No matter how much she hated him now, Jessie didn't think Dumond was stupid. He wouldn't be driving them so hard unless they were going to reach their destination in two or three days.

If they kept going in the direction they had been heading all day, Jessie had a pretty good idea what that destination was.

San Antonio.

The largest city in Texas and one of the oldest, San Antonio de Bexar dated back to the Spanish colonization of the area a couple of hundred years earlier. Jessie had been to San Antonio many times. It was an appealing combination of Old World grace and a raw, bustling frontier settlement.

The kidnappers had circled well to the west around Victoria, following the San Antonio River through rolling, brushy hills. The level of the river was up because of the rain, but it wasn't out of its banks. It continued to rise as the day went on, however, telling Jessie that even though the sky had begun to clear where they were, farther inland the remnants of the hurricane were still dumping rain on the Texas hill country. It might be several days before the rivers crested downstream along the storm's path.

As night approached, the riders still hadn't reached Cuero. It didn't matter anyway, Jessie thought, because the kidnappers weren't going to ride boldly into any settlement while she was such an obvious prisoner. They would be afraid she would start screaming for help. If they were taking her to San Antonio, she expected them to stop somewhere before they reached the city and somehow try to disguise the fact that she was their captive.

They had seen very few people during the day: a couple of riders in the distance, an old Mexican tending to a flock of sheep. Dumond wanted to avoid meeting anyone, and that wasn't hard considering that the vicious storm had driven everyone indoors as it passed through. Many of the people still hadn't emerged from their homes.

They found a clearing in a thick grove of cottonwoods and live oaks that lined the riverbank, and Dumond said, "We will make camp here for the night."

The man called Mullins registered a whining complaint. "I thought maybe we'd move on through the night. I gotta get a sawbones to look at this hand of mine. It's throbbin' like a son of a bitch."

Blood poisoning was already setting in, thought Jessie. She couldn't bring herself to feel sorry for him. Since he had thrown in with Dumond, he deserved whatever he had coming to him.

"I don't want to take a chance on running into any trouble in the dark," Dumond said with a note of impatience in his voice. "We will stay here."

"All right, all right," Mullins grumbled. "My hand hurts, that's all. Can't blame a fella for not wantin' to hurt."

They dismounted, and Dumond reached up to take hold of Jessie and lift her down from the saddle. As he did, she thought about kicking him in the balls and making another grab for his gun, but she didn't do it. So far, they hadn't treated her all that badly, but if she kept trying to escape, she didn't know how long that would last. Dumond might decide to turn his men loose on her, and she knew that wouldn't be a pleasant experience. Her next escape attempt *had* to succeed, so she was better off biding her time and waiting for a better opportunity.

Dumond set her on the ground and backed off a step. Jessie started making a beeline for some brush.

Dumond grabbed her arm and demanded, "Where are you going?"

She gave an angry toss of her head. "If you can't figure that out, then you don't know much about women, especially for a Frenchman."

"Oh. My apologies, of course, for not understanding . . . and for being forced to accompany you."

Jessie looked daggers at him. "You can't be serious."

"I assure you I am, *cherie*. But I will give you as much privacy as I possibly can."

"I suppose that's better than nothing."

But not much better, she thought as she took care of her needs. Dumond was right on the other side of the bush she was using to shield her, so that he could hear her if she tried to sneak away or bolt for the tall and uncut—and no doubt he could hear everything else, too.

When Jessie was finished, she stepped back out into the open and asked, "Are you planning to feed me, or do you starve your prisoners?"

"*Certainment*, we will share our rations with you. Some of them may be a bit waterlogged, but while we are traveling together, what is ours is yours."

"If that's true, I'll take a couple of Colts and a Winchester."

Dumond grinned at her audacity.

Dumond was true to his word. He had her sit down with her back against a tree trunk, and kept an eye on her while one of the other men found enough dry wood to build a fire, then fried some bacon and pan bread. The food was simple, but Jessie hadn't eaten since the night before, so she accepted the plate that Dumond gave her. She didn't thank him for it, though. She had to draw the line somewhere.

She forced herself to take her time and not wolf down the food. Dumond gave her a tin cup of coffee as well. The meal made Jessie feel halfway human again. She started thinking about ways to escape.

Dumond must have known what was in her mind, because he got a rope from one of the horses and said, "My apologies, *cherie*, but I cannot risk leaving you loose tonight. Too much depends on me delivering you to the one who sent me after you."

"And who might that be?" Jessie asked.

"You will find out in due time," Dumond replied as he started looping the rope around Jessie so that she was bound to the tree trunk. He also tied her wrists and her ankles. Being helpless like that made her seethe with anger, but for the time being, there was nothing she could do about it.

When Jessie was securely trussed to the tree, Dumond ordered his men to put out the fire, and picked several of them to take turns standing guard during the night. "With the storm just past, I do not believe anyone will bother us," he said, "but we cannot afford to take chances."

Even though her options were limited, she was turning them over in her mind when exhaustion caught up with her. The position she was in could hardly be called comfortable, but despite that, her head tipped back against the tree trunk, her eyes drooped closed, and sleep stole over her.

She had no idea how long she had been asleep when a hand roughly closing over her mouth so that she couldn't cry out suddenly jolted her awake. She tried to jerk her head away, but the cruel grip was too tight. The man's hand forced her head back painfully against the rough bark of the tree trunk.

Jessie opened her eyes. The night was so dark, she couldn't see anything except a vaguely darker patch of shadow looming in front of her. That was the man who had hold of her, she knew, kneeling in front of her. He leaned closer to her, and she wasn't surprised when she felt his other hand pawing at her breasts through her dress. Something felt odd about it, though, and when she smelled the ugly aroma of putrefaction, she knew what it was.

The hand that was mauling her left breast at the moment didn't have a thumb.

"You bitch!" Mullins whispered as he put his face next to hers, so close she wanted to gag from his sour breath. "Shoot my thumb off, will you? I'm gonna teach you a lesson for that, and I'm gonna have me a mighty good time doin' it."

Let him try to rape her, Jessie thought. He would have to untie her from the tree in order to do that, and untie her ankles as well. As soon as he did, she intended to put the son of a bitch down and take off into the night.

The analytical part of her brain still functioned despite

her fear and discomfort. She knew that Mullins must have been one of the men Dumond picked to stand guard. Everyone else was asleep, so he had seized this opportunity to molest her. Clearly, he hadn't thought things through, or he would have realized that even if he were successful in his sordid goal, in the morning Jessie could tell Dumond what had happened.

In which case, Dumond would probably just shrug and accept it, even though he might be angry. The Frenchman had made it clear that while they had to keep her alive, they didn't have to treat her with kid gloves. They could all take turns with her if they wanted to, and Dumond probably wouldn't do anything about it.

"Don't you make a sound," Mullins warned her. "You do and I'll cut your throat, I swear I will. Dumond won't know a thing about it until I'm long gone."

He eased up on her mouth enough for her to say, "If you do that, you won't get paid."

"I don't care anymore," Mullins said with a snarl in his voice. "I want to settle the score for what you done to me, bitch." He reached down to his groin, fumbled with his trouser buttons, and hauled out his stiff cock. As he drew a knife from his belt and pressed the blade's keen edge to her throat, he commanded, "Open that mouth o' yours . . . and if you're even thinkin' about bitin', just forget it. First time I feel you doin' anything but suckin', this knife's goin' right into your throat."

Jessie's heart pounded hard in her chest. Mullins wasn't going to untie her, so that hope of escape was gone. She said, "I'll tell Dumond what you did."

Mullins chuckled. "Go ahead. Once I'm done, there won't be a damned thing he can do about it, is there? My spunk'll already be in your belly."

The thought sickened Jessie. She closed her eyes as the world spun dizzily around her for a moment. Then Mullins dug the fingers of his mutilated hand into her cheeks and said, "Open up, bitch."

His erection was right in front of her face now. The musky smell rising from his groin, mixed with the stench of the putrid wound on his hand, turned her stomach. His fingers clawed at her face. She felt the warm trickle of blood down her neck from the cut that his knife had opened.

Suddenly, Mullins went flying backward. He cried out in alarm as he tripped and fell, sprawling on the ground near the faintly glowing embers of the campfire. A dark figure moved over him and kicked the knife out of his hand. Curses ripped out in French.

It looked like Dumond was more upset than Jessie had thought he would be.

Even though she hated him, she was grateful that he had woken up in time to stop Mullins from doing what he was trying to do. Dumond's loud, furious voice roused the other men as he cursed at Mullins.

The wounded man scrambled to his feet. "You can't treat me like that, you fuckin' frog!" Mullins yelled. With his good hand, he swept his duster back and clawed at the gun on his hip.

Dumond was faster. Jessie's eyes had adjusted to the darkness well enough so that she could see Mullins's gun had just slid out of its holster when Dumond's arm flashed up and the revolver in his hand roared. Flame licked from the barrel, the flash lighting up the clearing for an instant. Jessie saw Mullins knocked backward by the bullet that bored into his forehead, just above the left eye. She could only imagine what a bloody mess it made exploding out the back of his skull.

Mullins hit the ground hard, without firing his gun, and didn't move again. Dumond swung toward the others and demanded, "Well? Do any of the rest of you wish to defy my orders?"

One of the men laughed harshly and said, "If you think we're gonna risk dyin' over some crazy little shithouse rat like Mullins, Boss, you're on the wrong trail."

"Good," Dumond said. He lowered his gun part of the way.

"What'd he do, go after the woman?"

"That's right."

The hired gun shrugged and said, "She *is* mighty pretty . . . but there are pretty gals in San Antonio, too, and it won't get you killed if you try to bed down with 'em."

"You are a smart man, *mon ami.*" Dumond finally holstered his gun. "Now, I need someone to take over Mullins's turn standing guard, and someone else to drag his carcass away from the camp. I don't want him stinking the place up any worse than he already has."

Once those things were settled, Dumond came over to the tree where Jessie was tied and knelt in front of her. "My sincere apologies, *cherie.* I did not believe that even Mullins was foolish enough to attempt such a thing. I suppose I cannot blame him too much, however. Your beauty is enough to make any man's brain cease functioning."

Jessie worked her jaw back and forth for a second, trying to ease some of the soreness caused by Mullins grabbing it. Then she said, "Two things, Andre."

"Yes, *ma cherie?*"

"Thank you for what you just did."

"And the other?"

"Go to hell," Jessie said.

Chapter 21

When the light grew too dim for Longarm and Ki to see the tracks, Longarm called a halt and said, "We'll make camp for the night."

"What if those damned kidnappers keep goin' with Miss Starbuck?" O'Malley asked as the men dismounted.

"Then they'll get a bigger lead on us," Longarm replied with a shrug. "I don't like it any more'n you do, O'Malley, but we can't risk them heading off in some other direction and us losing the trail because we can't see it anymore."

Ki added, "We must be patient and careful right now."

O'Malley scowled. "What the two o' ye are sayin' makes sense, but 'tis drivin' me mad to think of the lady in the hands o' those bastards. There's no tellin' what they might—"

"Jessie is very good at taking care of herself," Ki said, cutting in. "You can rest assured, Captain, that she will make the best of any situation in which she finds herself."

O'Malley growled angrily, but didn't say anything else. He started unsaddling his horse.

Longarm found a small hollow and built a tiny fire in it

so they could boil coffee. Other than that, they would make
do with more jerky and stale biscuits for supper. As darkness descended, Longarm and Ki agreed to take turns
standing watch during the night.

"Is that really necessary?" O'Malley asked. "There are
no wild savages in this area, are there?"

"Nope," Longarm replied. "There are still a few bronco
Apaches way out west of here, in the Big Bend, but all the
Indians in these parts are tame. But you have men standing
watch on board your ship, don't you, even when you're not
expectin' trouble?"

"Oh, aye, of course. You can never tell when the sea will
hold a surprise or two."

"It's the same way on the frontier," Longarm assured
him. "It's always best to be ready in case all hell breaks
loose."

"In that case, it's volunteerin' I am to take a turn o' me
own."

"The marshal and I can handle it," Ki said.

"Maybe so, but 'tisn't fair. I can pull me own weight."

"All right, O'Malley," Longarm said. "You can stand the
first watch. You can tell time by the stars, right?"

The Irishman just snorted as if to say that was a foolish
question.

"Wake one of us at midnight," Longarm went on.
"Doesn't matter which."

With that, he and Ki rolled up in the blankets they had
picked up in Victoria and stretched out on the still-damp
ground, using their saddles for pillows. That was nothing
new for Longarm. He had learned to sleep that way during
the cattle drives he had joined as a young man, and many
times since he had slept on the ground while pursuing outlaws.

Like most frontiersmen, Longarm had also developed the knack of falling almost instantly into a deep, dreamless sleep whenever he got the chance. He did that here, and as a result he didn't know how much time had passed when he came awake to O'Malley's light touch on his shoulder.

"Midnight already?" he asked.

"No," O'Malley whispered as he leaned closer, "but riders are comin'."

Longarm sat up, reaching for the Winchester he had placed beside him as he did so. He heard the soft hoof-beats now. The riders weren't getting in any hurry. They approached the camp slowly and carefully, which could be good or bad. The fire was out, so the strangers might not even know that anyone was camped here.

But if they did know, their deliberate approach suggested that they were sneaking up on the place.

Longarm turned to Ki, but before he could say anything, Ki said, "I am awake, Marshal. I hear them as well."

Keeping his voice pitched low enough so that it couldn't be heard more than a few feet away, Longarm asked, "What do you think?"

"A cautious man does not necessarily seek trouble. You would approach a camp carefully at night, would you not?"

"I would," Longarm agreed, "but I'd sing out when I got close enough, too, so whoever was there would know I was comin'."

"Let's wait and see what they do," Ki suggested.

After a moment, the hoofbeats stopped, but no one called out. Instead, there was silence, broken occasionally only by small, faint crackles of brush.

One of the horses in the camp nickered. Longarm put his mouth close to Ki's ear and breathed, "Well, they know we're here."

"And they don't want us to know that they are here. They stopped their horses from responding to ours."

"Better spread out," Longarm told his two companions. "But be mighty quietlike about it."

It was a harrowing game of cat and mouse, Longarm thought as he bellied down and crawled away from the camp, pushing his Winchester ahead of him. He moved only a few inches at a time, being as silent about it as he possibly could, and then pausing to listen again. He tried to track Ki and O'Malley by the tiny sounds they made, but it was impossible to hear Ki's progress. He moved through the night as quietly as snow falling. O'Malley was a different story. Longarm could hear the crackle of brush and the scrape of boot leather against the ground.

So could the men skulking around in the darkness. Longarm wasn't surprised when he heard a man suddenly order, "Hold it right there, mister, or I'll blow your head off!"

Longarm came up on his knees, snapped the rifle to his shoulder, and fired at the sound of the voice. He heard a grunt of pain as he launched himself into a diving roll. More shots blasted as the lurkers aimed at the spot where they had seen his muzzle flash. Longarm wasn't there anymore, however.

More importantly, the other men had given away their positions to Ki, who struck out of the shadows with a silent, sudden fury. Longarm heard the solid thud of fists against flesh, then a yell of pain and alarm. "Stay down, O'Malley!" he called, then lunged up and moved to intercept someone who was crashing through the brush now, heedless of the noise he was making.

A dark figure loomed up right in front of Longarm. The big lawman swung the Winchester up and drove the rifle butt into the middle of where the man's face ought to be.

Sure enough, the blow landed with satisfying impact. The dark shape went over backward. Longarm stepped back and pointed the Winchester's barrel at the fallen man.

"Now it's your turn not to move, old son," he said. "Ki?"

"There are only four horses, Marshal," Ki's voice came back. "All the men are accounted for."

"Any of 'em done for?"

"Two are merely unconscious. A third is wounded and has passed out. The one who fled in your direction?"

"Out cold, I reckon. He ain't moved since I put him down."

"Can I get up now?" O'Malley asked in an angry voice.

"Reckon it'd be all right. See if you can get the fire started again, so we can figure out what we're dealin' with here."

Longarm was very curious to find out if the men who had tried to sneak up on the camp were wearing black dusters.

As it turned out, they weren't. They were dressed in ragged range clothes, and from the looks of their rough, unshaven faces, they were no more than small-scale desperadoes. The wounded man had a hole in his shoulder from Longarm's slug and had lost some blood, but Longarm didn't think the wound was too serious. Ki was patching it up when the men he had knocked out started to come to.

When they opened their eyes, they found themselves looking down the barrel of Longarm's Winchester. He had taken their guns away from them and had a cheroot clenched between his teeth. Around it, he said, "I wouldn't get too active there if I was you, boys. You go to jumpin' around and I'll get nervous enough to pull this trigger."

Both men gulped in fear and lay still. Now that the fire was brighter, Longarm could see a definite resemblance between them and the wounded man, as well as the hombre who was still out cold with shiners forming around his eyes from being clouted in the face by Longarm's rifle butt.

The man with the bullet hole in his shoulder, a burly, bearded gent, was considerably older than the other three. Longarm inclined his head toward that man and asked the others, "Is that your pa?"

"Yeah. He's gonna skin us alive when he wakes up," one of the men replied.

"You didn't have any call to start shootin', mister," the other man said. "We weren't gonna hurt you. We just wanted your horses and whatever else you got that's worth money."

"So you were just gonna rob us, not murder us," Longarm said.

"That's right!"

"How about lettin' us go?" the other one asked.

Longarm chuckled and shook his head, not so much in refusal as in amazement at their sheer audacity. "What's your names, boys?"

"I'm Calvin Gilfeather, this's my brother Joe, and the fella over yonder who's been knocked silly is my brother Mort. Our daddy is called Reuben."

Longarm ran the names through his memory. The Gilfeathers were clearly outlaws, but they had never been successful enough at it to draw the attention of the United States Marshals Service, at least not that Longarm recalled. He didn't have time to waste on them.

"Here's what we're gonna do," he said. "I want to get some more sleep tonight, so we're gonna tie you fellas up so you can't cause any trouble and gag you so you can't holler. Then, come morning, we're gonna leave you tied up here and take your horses."

"Damn it, you can't do that!" Joe Gilfeather exclaimed. "You can't leave us set afoot!"

Longarm prodded the owlhoot's nose with the barrel of his Winchester and snapped, "Shut up and let me finish. I don't believe for a second you would've left us alive if you'd got the drop on us, but I ain't in the habit of killin' folks in cold blood, not even no-account scalawags like you. We'll leave you so you can get loose after a while. Then we'll leave your horses far enough away that it'll take you most of the day to walk there."

"What about our guns?" Calvin asked. "Will you leave us our guns?"

"Nope," Longarm said. "Take it or leave it."

Calvin sighed. "We'll take it, I guess." When Joe started to protest, Calvin glared at his brother and went on. "Hush up. They could just kill us and be done with it, you know."

"That brings me to my next point," Longarm said. "I've had a good look at you boys now, and I don't never forget a face. If I ever see any of yours again, I'm gonna kill you. I won't ask questions, and I won't give you a chance to explain. I'll just kill you. Then I'll track down the rest of you and kill them, too. And then I won't ever give it another thought. You understand that?"

Calvin nodded, and after a second, so did Joe.

"All right then," Longarm said. "Let's get you fellas tied up and gagged so I can go back to sleep."

Chapter 22

Even gagged, all four Gilfeathers made quite a bit of noise during the night. The father, Reuben Gilfeather, tried to bellow curses through his gag when he regained consciousness. Longarm suppressed the urge to just shoot all four of them, and when Ki suggested cutting their tongues out, Longarm vetoed that as well. It would have made quite a mess, and probably would have taken him and O'Malley both to hold each of the owlhoots down while Ki did the cutting, and Longarm didn't figure the Irishman had the stomach for that.

In the morning, after they had eaten and saddled up their horses, Longarm loosened the Gilfeathers' bonds so that they could work their way free after a while. He had brought the outlaws' horses into camp the night before, and now he gathered up their reins. Ki and O'Malley were already mounted. Longarm swung up into the saddle and grinned down at the prisoners.

"Don't forget what I told you and Joe last night, Calvin," he said. "You'd better explain it to Mort and your pa and make sure they understand, too, since their lives are riding on it just as much as yours."

Reuben looked over at his sons and made puzzled, angry grunts through the gag. Calvin just rolled his eyes and shook his head.

"So long," Longarm said as he turned his horse. He rode away with Ki and O'Malley. He and Ki each led two of the extra horses.

When they were out of earshot of the outlaws, O'Malley asked, "Will ye really kill them if ye ever see 'em again, Marshal?"

"I just might," Longarm said.

Ki laughed. "I doubt it. The marshal may not always want to admit it, Captain, but he is a law-abiding man."

"Tell that to my boss," Longarm said with a smile. "He's all the time hoorawin' me about the way I do things."

"Bending a rule is not the same as breaking a law."

"I've been known to break a law or two when I had good cause."

"And ye used me as bait last night," O'Malley said, a note of anger in his voice.

"What do you mean?"

"Ye knew I couldn't move quiet enough to keep those rapscallions from hearin' me," the Irishman accused. "Ye wanted them to close in on me and give away where they were so you and Ki could jump them."

"Well, things sort of worked out that way," Longarm admitted, "but that don't mean I *planned* it."

O'Malley's disgusted snort showed how much he believed that claim.

They rode on, following the tracks left by Jessie's kidnappers. At least, they *hoped* the kidnappers had left those tracks. They didn't know that for sure, and the worry that they had guessed wrong gnawed at Longarm's guts. If it turned out that they weren't on the right trail, they would have lost days in the search for Jessie.

Around mid-morning, though, after leaving the Gil-feathers' horses miles from where they had left the outlaws, they got a break. They came upon an aged Mexican herding a flock of sheep, and Longarm signaled a halt. "Hello, Grandfather," he said to the old-timer in fluent Spanish. "Are you often in these parts?"

"Every day," the old man replied. He pointed a gnarled finger. "My hut lies over that hill, and the field where my sheep graze lies over there." He pointed in the other direction.

"Did you see six men ride through here yesterday?" Longarm didn't say anything about Jessie. He didn't want to plant any idea in the old-timer's head.

The Mexican nodded. "Yes, six men in long black coats."

Longarm's hopes rose.

They lifted even more as the old man went on. "They had a woman with them, riding with one of the men. A young woman, with hair like the sun when it rises in the morning, red and gold at the same time. She was so beautiful that she took away even the breath of an old man such as myself."

O'Malley asked, "What's he blatherin' on about?"

"He saw Jessie yesterday," Longarm said. "We're on the right trail."

"Saints be praised!" O'Malley exclaimed, and Ki looked pleased, but not surprised, at the confirmation.

"Did the beautiful woman appear to be unharmed?" Longarm put the question in Spanish to the old sheepherder.

"She looked unhappy, but not hurt," the man replied.

"Did you speak to her?"

The old-timer shook his head. "I feared to approach them. The men looked like devils. I did not even let them see my eyes."

Longarm nodded in understanding. He said, "I have no coins, Grandfather, or else I would reward you for the help you have given us."

"Do you wish to free the woman from those men?"

"We do."

"It will be payment enough if you succeed."

Ki spoke Spanish as well as Longarm did. He spoke up now, saying, "What is your name, Grandfather?"

"Manuel Torres."

"Know this, Manuel Torres," Ki said. "The friends of Jessica Starbuck are in your debt. Jessica Starbuck herself is in your debt. She—and we—always pay our debts. Someday we will return and reward you."

"If God wills it," the old-timer said, and made the sign of the cross.

"What was that last bit about?" O'Malley asked as they rode away, still following the tracks.

Longarm explained. "It's good to know that we're on the right trail."

"Have you figured out where they appear to be going, Marshal?" Ki asked. Longarm knew from the tone of the question that Ki already had a pretty good idea.

"Yep," Longarm said with a nod. "I'd say they're headed for San Antone."

Dumond's men buried Mullins in a shallow grave. They would have left the body for the buzzards and the coyotes if it had been up to them, but Dumond insisted. They stripped it of everything valuable first, though.

Just as Jessie expected, her captors circled wide around the town of Cuero, following the river toward San Antonio. To the south was Goliad, the scene of a brutal massacre during the Texas Revolution that had sparked a battle cry for the Texans, along with the Alamo.

Once again, Dumond set a fast pace. The sky had cleared and the weather was gorgeous now, although downed tree limbs, broken branches, and the swollen river were visible reminders that a terrible storm had passed this way a couple of days earlier.

Dumond tried to apologize again for what Mullins had almost done the night before, but Jessie stubbornly ignored him. Eventually, Dumond gave up, and they rode in silence for the most part.

Although she was too angry to allow herself to show it, Jessie was miserable. Mud still caked her clothes and her body. Her hair was tangled. She wanted to soak in a hot bath, to wash her hair and then comb it out, to slide between clean sheets and rest for hours. Instead, she was filthy and sore from the long hours in the saddle, and although she hoped that the situation would improve when they reached San Antonio, she knew she couldn't count on that.

Late in the day, they approached a large farmhouse that bore a resemblance to a Southern plantation, although it wasn't as elaborately built and had suffered some from neglect, as had the fields surrounding it. During the past two days, the kidnappers had gone to great lengths to avoid getting too close to any cabins or houses, so this was a change. They rode right up to this place and reined in.

A stocky man with graying, close-cropped hair came out of the house onto the columned porch. He wore a suit and looked out of place here, thought Jessie, an impression that was confirmed when he spoke in a guttural accent.

"I see you were successful in your mission, Herr Dumond."

The Frenchman dismounted and motioned for the others to do likewise. He reached up to help Jessie down, but she avoided his hands and slid to the ground by herself. She stalked toward the porch and demanded with a lot more assurance than she felt, "Are you the one who paid to have me kidnapped?"

"Me, Miss Starbuck?" The man shook his head. "*Nein*. But I have been charged with greeting you and making you comfortable here for the time being."

"Comfortable?" Jessie repeated. She laughed. "I'll never be *comfortable* as long as I'm a prisoner."

"That is indeed regrettable," the man said. He stood aside and gestured for her to come inside. "Please."

There was nothing else Jessie could do. She climbed the steps to the porch and allowed the man to usher her into the house. Dumond followed. The hired guns took the horses and went around toward the back of the house.

"I am called Reinhold, Miss Starbuck," the gray-haired man said, introducing himself. "I have a tub of hot water waiting for you upstairs, as well as clean clothing."

Jessie frowned at him. Had he read her mind somehow? Or had he just figured that those were the things she would want most after the long, miserable trip from Indianola?

She started to thank him, then stopped herself. She wasn't going to express any gratitude to any of these bastards, she told herself. All of them were her enemies.

"Show me the way," she ordered, not caring that she sounded a little imperious. When Dumond started up the staircase after them, she stopped short and wheeled around to face him. "Surely you don't think you're going to come with me?"

Dumond didn't answer her. Instead, he asked Reinhold, "Does the bedchamber have a good lock on its door?"

"It does," the man replied. "And the windows are nailed shut."

"In that case, then . . ." Dumond shrugged. "I think you can be allowed a little privacy, Jessie."

"It's about time," she said, scorn dripping from her voice.

She was putting up a good front, but inside, she was worried. She still hadn't found an opportunity to escape, and her chances to do so were narrowing even more. This old plantation house was going to be her prison, at least for the time being.

But a prison with a tub of hot water, she reminded herself. She might as well take whatever was offered to her, because there was no telling when the chance might come up again.

Inside, the house had the same air of faded, neglected gentility that it possessed outside. The musty smell in the air told Jessie that the place had been closed up, with no one living in it, until recently. Reinhold's boss, whoever that was, must have arranged for Dumond to bring her here. The hurricane had almost interfered with that plan, but Dumond had managed to overcome that unexpected obstacle.

With Reinhold in front of her and Dumond behind her, Jessie walked down a second-floor hallway. Reinhold opened a door into one of the rooms and stepped back. As he did, his coat swung open enough for Jessie to catch a glimpse of a gun butt. He had a pistol under his coat, and despite his polite attitude, he looked plenty tough enough to use it if he had to. In fact, he had an almost military air about him, to go with the Prussian accent.

Jessie stepped into the room, saw a huge, galvanized iron tub sitting in the middle of the floor. Tendrils of steam rose from the water in it. She almost moaned in anticipation of sinking down into that lovely heat, but managed not to. She didn't want to give them the satisfaction of hearing her express her feelings.

"There are clean clothes on the bed," Reinhold said, nodding toward the four-poster on one side of the room. "Someone will be waiting in the hall. Knock on the door when you are finished."

Jessie gave him a curt nod. Reinhold left the room, but Dumond lingered. "Jessie . . ." he began.

"Whatever you're going to say, I don't want to hear it," she told him. "I'm not interested in anything you have to say to me."

Dumond sighed. "A great pity, that. But have it your way . . . for now."

With that, he gave her a slight bow and left the room, too. Jessie wondered just how threatening he had meant that last comment to be.

She put that out of her mind and stepped over to the tub. A bar of soap and a large towel lay on a stool next to it. Jessie quickly stripped out of her dress, the first time she'd had it off since donning it before dinner three nights earlier. She dropped it on the floor, and then added her filthy undergarments to the pile. Kicking off her shoes, she lowered one foot into the tub, closing her eyes for a second at the feel of the hot water.

She climbed in and lowered herself into the water, relishing its heated embrace as it surrounded her. Closing her eyes again, she leaned back and felt her muscles relaxing. A long soak would work out all the kinks and soreness.

She dozed a little. The room was fairly dim, because

thick curtains over the windows shut out most of the late afternoon light and the wick of a lamp on a table next to the bed was turned low. Jessie let time pass without really paying attention to it.

Eventually, though, her mind began to work again. She considered everything that had happened. Someone wanted her in their power badly enough to pay Andre Dumond to come on board the *Harry Fulton* in New Orleans and seduce her, then kidnap her when they reached Indianola. Whoever was behind this had enough money to pay not only Dumond but also a dozen or so hired gun-wolves. And they had probably bought or leased this old farm with its plantation house, too, and sent Reinhold here to ready the place for her arrival.

Reinhold . . . a Prussian, and Dumond was French. The whole business had a definite European flavor to it, Jessie thought as she began soaping herself. She washed her hair first, then scrubbed the dirt off her skin. The water had begun to cool, so she didn't waste any time now. She got herself as clean as she could, then stood up and stepped out of the tub.

She was reaching for the towel on the stool when a key rattled in the lock and the door opened. With her hair hanging in wet, heavy loops around her head and water still beading and running down her sleek, honey gold skin, Jessie left the towel where it was and turned toward the door with a defiant glare on her face. She wasn't surprised at the identity of the person who stepped into the room and eased the door closed behind her.

"Hello, Katerina . . . you bitch."

Chapter 23

The woman was young and blond and beautiful, like Jessie, but that was where the resemblance ended. Unlike Jessie's mass of thick, reddish gold hair, Katerina von Blöde's fine-spun hair was a pale, pale blond, almost white, and arranged in delicate curls. Her complexion was milky, rather than having the golden tan Jessie's skin displayed. She wore an elegant blue gown with a low, square-cut neck that revealed the swelling upper thirds of full breasts. Icy blue eyes glittered with hate as she looked at Jessie, even though her full, red lips curved in a smile.

"There's no need for such animosity," Katerina said. "Have I not seen to it that you've been made comfortable since your arrival here?"

"All you people have an odd idea of comfort," Jessie snapped. She didn't like the way Katerina's eyes roamed over her body, so she picked up the towel and wrapped it around herself. "Anyway, a hot bath now doesn't make up for paying Dumond to betray and kidnap me."

Katerina moved closer and shrugged. "It was necessary. I regret any discomfort that was visited upon you."

"You mean like almost being raped by one of those gunmen you hired?"

Katerina's lips thinned as she pressed them together. "Who did that? I'll have him killed."

"No need," Jessie said. "Dumond already took care of that."

"Good. I'll have to commend him for saving me some trouble."

Jessie gave Katerina a defiant stare and demanded, "Just what is it you want from me . . . *Empress*?"

The scornful tone made anger flash even brighter in Katerina's eyes. "You don't need to know that now," she snapped. "I simply wanted to greet you and let you know that you'll be staying here tonight. Also, you'll be my guest for dinner this evening."

"I don't know how much of an appetite I'll have," Jessie said.

As a matter of fact, she realized that she was starving, and when Katerina had opened the door, she had let in some delicious aromas drifting up from downstairs. The smell of food cooking made Jessie's stomach clench with want. She tried to ignore the hunger pangs as she continued to glare at Katerina von Blöde.

"Come downstairs when you're dressed anyway," Katerina said. "Andre and I will be waiting for you."

"You mean the door won't be locked?"

Katerina shook her head. "There's no need. My men are all around the house, and they will be until we're ready to leave. You can't escape, Jessie. You might as well accept that."

"I wasn't raised to accept anything."

"Neither was I," Katerina said.

She turned and left the room. Jessie glared at the closed

door for a second before she realized it wouldn't change anything. She started drying her hair as she thought about Katerina—and about how she should have realized before now that the Outlaw Empress was behind her kidnapping.

Katerina's father had founded the Cartel, or at least had been one of the European master criminals responsible for its formation. To some extent, its origins were still shrouded in mystery. As the group began extending its evil reach around the world, it was inevitable that the plotters would run up against Alex Starbuck, who had business interests all over the globe. Jessie's father, a decent, honorable man, had resisted their efforts to recruit him and had become the Cartel's sworn enemy instead.

Alex Starbuck's battle against the Cartel had cost him his wife, and eventually had taken his life as well. With Ki's aid, Jessie had set out to avenge her father and smash his enemies. That had taken several years, and considerable assistance from Custis Long, but at last they had succeeded. Katerina's father had died in the epic struggle, and the Cartel was gone for good.

Or so they had all thought. It had been reborn in a Nevada ghost town, a city of outlaws called Zamora. That was where Jessie had met Katerina von Blöde and learned of her plans to bring the Cartel back to prominence. Although she and Ki and Longarm had ruined that particular plot, Katerina had remained active behind the scenes, pulling the strings on several other efforts to strengthen the new Cartel. Longarm had managed to break up those operations, and had written letters to Jessie detailing the encounters, so she would know what was going on.

She knew that Katerina harbored a special hatred for her, so it should have occurred to her right away that the self-styled Outlaw Empress was behind the kidnapping, Jessie told herself as she dressed. Katerina wanted revenge, not only for her father's death but also for Jessie's interference with her plans.

But she wanted something else, too, thought Jessie. Katerina wasn't going to devote so much time, money, and effort to something just to settle a personal score. She had to have some bigger goal in mind, some plan that needed Jessie's presence.

The best way to find out what that plan might be was to play along with Katerina, Jessie decided. She would continue to bide her time until it was clear what the Empress's real goal was.

Wearing the simple gray dress her captors had provided for her, she tried the door and found it unlocked, just as Katerina had said it would be. Nor was there a guard outside the door. Katerina really was confident that the men posted around the house were enough to keep Jessie from escaping.

She found Reinhold waiting for her at the bottom of the stairs. "This way, Miss Starbuck," the Prussian said, gesturing for her to follow him. He led her through an arched entrance into a dining room complete with a long table covered with a fine linen cloth. A sideboard and some of the other furnishings showed a thin layer of dust, more evidence of the house's formerly unoccupied state. The table was set with expensive, glistening china and crystal, though.

Katerina sat at the far end, sipping from a glass of wine. Andre Dumond was seated midway along the table on Katerina's right. He got to his feet as Reinhold led Jessie into the room.

"You look lovely, Jessie, as always," Dumond said.

"I didn't look too lovely when we got here," Jessie said.

For a second, she had considered ignoring Dumond and his flattery, but if she were going to be around these people for a while, such stubborn defiance would soon get tiresome.

Dumond shook his head. "I beg to disagree. Even covered with mud and exhausted, you were still a beautiful woman, *cherie.*" He glanced toward Katerina. "*One* of the most beautiful women in the world."

Katerina smiled as she placed her wineglass on the table. "You don't have to try to spare my feelings, Andre," she said. "I'm well aware of the fact that Jessica Starbuck is quite lovely. But I know how you feel about me . . . and my bank accounts."

Dumond cocked an eyebrow, and eloquently shrugged one shoulder.

Reinhold pulled out the chair at the far end of the table from Katerina. "If you would please be seated, Miss Starbuck . . . Dinner will be served in a moment."

Jessie sat down, as did Dumond. She glanced toward the big windows on one side of the dining room. The curtains were pulled over them, too, but enough of a gap remained so that she could see the fading roseate sky outside. The sun had set.

Reinhold brought a bottle of wine and filled the glass beside Jessie's plate. She picked it up and took a sip, then nodded her satisfaction to him as he stood by, holding the bottle and obviously waiting for her reaction. She wondered if he was an old family servant. For all she knew, he might have even worked for Katerina's father. It hadn't been that long ago that he had still been running the Cartel.

"I'm glad to see that you've decided not to be stubborn," Katerina said. "As long as you cooperate, you're in no danger."

Jessie didn't believe that. She and Katerina were natural

enemies. As long as Katerina was alive, Jessie knew she would be in danger.

She said, "I'll cooperate . . . as long as it suits me."

Katerina laughed. "I would expect nothing less from Jessica Starbuck." Her voice sharpened. "You've always been accustomed to getting your own way, haven't you?"

"Yes, and people who try to stop me usually regret it," Jessie shot back.

Dumond looked uncomfortable. "Ladies, ladies," he said. "Surely you can sheathe your claws long enough to have dinner."

"Mind what you say, Andre," Katerina snapped. "You still work for me."

"*Certainment,*" he murmured. "I just hoped that we could put aside our differences long enough to have a pleasant meal. Engaging in disputes while eating is very bad for the blood."

Katerina shrugged. "As you wish."

Dumond looked at Jessie, who also shrugged and said, "Why not?"

A moment later, several women emerged from a swinging door that led into the kitchen, bearing platters loaded down with hot food. The tantalizing smells made Jessie's stomach contract again. Roast beef, mashed potatoes, bowls of savory vegetables, a tureen of gravy, a plate piled with fresh-baked rolls . . . The meal was distinctly American, not German or French, as Jessie might have expected from the company she was keeping. The female servants were American, too, attractive women who spoke with soft Southern accents. Katerina addressed them by their married names—Mrs. Palmer, Mrs. Rutledge, Mrs. Harrison, and the like—confirming that she hadn't brought them with her from Europe.

Jessie couldn't help but wonder what American women were doing working for Katerina von Blöde. That was just one of many questions nagging at her, and she hoped to get answers to all of them by playing along with Katerina—for now.

The food tasted as delicious as it smelled. After being hungry for so much of the time the past few days, Jessie had to be careful not to eat too much and make herself sick. The wine was good, too, and she probably drank a bit too much. The warm feeling that came over her didn't make her hate Katerina any less, but it made that hatred perhaps a bit less urgent.

After they had eaten, Katerina swirled her wine in her glass and peered over the top of it. She smiled at Jessie and said, "Andre tells me that Custis Long was in Indianola before the hurricane hit. I didn't intend for him to be involved in this affair. But his presence was a bonus, I suppose you could say."

Jessie stiffened. Longarm had earned Katerina's hatred by ruining her plans on more than one occasion, and if she was bringing him up now, it couldn't be because of anything good.

Since Dumond had already told Katerina about Longarm, Jessie didn't see any point in denying it. "That's right, he was there," she said.

"As was your friend Ki. He came to Indianola to meet you when your ship arrived."

The glow from the wine had disappeared. Jessie nodded.

Katerina took a sip from her glass. "Do you know if they survived the storm?"

"How could I know?" Jessie asked. "I was dragged out of town by your lackey here."

"Lackey?" Dumond repeated. He pressed a hand to his

chest and laughed. "You call me a lackey? You wound me, Jessie!"

"What would you call it when you're at her beck and call and do everything she tells you to do?" Jessie asked coldly.

Dumond flushed, but before he could say anything else, Katerina raised her voice slightly and went on. "Until I have evidence to the contrary, I'm going to assume that Marshal Long and Ki are still alive. They are both extremely capable, stubborn men, and if anyone is likely to have come through a hurricane without being hurt too badly, it's them. So, Andre, I have new orders for you."

From the look on his face, Dumond didn't care for her telling him what to do in front of Jessie. But he said, "I am at your service, Empress, as always."

"You and the men who brought Miss Starbuck from Indianola will ride back along the trail you followed while the rest of us head west with the wagons."

Wagons, Jessie thought. She filed that bit of information away in her brain. They were going somewhere in wagons.

Katerina went on. "If you run into Marshal Long and Ki searching for Miss Starbuck, kill them. When you have made certain that both men are dead, then you can follow us. You should be able to catch up without much trouble and join us for the final part of the plan."

"The other men can handle that assignment without me—" Dumond began.

"No!" Katerina cut in. "I've given you your orders, Andre. Now it's up to you to follow them. Anyway, I don't trust those men to carry out their mission alone. Long and Ki are very resourceful . . . but so are you."

"As you wish," Dumond murmured, clearly unhappy about the orders, but reluctant to disobey. "I think it very likely, however, that they are already dead, and not necessarily from the hurricane. I sent men after Long, and Ki was heavily outnumbered as he battled our men in the hotel."

Jessie had been listening with a growing feeling of cold horror as Katerina talked so casually about having Longarm and Ki killed. Now she forced herself to laugh. "You'd need a whole army to outnumber Longarm and Ki," she said.

Katerina just smiled along the table at her. "If it comes to that, Jessie," she said, "that is exactly what I'll use."

Chapter 24

After dinner, Dumond escorted Jessie back up to her room. While she was downstairs, someone had removed the bathtub. Dumond lingered at the door. Jessie gave him a scathing look and said, "After everything that's happened, you don't honestly imagine that I'll invite you into my bed, do you?"

"I think I would be satisfied to know that you don't hate me, Jessie," he said.

"Too bad," she said. "Go see what you can get from the Empress."

With that, she closed the door in his face.

As soon as she was alone, everything caught up with her. She clenched her hands into fists at her side and took several deep, shuddery breaths as she battled to control her raging emotions. Ever since the kidnapping, she had wondered and worried about Longarm and Ki. Had they been killed in the hurricane, or had they survived somehow? If they were alive, did they know what had happened to her?

Many times in the past, she had found herself in deadly danger, only to have one or both of them show up and save her. Of course, to be fair, she had saved their lives on numerous occasions, too. The partnership she had with each man was different, but they were equally special.

And in her heart of hearts, Jessie couldn't bring herself to believe that they were dead. She knew somehow that Longarm and Ki were alive—and that they were coming for her.

But if that was true, they would be riding right into an ambush, she thought. Dumond and those hired gunmen would be waiting for them, waiting to cut them down. Jessie had confidence in her friends, but despite her bold statements to Katerina, she knew that sooner or later Longarm and Ki would run into a trap they couldn't escape.

If that happened while they were trying to save her, she knew she couldn't live with herself. She had to forget her plan to play along with the Outlaw Empress and find out what sort of scheme Katerina had hatched.

She had to get out of here, so she could warn Longarm and Ki.

She blew out the lamp and went to the window, pushing aside the curtains so she could look out. Night had fallen, and it was completely dark outside except for starlight. Jessie was looking back to the east, the direction she and her captors had come from—and the direction Longarm and Ki would come from as well if they were on her trail.

Reinhold had said that the window was nailed shut. Jessie tried it to make sure, getting a tight hold on the frame and heaving upward with all her strength. It didn't budge. She wasn't really disappointed, because she hadn't expected any other result from the experiment.

The room had a chair in it. She could pick it up and use it to break out the glass, but that would make such a racket, everyone all over the house would probably hear it. It would alert the guards posted outside, too, and even if she

managed to climb out without slicing herself to ribbons on
the broken glass, they would be waiting for her on the
ground below.

Feeling her frustration growing, Jessie went to the door.
She tried the knob, halfway expecting to find that Dumond
had locked it anyway. However, the knob turned easily in
her grasp, and the door swung open.

She stepped out into the hallway, which was dimly lit now
by a single lamp in a wall sconce. She didn't know which
room was Katerina's, or even if the Empress was staying
here in the old plantation house. The place had quieted down
quickly after dinner. No one was moving around. Jessie's
eyes searched the shadows in the hallway, thinking that she
might find Reinhold lurking there in the gloom.

No one challenged her as she cat-footed away from her
room. She went to the landing and looked down the big,
winding staircase. A man sat in a chair at the bottom of the
stairs with a rifle across his knees. He wasn't wearing a
duster like the kidnappers. Instead, he wore black whipcord
trousers, a red shirt, and a black leather vest. A black Stetson was pulled down on his head. From where she was,
Jessie could only see his profile, but he looked like a typical
hard case. She was sure she wouldn't be able to get past
him.

She prowled the other way along the hall, thinking that
there might be a rear staircase. She knew there were guards
around the house, but she would take her chances on getting past them if she could just make it outside.

The rear staircase was there, but the aroma of tobacco
smoke drifted up it. Jessie edged an eye past the corner to
peer down the stairs. She caught sight of a man sitting at
the bottom of them in the shadows. She might not have
known he was there if not for the scent of the quirley and the

ember that glowed orange when he sucked on the cigarette. She pulled back and took a deep but silent breath.

All right. So she couldn't go down.

What about up?

There had to be some way to get into the attic of this old house. The rear staircase just went down, not up. Jessie moved as quietly as possible along the hall. The doors were unlocked, the rooms behind them empty. She checked each of them, but didn't find any way out. The windows in each had been nailed shut, just like the one in the room where she was supposed to stay.

When she reached the far end of the corridor, she found a narrower door, and when she opened it, she found an empty linen closet. Since it was too dark in there to see very well, she stepped into the closet and felt around, searching for another door that might lead to some stairs going up to the attic. Nothing, just empty shelves. Jessie felt desperation growing inside her as she started to step back out into the hall.

As she did, something brushed against her cheek. Instinctively, she lifted a hand to brush it away, thinking it was a cobweb. Instead, her fingers touched a cord .

Jessie closed her hand around the cord, which ended at the level of her face. It hung from the closet's ceiling. She tugged carefully on it, felt it give a little. She pulled harder, but stopped short when she heard hinges begin to creak.

There was a trapdoor in the ceiling, she realized. The cord was attached to it so that it could be pulled down.

Her heart began to beat faster. The only reason anybody would put a trapdoor in the top of a closet was because it led into the attic. The guards at the bottom of the two staircases might not hear the squeaking hinges if she opened the door all the way—but they might. She had to silence them somehow.

Still moving as quietly as she could, Jessie hurried back to her room and picked up the chair. Throwing it through the window might not do her any good, but maybe it could help her in another way. She carried it back to the closet and set it down inside the little storage room. Then she pulled the door closed behind her.

She was in pitch-darkness now. Working by feel, she stepped up onto the chair and reached above her head, sliding her fingers along the cord until she found the place where it attached to a ring that was screwed into the trapdoor. Balancing carefully on the chair, she located the door's hinges, then kept one hand on a hinge while she spat on the fingers of the other hand. She wiped the spit onto the hinge, rubbing it into the metal in an attempt to work in the makeshift lubrication.

Jessie kept that up for several minutes, trying to loosen up the hinges. Her hands grew slick with her own spit. She dried them on her skirt, then took hold of the cord again and gently pulled down on it. She heard the hinges rasp a little, but she didn't think the sound could be heard outside the closed door of the closet.

A ladder unfolded from the other side of the trapdoor once it was lowered. It was stiff, probably from rust and disuse, and Jessie had to feel around until she found the joints where it folded and to use her spit to loosen them up, too. It was a good thing she didn't mind being a little unladylike in a good cause, she thought with a faint smile. She had probably spat more in the last five minutes than she normally did in a month.

When she had the ladder unfolded, she scrambled up it, a little unnerved because she was climbing into stygian blackness. Suddenly she felt something all over her face and recoiled. She had run into a cobweb for real this time.

One hand tightened on the ladder as she almost slipped; the other pawed at her face to wipe the spiderweb away—and hopefully any spiders that went with it.

She shuddered in revulsion as something skittered across the back of her hand. She flung it away, wishing for some light so that she could see what she was getting into. Then, as she paused there on the ladder, she realized that there *was* some light in the attic. Not much, but a faint grayness that drew her eyes to a lighter oblong in the darkness.

A dormer window, Jessie thought. That was exactly what she had hoped to find.

She climbed into the attic, which had a sturdy plank floor. Whoever had built this house had probably used this space up here for storage. It might be empty, or it might still hold some of the detritus of departed lives. Carefully, Jessie started making her way toward the window. She bumped into something that felt like an old trunk, and reached down to feel her way around it—then ran right into someone standing there waiting for her.

Jessie stifled a cry of alarm and struck out, shooting a fist toward the spot where the person's head should be. The punch didn't hit anything. Off balance because of the miss, Jessie stumbled forward and grappled desperately with her opponent. She felt the thrust of a bosom against hers.

Katerina? What would the Outlaw Empress be doing up here in the attic?

As Jessie grabbed hold of the lurker in the dark, she suddenly felt foolish. She was wrestling with a dressmaker's dummy. That was why it didn't have a head. Stifling a laugh of relief, she moved the dummy aside. She was lucky it hadn't gone crashing over and alerted everybody that somebody was skulking around the attic.

Only a few more feet separated her from the window. Jessie covered that distance carefully, but finally she was there. Surely, no one had climbed all the way up here to nail the dormer window closed, she thought.

She took hold of the window and tried to slide it up. Her heart sank when it didn't move. The window had no curtain, so she leaned closer to the glass and peered through it, trying to see in the starlight if she could spot the nails holding it closed. As far as she could tell from studying the outer sill, there weren't any nails.

It was just stuck then, she told herself. She could deal with that.

While she was feeling her way around the trunk, her hand had brushed one of the metal straps that held it closed. The strap had swayed back and forth as she touched it. It wasn't attached well, the nails that held it having loosened as the wood of the trunk rotted. No telling how old the thing was.

Jessie went back to it, being careful not to knock over the dress dummy, and found the metal strap. She worked it back and forth, trying to loosen it even more, and then started wrenching on it. After a minute or so, it came free.

She went back to the window and worked the end of the strap into the little gap between the window frame and the sill. Once she was satisfied that it was wedged in securely, she heaved back, putting her weight against the strap in an attempt to pry the window up.

At first, the window didn't move. Jessie tried again, and this time she thought the window shifted a little. She adjusted her grip on the metal strap, which was cutting into her palms a little. Taking a deep breath, she heaved on it again, and this time the window definitely slid up a fraction of an inch.

Jessie was able to work the strap farther into the gap, giving her more leverage. This time, she pressed down on the other end of it, using her weight as well as her strength. With a rasping sound, the window slid up a couple of inches.

She hoped no one outside had heard that noise, but she had come too far to turn back now. She set the metal strap on the sill and slid her fingers underneath the window. Setting her feet, she put a firm, steady, upward pressure on it. The window resisted, but Jessie was able to raise it slowly without making too much noise. She stopped when she had it high enough for her to fit through it.

Bending over, she stuck her head and shoulders through the opening and looked around. The dormer was on the front side of the house, facing toward the road, but no one was out there. The guards were all closer to the house. She couldn't see or hear any of them, but she knew they were there.

Jessie crawled out onto the roof. Her dress caught for a moment on a rough spot in the window frame. She reached back and worked it loose, ripping it only a little.

Once she was out, she made her way on hands and knees toward the roof peak. When she got there, she stretched out to take a look around.

Not surprisingly, there were quite a few buildings behind the plantation house. She saw a large barn with a corral next to it, a couple of smaller buildings near it that were probably a blacksmith shop and a smokehouse. A long, low building she pegged as a bunkhouse. Smaller huts and cabins in the distance must have been the slave quarters in the days before the Civil War.

Lights burned in the windows of the bunkhouse. Katerina's gunmen were in there, Jessie thought. More than likely playing cards, drinking, or both.

What she saw next might have really shocked her had it not been for Katerina's comment at dinner. A large number of covered wagons were arranged in a circle in what had once been a field. They were Conestogas, the sort of prairie schooners that had carried thousands of immigrants westward during the country's great expansion into the frontier a few decades earlier. Up until the completion of the transcontinental railroad, such wagon trains had been common. These days, most immigrants used the railroad, but from time to time the wagons still rolled, taking new settlers to areas where the steel rails hadn't reached yet.

Now Jessie realized that Katerina hadn't been talking about a few wagons, but rather a whole wagon train. Jessie saw campfires burning in the area enclosed by the wagons and people moving around those fires. Based on the number of the canvas-covered vehicles she could see, she estimated that there might be close to a couple of hundred immigrants over there.

What in the world was going on here?

She could try to find out the answer to that question later, Jessie decided, once she was reunited with Longarm and Ki. She wasn't going to allow herself to even consider the possibility that they might be dead.

But if they were, she was acquainted with the commander of the army post at Fort Sam Houston in San Antonio. She would get the cavalry to take care of whatever deviltry the Empress was planning.

First things first, though. She had to get away from here. She started crawling again, this time toward the back of the house.

Most of the roof was too high for her to drop from it. But a single story extended out from the rear of the house. That would be where the kitchen was located. There shouldn't be anyone in there at this time of night, thought Jessie. She was able to hang from the edge of the higher roof and drop onto the lower one. All she could do was hope that no one, inside or out, heard the soft thump she made as she landed.

She could reach the ground from this kitchen roof. But it wouldn't do her any good if she landed right in the lap of a guard.

Or maybe it would, she suddenly thought. The guards were probably spaced at intervals around the house. If she could eliminate one of them, that would create a gap in Katerina's defenses.

Still moving as quietly as possible, Jessie made her way along the edge of the roof, pausing every couple of seconds to listen. And not only to listen, because Ki had taught her to reach out with all her senses. Because of that, after a few minutes, she not only heard someone shifting around slightly below her, she also smelled leather, tobacco, and sweat.

One of the sentries was right underneath her on the house's back porch.

Jessie froze in place. The man coughed softly, cleared his throat. Boot leather scraped on the ground as he shuffled his feet. Not surprisingly, he was bored. Standing watch was a tedious job. Sooner or later, he would have to move around some, just to stay alert.

Jessie was ready when he did.

She came up in a crouch as the man ambled out from under the porch's overhang. She raised her dress around her hips, not only baring her legs, but freeing them from the garment's constraints as well.

Then, without pausing to worry about what might happen if this went wrong, she leaped out into space.

Chapter 25

By nightfall, Longarm, Ki, and Seamus O'Malley were only about ten miles outside of San Antonio. That was what Longarm estimated anyway, and Ki agreed.

"Why don't we just ride on into town?" O'Malley suggested. "We could start lookin' for Miss Starbuck."

"San Antonio's a big place," Longarm said. "Biggest town in Texas, I reckon."

"I know that." O'Malley rubbed his jaw. "You're sayin' ye wouldn't know where to start lookin'."

"We can't knock on every door in town. That'd take too long."

O'Malley sighed. "Aye, that makes sense, I reckon. I'm just anxious to find Miss Starbuck."

"So are we, Captain," Ki said. "As impatient as we all are, it will still be better to wait until morning so that we can continue following the trail."

They made camp not far off the trail, under some trees. Ki built a small fire to cook their supper, and when that chore was finished, Longarm said softly, "Let it burn."

Ki was hunkered next to the fire. He glanced up at Longarm and cocked an eyebrow. "You think so?"

"I do," Longarm said with a solemn nod. "I got a hunch again."

O'Malley looked back and forth between them. "What are the two o' ye talkin' about?"

"You'll see," Longarm told him. "Just be ready for trouble if any crops up."

O'Malley frowned, but didn't press the issue. The three of them ate their supper, then spread their bedrolls at the very edge of the gradually dwindling circle of light cast by the fire as it died down naturally.

In the thickening shadows, Longarm rolled up one of his blankets and thrust it under the other. With his saddle at the head of the blanket roll, in poor light it looked like someone was sleeping there. Without saying anything, he motioned for O'Malley to do the same. The sea captain followed the order, as a look of comprehension dawned on his face. On the other side of the camp, Ki was doing likewise.

Carrying his rifle, Longarm gestured for O'Malley to follow him, and faded back into the darkness under the trees. Ki circled to join them. As they looked back at the fire and the shapes on the ground around it, O'Malley whispered, "It looks like we're sleepin' there . . . but that's how 'tis supposed to look, isn't it?"

"That's right. If those fellas who grabbed Jessie work for the Empress, I wouldn't put it past 'em to double back and try to ambush us. We're gonna make it easy for 'em if they do."

"So that *we* can ambush *them*."

"You're starting to get the hang of this, Captain."

O'Malley hefted his rifle. "Just give me a good shot at the scalawags. That's all I ask."

The three of them settled down to wait silently in the darkness. Longarm had no idea how long it would take for the trap to spring closed, or if it even would. All he knew was that he and his companions were ready.

After a while, Ki whispered, "I'm going to scout the area."

"Be careful," Longarm told him. He didn't see or hear Ki leave. One second he was there; the next he was gone. That didn't surprise Longarm. He knew that Ki could move in the shadows as if he were one of them, as insubstantial as mist.

Half an hour went by, and then Ki was there again, appearing as suddenly and silently as he had vanished. "Six riders coming from the direction of San Antonio," he said.

"Our friends in the black dusters?" Longarm asked.

"That's right."

Longarm looked at the campfire. It had burned down to the point that it was little more than embers, but it still cast enough of a glow for the blanket-shrouded shapes to be visible. He hoped that bait would be enough to draw in their enemies.

O'Malley asked, "Do we wait for them to sneak up on the camp?"

"That's the idea," Longarm told him. "Let's spread out. Wait for them to open the ball. They'll be blazing away so much, they may not notice our shots until we've already downed a few of 'em." Longarm paused, then added, "I'd like to take one of the bastards alive, if we can."

"Leave that to me," Ki said.

Longarm nodded. He had confidence in Ki's abilities.

"You stay here, so we'll know where you are," Longarm

told O'Malley. "Ki, you go right, I'll go left. Be careful where you're shootin', Captain. You don't want to hit one of us by mistake."

"This isn't the first fight I've ever been in, Marshal," O'Malley replied with a touch of annoyance in his voice.

"Let's hope it ain't your last one."

With that, the group split up, O'Malley staying where he was, Longarm and Ki going in different directions. Longarm couldn't move like a phantom, the way Ki did, but he was pretty damned stealthy, he thought as he glided through the darkness.

He circled around the campfire, stopping when he had put about a hundred feet between himself and O'Malley. Ki was over there somewhere in the shadows on the far side of the fire. They were well away from the camp, leaving an open space so that the would-be bushwhackers could approach it. Longarm had seen enough ambush attempts to have a pretty good idea what the duster-clad killers would do. They would spread out, too, and close in on the camp, then open fire on what they thought were the sleeping forms of Longarm, Ki, and O'Malley.

Longarm's gut had told him that something like this might happen tonight. If the kidnappers were taking Jessie to San Antonio, they had had enough time to reach their destination, turn her over to Katerina von Blöde, and double back to get rid of any pursuit. The Empress was good about trying to cover her tracks.

Of course, those hombres in the black dusters couldn't be sure that the three men who appeared to be sleeping around the fire were really after them. They might be murdering innocent bystanders.

Somehow, Longarm didn't figure they would worry too awful much about that.

He didn't hear any horses, but the skin on the back of his neck suddenly prickled anyway. Instinct told him that the bushwhackers were here. He had already levered a round into the Winchester's firing chamber. He lifted the rifle to his shoulder now and peered over the barrel, waiting for the first muzzle flash.

With no more warning than that, a man's voice abruptly yelled, "Wait! It's a—"

But trigger fingers were already tightening. It was too late to stop the ambush. Shots blasted, and flame spurted from rifle barrels to light the night with bright orange flashes.

One of the bushwhackers had already tumbled to the fact that this was a trap. Longarm knew he couldn't afford to wait. He started firing as fast as he could work the Winchester's lever, spraying the area around the campfire with lead. Off to his right, O'Malley did likewise. Ki didn't open fire, because he was closing in on one of the killers, targeting him for capture. That meant Ki was in extra danger, because he might be placing himself in the path of the bullets fired by Longarm and O'Malley, but that couldn't be helped.

Longarm cranked off ten shots, leaving five rounds in the Winchester. As he stopped firing, O'Malley did, too. Longarm heard a wounded man screaming somewhere in the darkness, a high, thin screech of agony. The cry choked off in a grotesque bubbling sound that signified death.

Someone started crashing through the brush. Longarm knew it couldn't be Ki making that much racket, so he wasn't surprised when Ki called, "Coming your way, Marshal!"

Longarm dropped to a crouch. The fleeing man opened fire in an attempt to clear the way ahead of him, using a handgun from the sound of the shots. Bullets whipped through the trees, going well over Longarm's head. Shots fired in haste while on the run nearly always went high.

The noise and the muzzle flashes gave Longarm plenty at which to aim. He kept his shots low as he squeezed off two rounds, hoping to knock one of the bushwhacker's legs out from under him and take him alive, since he didn't know if Ki had succeeded in grabbing a prisoner. Luck wasn't with Longarm, however, and suddenly the duster-clad figure was practically on top of him, still moving fast.

Longarm uncoiled from his crouch and thrust his rifle out ahead of him, driving the barrel into the man's belly. The blow made the man double over and grunt in pain. His momentum carried him on into Longarm, and the collision sent both men tumbling to the ground.

Longarm's rifle slipped out of his hands as he rolled over and came back to his feet. The bushwhacker was already back up, too, lunging at him. Longarm swung a punch that glanced off the hombre's shoulder. Then the bushwhacker rammed him again, this time against the trunk of a tree behind him. Longarm's head bounced painfully off the trunk. The impact made brightly colored rockets flash behind his eyes.

He flung out his arms, grappling with the man. The man got a hand on his face and tried to stick a thumb into his eye. Longarm twisted away from the gouging thumb, and brought his left fist up in an uppercut that landed on the man's jaw and knocked him back a step. That gave Longarm the room he needed for a roundhouse right that landed with a sound like an ax blade chopping into a stump. The bushwhacker went down and stayed down.

The night was quiet now. The shooting was over. Ki called softly from somewhere nearby, "Marshal?"

"I've got the son of a bitch," Longarm replied.

"He never should have gotten away from me," Ki said. "He broke and ran when the others started shooting, and he happened to be the one I had picked to capture. I was too far away from the others to reach them in time."

"What about the rest of them?"

"Four are dead. You captured one." Bitterness edged Ki's voice as he added, "One got away."

Longarm bit back a curse. He didn't doubt for a second that the varmint who had gotten away would run right back to the Empress and tell her that the ambush attempt had failed. Now she would *know* that someone was after her.

But she would have been prepared for such a thing anyway, he told himself. In the long run, it wouldn't make much difference.

There were still some things he wanted to find out. He bent down, grasped the collar of the man he had knocked out, and hauled the hombre back to his feet, where he swayed in groggy semiconsciousness. Longarm pressed the barrel of his Colt into the man's back and growled, "Move, you bastard. And if you try anything funny, I'll blow your backbone in half."

As Longarm marched the man toward the fire, he called out, "Come on in, O'Malley!" A racket in the brush told him that the captain was doing as he was told.

O'Malley reached the camp about the same time as Longarm and the prisoner. Ki came in a moment later, dragging one corpse and carrying another draped over his shoulder. He dumped the one he was carrying next to the other body and said, "I'll bring in the other two."

In the dim light of the fire, the captured bushwhacker looked at the sprawled corpses with an expression of dull shock on his face. "You killed 'em," he muttered. "You killed 'em all."

"And just what was it you and your pards were intendin' to do to us, old son?" Longarm asked.

The man's hat had come off during the fight. He was a heavy-featured gent with a mostly bald head. Longarm told him to sit down, adding, "If you move, I'll shoot you. Or rather, O'Malley will. You got that, Captain? Keep him covered."

"Aye," the Irishman agreed.

Longarm knelt by the fire and pushed some broken branches into it. The flames began to leap higher and cast more light. When he had it burning steadily, he turned toward the dead outlaws and studied their faces in the light. He had never seen either of them before.

Ki brought in the other two a minute later and added their bodies to the grim display. All four of the bushwhackers had been shot several times. Longarm checked the faces of the other two men and shook his head.

"What's wrong?" Ki asked.

"I thought I might see a face that I recognized," Longarm said. "The fella who yelled just before the shooting started, the one who figured out what was going on, sounded familiar to me."

"To me as well," O'Malley said. "'Tis mistaken I might be, I would have sworn 'twas that Frenchman . . ."

"Andre Dumond," Longarm said. "And since he's not here, that can only mean one thing. He's on his way back to the Empress right now to warn her that we're after her."

Chapter 26

Jessie plummeted through the darkness, straight at the unsuspecting guard below her. She landed on his shoulders, and as she did so, her bare legs scissored around his neck in a wrestling move that Ki had taught her long ago. Her weight sent the man stumbling forward.

She locked her legs as tightly as she could, choking off any outcry he might make. At the same time she knocked his hat off and wrapped her fingers in his hair, hanging on. Unable to catch his balance, after a couple of steps, he pitched forward to the ground. Jessie's legs released their grip and shot out to take her weight as she landed. She used her momentum to drive the guard face-first into the ground.

That stunned him and kept him quiet long enough for Jessie to snatch his gun from the holster on his hip and bring the butt down on the back of his head with a soggy thud. The guard quivered and then went completely still.

She picked up the Winchester he had dropped and got to her feet. She was free, she was armed, and from here on out she would take her chances. From the roof, she had seen horses in the corral next to the barn. That was her next goal, to get a mount and start putting some distance between her and her enemies.

It would have been nice if there were more trees to use for cover, but she would have to make do with what she had, she told herself as she darted behind a willow. She waited there in the shadows to see if any of the other guards had heard the brief scuffle, but everything still seemed to be peaceful and quiet around the old house.

After a moment, Jessie headed for the corral. The horses milled around a little as she approached. She had lived on a ranch for most of her life, so she knew how to calm frightened horses. She spoke to them in a soft, gentle voice, and as she came up to the fence, the animals settled down slightly. She felt for the latch on the gate.

Before she could open it, someone up by the house yelled, "Son of a bitch! Roscoe!" Then: "She's loose! The Starbuck woman is loose!"

Well, hell, Jessie thought as she slapped the latch up and shoved the corral gate open. No point in trying to be quiet now.

She couldn't jump on a horse carrying both the rifle and the Colt, so she whirled toward the house, thrust the revolver in that direction, and started firing. The Colt was a double-action, so she was able to empty it in a matter of heartbeats. She didn't care if she hit anything; she just wanted to send the guards diving for cover and slow them down.

The shots roaring so close by spooked the horses again. Some of them bolted through the open gate. Jessie didn't try to stop them. Their bodies screened her from the house, at least to a certain extent. She tossed the empty pistol aside and ran into the corral, carrying the Winchester.

Some of the guards began to shoot, but only a few reports had sounded before a voice Jessie recognized as belonging to Reinhold bellowed, "Cease fire! Cease fire! The prisoner must not be hurt!"

That was good to know, thought Jessie with a grim smile as she tried to grab one of the horses. It meant they couldn't just blaze away indiscriminately at her. That gave her a better chance to get away.

She managed to grab one of the horses by the mane and pull its head down, bringing it under control after a second. It was a struggle to maintain that control, because the other horses in the corral were still milling around skittishly. Jessie led the one she had grabbed over to the fence, and stepped up onto the bottom rail with one foot. That brought her up high enough that she was able to throw her other leg over the horse's back.

Luckily, she'd been able to ride before she could walk, so she was able to use her knees and one hand tangled in the horse's mane to bring it around. Then she kicked its flanks and sent it lunging toward the open gate. A number of the other horses dashed out with it.

Several of Katerina's men were running toward the corral, but they had to scatter to avoid being trampled by the stampeding horses. One man got close enough to make a grab for Jessie. She swung the rifle one-handed and caught him in the head with the barrel, sending him spinning off his feet.

Then she leaned forward on the horse's back and urged it into a hard gallop. She was headed west, and she could see the lights of San Antonio glittering a couple of miles away. This late, only the saloons were still open, but there were enough of them to make the city visible in the darkness.

It was going to take the Empress's men several minutes to catch and saddle their horses, she thought. That delay would give her enough of a lead to reach San Antonio, and once she was there, she could find someone to help her. The law, the army, somebody. Right now, Jessie didn't care who it was.

And as quickly as possible after that was taken care of, she had to send someone to warn Longarm and Ki that Andre Dumond and the Empress's hired gun-wolves were going to ambush them. If it wasn't too late already.

Jessie forced that thought out of her mind. Right now, she had to concentrate on her own escape. She cut across an open field, hoping that the horse wouldn't step in a hole or anything like that. From the corner of her eye, she could see the covered wagons drawn up in their protective circle. Even though there was no longer any danger of being attacked by Indians in this part of the country, wagon camps were still formed that way.

Sudden movement caught her attention. Several riders left the camp and angled toward her. She hadn't counted on pursuit coming from the wagons. She bit back a curse. She thought she could outrun the riders, but it was going to be more difficult than giving the slip to the men who'd be chasing her from the plantation house.

"Come on, horse," she urged as she practically lay flat on the animal's neck, clinging to its mane and banging her heels against its flanks. The horse stretched out, legs flashing in the night as it ran for all it was worth.

Jessie was a good judge of horseflesh, and knew this mount had both strength and sand, but that might not be enough. Not the way those riders from the wagons were cutting across the fields toward her.

She veered to the left, away from them. Now it was more of an out-and-out race, but she wasn't headed directly toward San Antonio anymore.

She looked back over her shoulder. It was hard to tell in the darkness, but she thought the pursuers were gaining on her. Her heart tried to sink, but she wouldn't let it. After working as hard as she had to escape, she wasn't going to give up now. Not without giving it everything she had.

Unfortunately, everything she had wasn't enough. Her luck ran out a moment later as the horse running so gallantly beneath her suddenly stumbled. Jessie cried out in alarm as she felt the horse falling. At least, she didn't have to kick her feet free from any stirrups. There was nothing to hold her as she went sailing through the air.

She managed to land on one foot and used it to lever her momentum into a roll that broke some of the force of her fall. She went over and over on the ground, the plants and rocks tearing at her flesh through the dress. As hoofbeats pounded somewhere close by, she came to a stop and realized that instinct had prompted her to hang on to the rifle. One hand was still wrapped around its stock.

Fighting off weariness and the pain she felt from the fall, she forced herself to her feet, swinging the Winchester up as she did so. Riders were all around her. She wouldn't have any trouble finding targets.

Before she could pull the trigger, one of the men left his saddle in a leap that sent him crashing into her. Jessie stumbled back and managed to stay on her feet, but the man grabbed the rifle and ripped it out of her hands. As he tossed the weapon aside, Jessie turned to run. She knew it was hopeless, but she couldn't stop fighting.

She made it only a few steps before his arms closed around her from behind. She cried out in a mixture of rage and despair as he jerked her back and then swung her around so that her feet left the ground.

"Might as well stop fightin', ma'am," he said into her ear in a soft Southern drawl. "I've got y'all."

"Let go of me, damn you!" Jessie raged. "You've got no right—"

"You're correct, ma'am," he said, surprising her with his agreement. "We don't have any right, and we'd never think of harmin' y'all if we hadn't been forced to it. So please don't make things any worse for all of us than they already are."

Something about his voice calmed her despite the anger she felt. She wanted to keep fighting, but sheer logic told her it was wasted effort. He was bigger and stronger than her, and several other men surrounded them. As bitter a pill as it was to swallow, she knew her escape had failed.

"All right," she said, letting her muscles go limp as she stopped struggling. "Let me go. You're hurting me."

The tightness of his grip eased, but he didn't release her. "Sorry, Miss Starbuck. It's late and I'm tired. I don't really feel like havin' to chase you down if y'all decide to run again."

"I'm not going to run," Jessie snapped. "Where would I go?"

"Well, I reckon that's true." He finally let go of her and moved back a step. She turned to look at him in the moonlight, saw the short, grizzled beard and the craggy features. He was older than he had sounded, and he had the strength of a younger man as well.

The man turned to look at one of his companions and went on. "Corporal, check on the lady's horse."

"Yes, sir, General," the man responded. He raised a finger to the bill of the forage cap he wore in a casual salute.

Soldiers, she thought in amazement. She had been re-captured by soldiers.

"Who *are* you people?" she asked.

The older man reached up and touched the brim of his hat as he gave her a polite nod. "Brigadier General Arthur Tennyson, Miss Starbuck," he said, introducing himself. "Fifth Georgia Cavalry, Confederate States Army."

Chapter 27

Ki tied the prisoner's hands behind his back so that they wouldn't have to worry about him getting away; then Longarm began to question him.

"Andre Dumond was the leader of your bunch, right?"

Sitting on the other side of the fire, the hard case just stared sullenly at him and didn't say anything.

Longarm reached across his body and drew his gun, taking his time about doing it. He leveled it at the man's nose and said, "I already know you were working for Dumond and Dumond is working for Katerina von Blöde, so if you don't want to talk, I can just go ahead and shoot you and get it over with."

The man paled and swallowed hard. "You . . . you can't do that!" he blustered. "You're a lawman. It wouldn't be legal to just shoot me!"

"Well, one way of lookin' at it is that something ain't a crime if nobody reports it," Longarm mused. He looked at Ki. "You plan on saying anything about what happens here?"

"You know better than that, Marshal," Ki replied with a faint smile.

"How about you, O'Malley?"

"'Tis silent as a lamb I'll be," the Irishman promised.

Longarm looked at the prisoner again and eared back the Colt's hammer. "It's up to you, friend."

The outlaw looked so scared, he might piss himself at any moment. He grimaced and burst out, "All right, all right! I'll tell you whatever I can, but I warn you, it ain't that much. Just don't kill me!"

Carefully, Longarm let the Colt's hammer back down. Then he lowered the gun. "You work for Dumond?"

"Dumond was in charge, but I work for the Empress. So does he, just like you said."

"You know who she is?"

"You called her by name. I reckon you already know who she is. But I don't know anything *about* her except her name . . . and that she's got plenty of money and she's used to gettin' her own way."

"You ever hear of the Cartel?"

The prisoner licked his lips. "Sure. Just about everybody who hires out his gun has heard of the Cartel at one time or another. They've hired a bunch of us over the years. But they're gone now."

"They're coming back," Longarm said. "The Empress is in charge. She's trying to rebuild the organization."

"That's news to me, Marshal. All I know is that I was paid to help Dumond snatch Miss Starbuck."

"What about ambushing me back in Indianola?"

"That was all Dumond's idea," the gunman insisted. "We were just after the woman. But when Dumond found out who you were, he figured you might try to interfere and that it'd be better if we got rid of you."

"But you were in the bunch that grabbed Miss Starbuck?"

"Yeah."

"Where did you take her?"

The prisoner hesitated, and Longarm could tell that he was weighing his chances of getting away with a lie. Chances were, he was afraid of what the Empress might do to him if she ever found out that he had put Longarm, Ki, and O'Malley on her trail. To impress upon him that he had other things to worry about, Longarm raised the gun again.

It wasn't enough. With a touch of bravado creeping back into his voice, the man said, "You're bluffin'. You won't shoot me."

Longarm sighed. "You're right, old son," he admitted. "I don't reckon I could live with myself if I killed a man in cold blood, even a snake-blooded hombre like you."

He pulled the trigger. The Colt roared. The prisoner screamed as he jerked back. Dirt had exploded into the air as a bullet slammed into the ground no more than an inch from his knee.

"But I don't reckon I'd lose more than one night's sleep if I blew your knee apart, and I figure I can live with that," Longarm went on.

"There's a b-big house a couple of miles east of San Antonio!" the gunman blurted in terror. "It was an old plantation, looks like it's been deserted for years until now! We took the woman there. The Empress ordered Dumond to take some of us and double back to make sure nobody followed us!"

"How do we find this old plantation house?" Longarm asked.

The man babbled on, telling them all the landmarks he could think of. Longarm made mental notes of all of them, and knew that Ki was doing the same thing.

"Now," Longarm said when he was confident of being

able to find the plantation house, "what's the Empress's plan? Why did she have Jessie Starbuck kidnapped?"

"Well, hell . . . I don't know. She don't confide in me, not by a long shot! Maybe she just wanted to settle old scores with the Starbuck woman."

Longarm shook his head. "I don't doubt that Katerina's got a grudge against Jessie. But she don't strike me as the sort to go to this much trouble because of a grudge. She's got something else in mind, and Jessie Starbuck plays into it somehow."

"That may be true, Marshal," the prisoner said, "but I don't know one damned thing about it, and that's the truth. I swear it."

Longarm believed him. He had already spilled too much to start hedging now.

Ki spoke up, asking, "How many men does the Empress have at the plantation?"

"Well . . . I don't rightly know. We weren't there all that long. I saw maybe a dozen fellas. Of course, that's not countin' the ones with the wagon train."

"Wagon train?" Longarm repeated sharply. He lifted the Colt again. "You been holdin' out on us, old son."

"Wait, wait! I was gettin' to that part, I swear!" The gunman gulped. "There was a bunch of covered wagons in one of the fields close to the house. You know, prairie schooners like the ones that folks headin' West used to travel in. They were even parked in a circle, like the old wagon trains."

"There were quite a few men with those wagons?" Ki asked.

"Yeah. And women and kids, too. Families."

Longarm frowned as he glanced at Ki and O'Malley. They looked just as puzzled as he felt. What was the Empress's connection to a wagon train full of immigrants?

"Did you talk to any of those folks?" Longarm asked.

"No. Some of the women from the wagon train handled the cookin' for everybody. They brought our food to us in the bunkhouse. The fellas who were already there warned us about 'em, though. They weren't whores. They were married to some of the gents with the wagon train, and we had to treat 'em properlike."

This was getting more puzzling all the time, thought Longarm. The one thing he knew for sure was that whatever Katerina von Blöde was up to, it couldn't be anything good.

After a moment of silence, during which Longarm mulled over the situation, the prisoner asked nervously, "What are you gonna do with me?"

"You're guilty of all sorts of things," Longarm pointed out. "Kidnapping and the attempted murder of a federal officer, for starters. I figure we'll turn you over to the law in San Antonio. Then I'll wire my boss and let him figure out what to do with you in the long run. I'd start gettin' used to the idea of spending the rest of my life in prison, if I was you."

The man sighed in despair.

"Before that, though," Longarm went on, "you're gonna lead us to that plantation house."

"Me? What for? I told you how to find the place."

"Yeah, but we might as well take advantage of having you for a guide. And you're gonna take us there tonight. Dumond got away, and I know damned good and well he's gonna run right back to the Empress. Once she finds out for sure that we're still alive and on her trail, she won't stay there."

Ki asked, "How do we know that whatever she's planning isn't going to take place there at the plantation?"

"Well, I thought about that," Longarm admitted. "But it

seems mighty unlikely to me that she could do anything
worthy of the Cartel right there just outside a town as big as
San Antone. Especially if she's got a whole wagon train's
worth of pilgrims with her. I'll bet they're headed somewhere else. That plantation was just a rendezvous point."

Ki thought it over and then nodded. "What you say
makes sense, Marshal." He stood. "I'll start getting the
horses ready."

The prisoner said, "I'd appreciate it if you'd take me to
jail first, Marshal. I'd rather be in a nice, safe cell somewhere."

Longarm shook his head. "Sorry, old son. Like I said,
you're gonna lead us to that plantation."

The gunman didn't say anything else. He just sat there
with his head down and a look of defeat on his face while
Longarm, Ki, and O'Malley got their mounts ready to ride.
Ki said, "There should be several of the horses that belonged to the dead men still in the area. I'll go find one of
them."

He swung up into the saddle and rode off. The gunman
finally lifted his head again. He nodded toward the corpses
and asked, "What are you gonna do about them?"

"As soon as I get a chance, I'll let the local sheriff know
that they're here," Longarm replied. "He can send out the
undertaker with a wagon."

"The buzzards are liable to be at 'em before then," the
prisoner said bitterly.

Longarm shrugged. "That's a shame, but I'm more concerned about folks who are still alive, instead of those
who've already crossed over the divide."

Ki was back, leading a saddled horse. He hung on to the
reins while Longarm took hold of the prisoner's arm and
hauled the man to his feet.

"I can't get on a horse with my hands tied behind my back," he complained. "You got to cut me loose so I can ride."

"I don't reckon that's necessary," Longarm said. "I'll hang on to you and steady you while you're mounting."

"And I'll lead your horse," Ki said, "so you don't have to worry about that."

"All right, all right," the man grumbled. He got his left foot in the stirrup and started to step up.

As he rose, though, he suddenly lurched at Longarm, lowering his head as he did so. He rammed the top of his head into Longarm's face and knocked the big lawman backward. Longarm's grip on the man's arm slipped. The hard case kicked his foot out of the stirrup and landed running. Sheer desperation gave him speed.

He couldn't outrun a horse, though. Ki said, "I'll get him!" and sent his mount leaping after the fleeing gunman. He left the saddle in a diving tackle, crashing into the prisoner and sending both of them to the ground. Ki was back on his feet almost instantly. He reached down, grabbed the stunned gunman, and lifted him upright. The man shook his head groggily and groaned, "Oh, shit." He looked around at Longarm, Ki, and O'Malley and added, "You can't blame a fella for tryin', can you?"

Longarm rubbed his jaw where the man had butted him and said, "No, and you can't blame me for wantin' to blow your kneecap off so you can't try anything that foolish again."

The gunman blanched.

"But you might up and bleed to death, and I don't want to take a chance on that," Longarm continued. "Just don't try it again, or I'm liable to decide that it's worth the risk." He took hold of the man's arm and shoved him toward the horses. "Mount up. We got places to be."

Chapter 28

Jessie was still surprised and confused, but had recovered her wits somewhat by the time General Tennyson got her back to the plantation house. Reinhold was waiting for them.

"Is Miss von Blöde here?" Tennyson asked.

The Prussian shook his head. "She has returned to San Antonio, but I have sent a rider to alert her to the news of Miss Starbuck's near-escape. Also, Herr Dumond has returned with news that she needs to hear."

Jessie felt her heart sink at that comment. If Dumond was back, did it mean that his ambush of Longarm and Ki had succeeded?

Reinhold stepped aside and gestured toward the door, as he had earlier in the day when Jessie first arrived. "Miss Starbuck, please. And General Tennyson, if you could come in, too, and wait, I'm sure the Empress would like to speak to you as well."

Tennyson hesitated, then nodded. "That would probably be best."

Discouraged, Jessie went into the house. Tennyson followed right behind her, with Reinhold bringing up the rear.

The Prussian moved around them and ushered them into a parlor. Dust lay heavily on some of the furnishings. Some of the chairs still had cloths draped over them.

"Would either of you care for something to drink?" Reinhold asked.

"If you've got some good bourbon, that might be nice," Tennyson said.

"Miss Starbuck?"

Jessie shook her head. "No." She didn't add any thanks. She didn't feel much like being polite at the moment. She was too worried about Longarm and Ki.

Reinhold left the room, and came back a minute later with the drink for Tennyson. The general removed his hat and set it on a small table, then took the glass and said, "Much obliged, suh." Reinhold bowed slightly in acknowledgment of the thanks. Jessie halfway expected him to click his heels together, but he didn't.

"I assume you can watch over Miss Starbuck?" he asked Tennyson.

"I reckon we'll be fine. Won't we, Miss Starbuck?"

Jessie looked away and didn't answer. From the corner of her eye, she saw Tennyson shrug after a moment.

"I'll let the Empress know that you're here as soon as she arrives." With that, Reinhold left the parlor.

"I'd appreciate it if y'all didn't try to get away again," Tennyson said. "I'm not as young as I used to be, and it's gettin' late."

Jessie finally turned to face him. "General—I assume you *are* a real general? Or at least were?"

"I am indeed a real general."

"In the Confederate States Army."

"That is correct."

"Which doesn't exist anymore."

Tennyson smiled at her. "A noble cause never truly dies, Miss Starbuck."

"Some would say the Confederacy wasn't all that noble."

"More learned men than me have been arguin' about that for years, and I suspect they will continue to do so for the foreseeable future. I'm just a soldier, ma'am . . . a soldier who never surrendered, who never agreed to lay down his arms to the Yankees."

"General Lee surrendered," Jessie said. "That was the end of the war."

Tennyson sipped his drink and then said, "Now that's where y'all are wrong, but don't worry . . . it's a common mistake. General Lee, rest his soul, surrendered the forces under his command at Appomattox, but that's all he did. It was up to the other commanders to decide if they wanted to follow suit. It was several months before some of them did so." He took another drink. "And some of us never did."

"So you're still fighting the Civil War?" Jessie asked in disbelief.

"No, ma'am. We're not fools. For all practical purposes, the war ended almost twenty years ago. Those few of us who are left would stand no chance of defeating the Union. It's ludicrous to think so."

"Well, I'm glad you can see that anyway," Jessie said.

"But that doesn't mean that we will ever bow down to the Yankees. It's simply not in our blood to do so."

"So what are you going to do? Try to fight back somehow, even if it's not an outright war? Is that why you've allied yourselves with an evil bitch like Katerina von Blöde?"

Tennyson frowned as if he were offended by the question, but before he could answer it, a silky voice said from the doorway, "Such language, Jessie. Alex Starbuck would be ashamed of you."

Jessie turned sharply toward the door and saw Katerina walking into the parlor, wearing a stylish traveling outfit including a blue hat with a feather on her upswept crown of blond curls.

"Don't dishonor my father's name by speaking it," Jessie said coldly. "*Your* father and his associates murdered him."

Katerina reached up, unpinned the hat, and took it off. "I'd say that we're both our fathers' daughters. Strong-willed women accustomed to getting what we want. To *taking* what we want if it comes to that." She set the hat on a table and then shook her head. "I should have known you'd try to escape. That man you hit on the head died, you know. What did you use, a pistol?"

"That's right. And for what it's worth, I wasn't trying to kill him."

"But you don't care that he's dead, do you?" Katerina shot back.

"I'd be lying if I said that I did," Jessie replied. "I figure if somebody goes to work for you, he knows what he's getting into."

"And what exactly is that?" Katerina asked with a note of challenge in her voice. "Just what do you think I'm planning?"

"I don't know, but it can't be anything good."

Katerina smiled and shook her head. She turned to Tennyson. "Reinhold told me that you're the one who captured Miss Starbuck when she tried to escape, General. You have my gratitude."

Tennyson shrugged. "I won't say it was my pleasure, ma'am. I don't like treatin' a lady so rudely. But I reckon it was necessary."

"Indeed it was. How soon can you have your people ready to travel?"

"First thing in the mornin'. That was the plan, wasn't it?"

"Yes, but tonight's developments indicate that we should depart sooner."

"Y'all can't mean to pull out tonight," Tennyson said with a frown.

"That's exactly what I mean," Katerina said. "I don't believe we can afford to wait until morning to get away from here."

Tennyson's frown deepened. He pulled a watch from his pocket and opened it. "It's nearly ten o'clock. We might be able to have the wagons ready to roll by midnight."

"Very good. I'd like to leave even sooner than that if possible."

Tennyson sighed and nodded as he closed the watch and put it away. "I'll see what I can do." He threw back the little bit of whiskey still in his glass and then set the empty glass on the dusty table. He picked up his hat and put it on. After polite nods to both Jessie and Katerina, he turned and left the room.

Jessie had been thinking about what Katerina had said, and when Tennyson was gone, she smiled and said, "Longarm and Ki are still alive, aren't they? Dumond's ambush failed."

Katerina lifted her chin defiantly, but Jessie caught the flicker of surprise in the other woman's eyes. "What makes you believe that?" Katerina asked. "You shouldn't get your hopes up."

Jessie laughed. "You wouldn't have told General Tennyson to get his people ready to leave if you weren't in a hurry to get out of here. You're running scared, *Empress*."

She didn't try to keep the scorn out of her voice. "The only people I can think of who'd make you take off for the tall and uncut like this are Custis Long and Ki."

"Think whatever you want," Katerina snapped. "I don't care. Just don't try to escape again. You won't get off so easily next time."

"You can't afford to kill me," Jessie replied mockingly. "I heard Reinhold say so."

"Reinhold was aware of my order that you not be harmed. But I can countermand that order any time I want to." Katerina reached into the bag she was carrying and took out a derringer. As she pointed the little pistol at Jessie, she said, "I can kill you right now if I want to. It's my decision, and mine alone."

Jessie felt an icy finger trace a path along her spine. She saw the light of madness lurking in Katerina's eyes. If the other woman had been closer, Jessie might have risked jumping her and trying to take that derringer away from her. Katerina played it safe, though, and kept plenty of distance between her and Jessie.

After a tense moment ticked by, Katerina gave a little shrug and lowered the gun. "You're safe . . . for the time being," she said. "But don't push me, Jessie. My plan can proceed without you if it has to."

"What plan is that?"

Katerina smiled. "You'll find out when I'm good and ready to tell you. In the meantime, if you know what's good for you, you'll do as you're told. Right now, that means you stay here and don't cause any more trouble."

She turned and left the parlor. Less than ten seconds later, Reinhold stepped back into the room, crossed his arms over his chest, and stood there blocking the entrance to the parlor. Jessie didn't know how good her chances would be against him in a fight, and she recalled that he carried a gun under his coat and no doubt knew how to use it. For the time being, she would just have to cooperate, whether she liked it or not.

After a few more minutes went by, Andre Dumond appeared in the doorway and told Reinhold, "I'll keep an eye on Miss Starbuck. You can go help Miss von Blöde with her preparations."

Reinhold nodded and left without saying anything. Dumond leaned against the doorjamb and looked at Jessie as if waiting for her to speak to him. Stubbornly, she just glared at him and remained silent.

He looked tired, and his clothes were covered with trail dust. He must have grown weary of the standoff, because he finally said, "I hear you caused some trouble tonight."

"And I hear *you* failed in your mission for the Empress," Jessie said. "Longarm and Ki are still alive."

Dumond straightened from his casual pose. His face darkened with anger. "She told you about that?"

"Not really." Jessie smiled. "It was a hunch. But you just confirmed it for me."

Dumond took a step toward her, his hands clenching into fists. Jessie set herself, ready to fight back if she needed to, but Dumond stopped after that single step. With a visible effort, he brought his anger under control.

"You are a very intelligent woman, *cherie*," he said. "Perhaps, at times, too smart for your own good, as they say. But none of it will help you now. Before the night is over, we will leave this place and set out for our final destination."

Final destination . . . That didn't sound too promising, Jessie thought.

She said, "You don't really think there's anywhere you

and the Empress can hide where Longarm and Ki can't find you, do you?"

"Soon, it will not matter what your friends do. Things have been set in motion that cannot be stopped."

"We'll see," Jessie said with a serene confidence. If there was anyone who could break up whatever Katerina was planning, it was Longarm and Ki.

"You might be interested to know," Dumond said, "that Marshal Long and Ki were not alone. Captain O'Malley was with them."

"Seamus?" Jessie exclaimed. "He's alive?"

Dumond nodded. "I heard the marshal call his name. I have no idea how he survived that hurricane, but evidently he did."

Jessie didn't understand it either. O'Malley had been determined to ride out the storm on the *Harry Fulton*. He must have changed his mind. Regardless of the explanation, Jessie was glad to hear that the Irishman was alive.

"So now there are three of them after you," she said.

"Three men or thirty, it doesn't matter," Dumond said with a shrug. "They are no match for the Empress's men. Soon, she will have an army at her command, and an arrogant nation will be brought to its knees."

That was a mighty big claim to make, and Jessie couldn't keep a flash of surprise from showing on her face. Dumond grimaced as if realizing that he might have said too much.

Things had gone back to the way they were before, Jessie thought. Based on what Dumond had just said, it might be more important than ever for her to find out what Katerina von Blöde's plan was. From the sound of it, it was something that might threaten the entire country.

And, thought Jessie, in the end it might come down to her being the only one who could stop it.

Chapter 29

The prisoner's name was Otis Sewell. The name wasn't any more familiar to Longarm than the man's face was. No doubt Sewell was an experienced gunman who had probably been on the wrong side of the law for years, but he hadn't ever been mixed up in anything to bring him to the attention of the federal star packers.

Until now.

Sewell was unhappy and sullen about it, but he did as he was told and led Longarm, Ki, and O'Malley to the old plantation that Katerina von Blöde was using as her headquarters in the San Antonio area. It was well after midnight when Sewell reined in and said to Longarm, "You told me to stop you when we got within a mile of the house, Marshal. It can't be much more'n that now."

Longarm had brought his mount to a halt as well, as had Ki and O'Malley. "You're bein' smart now, Otis," he said. "How are the guards set up?"

"I don't rightly know. We just got here earlier today . . . yesterday, I should say. I never spent a night here, so I don't have any idea where the guards are, how often they change, or anything like that."

That answer made sense, Longarm decided. Sewell couldn't tell them what he'd had no chance to learn.

"All right," Longarm said. He looked over at Ki and gave a curt nod. Ki pulled his knife from his belt and edged his horse over closer to Sewell's mount.

"Wait a minute!" Sewell said, fear and desperation giving his voice a high, strained quality. "You can't kill me. I've done everything you told me to do!"

Ki reached behind Sewell's back with the knife and quickly cut the bonds holding the gunman's wrists together. Sewell sagged forward in the saddle, obviously so relieved that he nearly fainted. He pulled his arms in front of him and began massaging the feeling back into his numb hands.

"That'll teach you to eat an apple one bite at a time, Otis," Longarm said with a smile. "If we haven't ventilated you by now, it ain't likely we're gonna."

"Th-thanks," Sewell muttered. "I thought I was a goner for sure."

"Well, you've been wrong about a heap of things," Longarm pointed out, "first and foremost among 'em being signin' on to work for Katerina von Blöde. The Empress don't care about any of you fellas. You're just so much cannon fodder as far as she's concerned."

Sewell continued rubbing his wrists. "Maybe so, maybe so," he admitted. "But we always got paid good."

Longarm could see a scattering of lights in the distance that he took to be San Antonio, but where Sewell said the plantation was, no lamps burned. That wasn't too surprising, considering the hour. Everybody was probably asleep, except for the guards. The number of guards might have increased tonight, because Dumond had probably made it back by now with the news that the ambush had failed. Katerina would have to expect Longarm and Ki to try to rescue Jessie.

"Why don't I go take a look around?" Ki suggested.

"That's a good idea," Longarm said with a nod. "Just don't get yourself nabbed. We don't want to have to rescue two prisoners instead of one."

"I'll try to be careful," Ki said, his voice dry. When he was scouting, the chances of anybody seeing him if he didn't want to be seen were mighty remote. He dismounted and went ahead on foot, vanishing into the shadows in seconds.

Longarm looked over at Sewell and said, "Don't go gettin' any ideas in your head about warning your pards. For one thing, I reckon you could yell your lungs out, and at this distance they wouldn't hear you."

"Don't worry," the gunman muttered. "I'm done with 'em. I don't have any choice but to throw in with you fellas now."

Longarm didn't believe that for a second. Sewell would betray them without hesitation if he got the chance. Longarm didn't intend to give him that chance.

The three of them sat there silently on their horses, waiting for Ki to get back from scouting the plantation. Time dragged by. Longarm stifled a yawn. He didn't want Ki to get in a hurry or be careless. Better to take their time and not waltz into a trap.

Finally, after more than an hour, Longarm heard the cry of a night bird. It wasn't really a night bird, though, he realized. It was Ki signaling that he was coming in.

"Marshal?" Ki called softly a few moments later.

"Come ahead," Longarm told him, equally softly.

Ki seemed to materialize out of the shadows. He took the reins that Longarm handed him and swung up into the saddle.

"They're gone," he announced.

"Gone?" Longarm repeated in surprise.

Ki nodded. "The plantation is deserted. I checked all the buildings, once I was certain there were no guards outside. No one was inside either."

"What about all those wagons I saw?" Sewell said. "They got to be there."

"They're not," Ki replied with a shake of his head. "I could tell where the wagon train was camped, because I found plenty of fresh droppings from their livestock. But they're all gone now."

"Well, if that don't beat all!" Sewell's surprise sounded genuine. "What happened to 'em?"

"They ran out on you, old son," Longarm said. He felt a keen disappointment that Jessie was still in the hands of her captors and out of reach for the moment, but he couldn't help but be a little amused by Sewell's consternation. "I guess they figured it wasn't worth waiting to see if you'd show up before they left."

O'Malley said, "I don't understand. This so-called Empress, with her army of hired gunmen, is running from the three of us?"

"That's what it looks like," Longarm said. "We'll have to wait until morning, but it shouldn't be hard to track that many wagons. Shouldn't take too long to catch up to them either. Those prairie schooners don't travel very fast."

Ki nodded. "I agree. It was all right for us to come this far tonight, because we had the prisoner to lead the way. We can't risk trying to follow the trail from here in the darkness, though. At any rate, the horses need more rest."

"That they do," Longarm agreed. He hitched his mount into motion. "Come on. I want to take a good look around that plantation and see if we can find anything that might tell us where they're goin'."

The big house was dark as they approached it. Longarm was confident that Ki was right about the place being deserted. Ki didn't make mistakes when it came to things like that. Ki didn't make very many mistakes, period. He would have made a heck of a deputy U.S. marshal, if he hadn't already found his life's work siding Jessica Starbuck.

"Don't go gettin' any ideas, Otis," Longarm warned as they pulled up in front of the house. "You're still my prisoner. The only reason I had Ki cut you loose is because you've played square with us since that stupid stunt you tried to pull back at our camp. You'd be better off to keep on playin' square."

"Don't worry about that, Marshal." Sewell sounded bitter now. "I don't like bein' abandoned like this. If there's anything I can do to help you, you can count on me."

Longarm didn't point out that Sewell had broken and run as soon as the shooting started earlier, instead of staying behind to help his fellow gunmen in their failed ambush. Nor did he believe the man's declaration of loyalty. Sewell would remain trustworthy only for as long as he thought it would benefit him.

Longarm dismounted. "Come on," he told the others. "We're all goin' in." As they climbed onto the porch, he glanced over at Ki. "You didn't find any traps waiting for us?"

"No. It appeared that everyone left in a hurry. No one took the time to try to booby-trap the house."

They went inside. Longarm struck a lucifer on his thumbnail and looked around until he found a lantern. He lit it. When the wick caught and the flame welled up, its glare revealed a former elegance that had dulled into a drab, dusty neglect. Marks in the dust on the floor told him that quite a few people had been in here, though. The faint smell of food lingered in the dining room. People had eaten dinner here tonight. They must have brought all their food and other supplies with them, however. The pantry and the larder were empty.

Longarm searched the rest of the house, carrying the lantern with him, while Ki and O'Malley kept an eye on Sewell. The lawman wasn't sure what he hoped to find. He doubted that Katerina was going to leave behind a letter detailing her plan, or a map showing where she was going with that wagon train, or anything like that. Still, it wouldn't hurt to check.

The only thing he found was in the parlor, and he almost missed it because someone had kicked it under a small, round table next to the wall. A ring in the dust showed where someone had set a glass on the table, and there were some other marks that Longarm couldn't decipher. He caught a gleam of light on something metal under the table, though, and knelt to pull out a military insignia. Crossed sabers—that indicated the cavalry. Longarm had seen plenty such insignia over the years, on the hats of cavalry officers.

There was something different about this one, though. He turned it over and peered at the back of it in the lantern light. Etched into the back of the insignia were three initials.

CSA.

The war had been over for a long time, so long that most people didn't call it the Late Unpleasantness anymore. But this insignia belonged to a Confederate cavalry officer,

Longarm thought as he bounced the crossed sabers in the palm of his hand, and judging by how bright and shiny they were, the owner of the insignia took good care of it, polishing it on a regular basis.

Longarm didn't know what to make of that. He tucked the insignia away in his shirt pocket and went to rejoin Ki, O'Malley, and Sewell in the foyer.

"Did ye find anything?" O'Malley asked.

"Nothing that's going to help us," Longarm said. "We might as well go tend to the horses and get some sleep. There are a couple of divans in that parlor where two of us can stretch out while the other fella stands guard."

"What about me?" Sewell asked. "Do I have to sleep on the floor?"

"Be glad you ain't sleepin' the big sleep," Longarm told him. "Let's go."

The four men moved toward the door. Sewell stepped out onto the front porch first.

A bullet slammed into him and threw him backward as a rifle cracked in the darkness.

Chapter 30

Sewell reeled across the foyer, gasping in pain as he pawed at his chest. Longarm grabbed him by the collar and flung him to the floor as more shots rang out. "Everybody down!" Longarm called.

Bullets thudded into the walls and shattered glass. The shadows outside were lit by orange muzzle flashes. Longarm used the barrel of his Winchester to push the heavy door closed. He, Ki, and O'Malley hugged the walls of the foyer and waited for the shooting to stop.

When it did, a man somewhere outside yelled, "Damn it, Mort, you jumped the gun! We should'a waited until all three of the bastards were outta the house!"

"Sorry, Pa!" another man called back. "I was just so anxious to plug one o' those sons o' bitches—"

"Now we got to root 'em outta there," the first voice replied. "Calvin! Joe! Get around back so's they can't sneak out that way!"

"The Gilfeathers," Ki said quietly.

"You mean the bunch that tried to ambush us last night?" O'Malley asked. "The father and his three sons?"

"That's right," Longarm said. "That Reuben Gilfeather must be one stubborn son of a bitch. They found their horses, got their hands on some guns, and trailed us here to settle the score."

"He sent two of the boys around back," Ki said. "I had better go back there myself, to keep them from getting into the house and attacking us from that direction."

Longarm nodded. "Good idea. They may have us pinned down, but I'll bet a hat we've got better cover than they do. O'Malley, find a window, bust it out, and keep 'em busy out front while Ki's doin' the same thing in the back."

"What will ye be doin', Marshal?" the Irishman asked.

Longarm jabbed a thumb toward the ceiling. "I thought I'd go up."

"The high ground," Ki said.

"That's right. Or in this case, the roof."

A long, rattling sigh came from Otis Sewell, who had been lying there moaning softly. The moaning stopped, and so did the sound of his breathing. Longarm reached over, checked for a heartbeat, and didn't find one. The hired gun had been in the wrong place at the wrong time. His violent life had caught up with him.

Ki headed for the rear of the big house at a crouching run. Longarm took the winding staircase to the second floor. He heard glass break somewhere behind him, and then O'Malley's rifle began to crack. Longarm didn't care if the Irishman hit anything; he just wanted O'Malley to keep the Gilfeathers occupied.

It took him several minutes of searching once he reached the second floor to find an open trapdoor inside some sort of closet. A ladder attached to the door led into the attic. Longarm climbed into the darkness, grimacing as he felt a spiderweb brush across his face. He didn't like the eight-legged varmints.

The moon had set, but enough starlight remained for him to be able to make out a window. It formed a rectangle of paler darkness than the rest of the Stygian attic. As he went over to it, he saw that someone had raised the window. Some sort of metal strap lay on the sill. Longarm's gaze also touched on a tiny bit of cloth stuck on a nail head that hadn't been driven down completely in the window frame.

To a man used to tracking fugitives through the wilderness, little things told a story. These things that Longarm noted now had a yarn to spin, too. He couldn't be sure, but as he plucked the bit of fabric from the nail and rubbed it between his fingers, a grin spread across his rugged face. He had a hunch that Jessie Starbuck had pried that window open and then climbed out through it in an attempt to escape. That would be just like her.

Did that mean she had gotten away? If she had, where was she now? She would have headed for town, Longarm decided. She would have tried to get help from the law or the army in San Antonio.

That would be their next stop once he and Ki and O'Malley dealt with the Gilfeathers, thought Longarm. He would check first with the local law, then at the Menger Hotel, where Jessie always stayed when she was in San Antonio. He could talk to the post commander at Fort Sam Houston, too.

But if none of that turned up any sign of Jessie, then the only option left would be to follow Katerina von Blöde and that blasted wagon train, because chances were, Jessie was still a prisoner.

First things first, Longarm reminded himself. They had to do something about those pesky Gilfeathers.

The window wasn't open far enough for him to climb out. He shoved it up higher and then crouched to stick his head and shoulders through. It was a tight fit, but he climbed out onto the roof, and found himself lying just in front of the dormer where the window was located.

Longarm crawled closer to the edge and looked down at the area in front of the plantation house. The two Gilfeathers on this side of the building were still firing their rifles. They were hidden behind some trees next to the lane leading to the house. Even from this angle, Longarm couldn't get a good shot at them.

That left the two behind the house. Longarm scrambled to the top of the roof and slid over its peak. It took him only a minute to locate the riflemen on this side. One lay behind an old water trough, firing around the end of it. The other was crouched behind the wreckage of a wagon that had been abandoned years earlier, from the looks of it.

Longarm considered the angles. Even in the poor light, he could see the lower half of the man behind the water trough fairly well, forming a dark shape against the sandy ground, so he picked that one as his first target. Sitting on the roof, Longarm snugged the stock of the Winchester against his shoulder, drew a bead, and shot the hombre in the ass.

It sounded funny, but Longarm knew there was nothing humorous about it. The man screeched in pain, dropped his rifle, and rolled out from behind the water trough, slapping at his wounded posterior with both hands. Longarm had already levered another round into the Winchester's firing chamber. He put the man out of his misery by drilling him through the head.

That brought the other Gilfeather out from behind the wagon. He yelled, "Joe!" That was his last word because Longarm put a bullet through his body, spinning him off his feet.

The two remaining outlaws in front of the house wouldn't be able to see what was going on back here, so they probably didn't know that Joe and Calvin were dead. Longarm went back up to the top of the roof and waited for a lull in the firing. When it came, he shouted, "Gilfeather! Reuben Gilfeather!"

"What the hell!" Gilfeather sounded surprised that somebody was on top of the house.

"The boys you sent around back are dead, Gilfeather!" Longarm called. "You sent 'em straight to hell!"

Gilfeather howled in pain and grief. "You son of a bitch!" he screamed. "You fuckin' bastard!"

Then he charged out from behind the tree where he had been hidden, yelling in incoherent rage as he fired his rifle wildly toward the roof.

Longarm had thought that might draw Gilfeather out. He lined his sights and fired, and at the same time two shots rang out from down in the house. With the threat from behind the house eliminated, Ki had rejoined O'Malley, and both of them cut loose on Reuben Gilfeather, too. The man's burly shape flew backward as all three slugs slammed into him. Gilfeather landed on the ground and didn't move except for a couple of jerks of his right leg.

"Pa?" The voice wavered with fear and shock.

"You'd be Mort," Longarm called. "Throw your guns out and step into the open with your hands up where we can see 'em, and this can be over, Mort."

"You . . . you damned lawdog!" Mort Gilfeather was sobbing now. "You go to hell!"

He burst out from behind his tree and charged toward the house just like his father had done. In Mort's case, instead of a rifle he had two revolvers, one in each hand. They blossomed redly as he triggered shot after shot.

And like his father, he was cut down by bullets from Longarm, Ki, and O'Malley.

With all four Gilfeathers dead, Longarm climbed back into the attic through the dormer window. He went downstairs, and found Ki and O'Malley waiting in the foyer.

"Are we still goin' to stay here tonight?" O'Malley asked.

"Yeah. We don't have to worry about those two-bit desperadoes anymore, and we still need to wait until morning to track that wagon train."

"We can't just leave their bodies lyin' out in the open."

"We could," Longarm said, "but I don't reckon it'll hurt anything to drag 'em around to one of those sheds I saw in the back."

He was about to tell Ki and O'Malley about his idea that Jessie had tried to escape through the attic, when he heard a distant boom.

"What the devil was that?" O'Malley exclaimed.

Longarm thought it sounded like something he had heard before, on many occasions during the war and a few times since. He might disremember which side he had fought on, but he still recalled the sound of artillery.

The high-pitched whine he heard a second later was familiar, too. That was an artillery round screaming toward them, and just as he yelled, "Hit the dirt!" the whole world exploded around them.

Chapter 31

General Tennyson made good on his word. He had the wagon train ready to roll before midnight.

Andre Dumond escorted Jessie from the plantation house. He took her to one of the wagons and helped her climb onto the seat next to a burly, bearded, middle-aged man who nodded politely to her and said, "Ma'am."

"This is Sergeant Brackett," Dumond told her. "General Tennyson informs me that the sergeant is a highly competent man. You can ride there on the seat with him, *cherie*, or if you prefer to cause trouble, you can be tied hand and foot and ride in the back of the wagon."

"I'm not going to cause any trouble," Jessie said. She looked over at Brackett. "You have my word on that, Sergeant."

A grin appeared in the middle of the man's bushy beard. "I'm right glad to hear that, ma'am. I'll appreciate havin' some comp'ny for a change. You can help me stay awake, too. I ain't used to drivin' a wagon at night."

"I'll be riding nearby," Dumond added. "So don't get any ideas, Jessie."

"I'm fresh out of ideas," she said.

That wasn't strictly true. Her goal was to find out what Katerina was up to, and that meant cooperating—for now.

The wagon train pulled out not long after that. Sergeant Brackett's wagon was the second vehicle in the lengthy line. Up front rode more than a dozen men, led by General Tennyson. Directly behind them was a buggy driven by Reinhold. Jessie knew that Katerina was in that buggy. The Empress wouldn't lower herself to ride in an immigrant wagon. Then came dozens of wagons. There were even more of the prairie schooners than Jessie had estimated earlier.

She didn't know if Brackett would talk to her, but she didn't see any harm in trying. "I'll bet you rode with General Tennyson during the war, didn't you?"

"Yes'm," he answered without hesitation. "Most of us did."

"The men with the wagon train, you mean?"

"That's right. Most o' the fellas went back home after we stopped fightin', and when the general put out the call, they brung their families with 'em. Some of the boys have passed on, but their widows and kids showed up."

Obviously, no one had warned Brackett not to tell Jessie anything. Katerina might not have thought of it—but more likely, she just didn't consider Jessie enough of a threat to worry about what she might find out.

Katerina's arrogance had led her to make mistakes before. This might be another such occasion, Jessie hoped.

"So this is like a . . . reunion? Is that it?"

Brackett chuckled. "Well, sort of, but not really. General Tennyson got us together so's we can finish what we started."

"You mean the war?"

"I mean showin' the damn Yankees they can't run roughshod over folks, pardon my language, ma'am. But we had a right to do what we done when we seceded from the Union. Anybody who can read the dang Constitution can see that. Ol' Abe Lincoln's the one who busted the law by invadin' the Confederacy."

"The war's over and done with," Jessie pointed out.

"The side that wins ain't always the side that was in the right to start with." Brackett shrugged. "But I ain't gonna argue with you, ma'am. It wouldn't be polite, and it wouldn't do no good. All we want now is the chance to live the way we see fit."

"With slaves?" Jessie snapped. She couldn't help herself.

"You see any slaves in this wagon train?"

"Well . . . no."

"I never owned a slave in my life, and neither did anybody else in my family. Would'a been fine with me if they'd done away with the whole business a long time 'fore they did. But I can't abide a bunch of folks comin' onto my land with guns and tellin' me how to live, especially when they do things just as bad or worse'n what they're fumin' about us doin'." Brackett shook his head and sighed. "Ah, hell. Like you said, the war's over. Water under the bridge. Most of us would'a been glad to let it go if it hadn't been for them blasted carpetbaggers stealin' our land. Reconstruction, they called it. *Dee*-struction is more like it."

"I know you have some legitimate grievances," Jessie said, "but attacking the rest of the country isn't going to help. You can't win. You'll just get your families hurt or killed."

"I told you, we ain't goin' to war."

"Then what *are* you going to do?"

Brackett grinned again. "I reckon you'll find out when we get there."

"Get where?"

The sergeant just shook his head and didn't say anything else.

A short time later, the wagons came to a halt. Jessie hadn't expected them to stop so soon. They hadn't come more than a few miles from the plantation. She saw General Tennyson ride back to the buggy and rein in, then lean over to converse with Katerina. After a moment, he nodded, wheeled his horse, and rode back along the line of wagons.

"What's going on?" she asked Brackett.

"Durned if I know," the sergeant replied. "I didn't figure we'd be stoppin' until mornin', and then just to rest the livestock for a while."

Jessie had thought the same thing. She leaned over on the seat to look back along the wagon train. Brackett didn't try to prevent her from doing that.

Tennyson stopped at a wagon near the end of the line. Several riders had followed him. They dismounted and went to the rear of the wagon. From what Jessie could see, they were lowering the vehicle's tailgate and starting to unload something. In the darkness, however, she couldn't really tell what it was.

Oxen were hitched to the wagons, but a large number of mules had been driven along behind the wagon train, bringing up the rear. The men brought a couple of those mules forward now and hitched them to something they had unloaded from the wagon. As it pulled away, Jessie finally got a good look at it and realized what it was.

A cannon.

She felt a shock go through her. What in the world were they doing with a cannon? she asked herself.

Then she remembered that this was, in a way, a military unit. Of course they had a cannon. They probably had more than one. There was no telling what else might be loaded in the wagons. Rifles, Gatling guns, ammunition ... all that and possibly more. Katerina and Dumond had both dropped hints about an army. Where there was an army, there were bound to be munitions as well.

They were actually going to do it, despite their denials, Jessie thought. These ex-Confederates were going to declare war on the United States.

And from the looks of it, that cannon, along with a crew of gunners, was now heading back in the direction they had come from to fire the first shot.

The explosion threw Longarm off his feet and pounded his ears like a pair of giant fists. He landed in the doorway of the plantation house, lying half inside and half on the porch. He couldn't hear anything, but he felt the concussion of a second blast.

Somebody was shelling the house, and he felt certain that Katerina von Blöde had something to do with it. He pushed himself up on his hands and knees and looked around. Ki and O'Malley lay in the foyer, stunned just as he had been. Both of them had begun to stir, though.

Longarm staggered to his feet and grabbed Ki. He started dragging his old friend out of the house, but Ki struggled out of his grip and shook his head. Longarm saw Ki's mouth moving, but couldn't hear what he was saying. He guessed that Ki was telling him he was all right and urging Longarm to help O'Malley instead.

That hunch proved to be right. Ki was able to stand up as well. He and Longarm both hurried over to O'Malley. Each of them grabbed an arm and hauled the Irishman to his feet. With O'Malley between them, they ran toward the front door, just as another shell came screaming in through a hole that had been blown in the roof and exploded as it struck the staircase.

That detonation sent Longarm, Ki, and O'Malley flying through the door and across the porch as it filled the air around them with splinters. Longarm felt them stinging the back of his neck. All three men sprawled from the porch onto the ground.

They struggled up, and Longarm yelled, "Go! Go!" even though he couldn't hear his own words. They broke into a stumbling run away from the house as more explosions behind them shook the earth under their feet.

They made it into the trees along the lane and collapsed. Longarm looked back and saw that less than half the plantation house was still standing. The rest of it had been blown to smithereens. As he watched, the bombardment continued. In a matter of minutes, he thought, there wouldn't be anything left of the house.

He looked around for their horses, but didn't see the animals. Chances were, the horses had bolted when the explosions started. Horses didn't have much common sense, but they generally took off for the tall and uncut when things started blowing up. Longarm couldn't blame them for that.

After he and Ki and O'Malley had leaned against the trees for a few seconds, catching their breath, Longarm said, "We gotta get out of here!" He surprised himself by being able to hear the words, at least faintly.

"What . . . what the hell is happenin'?" O'Malley asked. Even though he was probably shouting, to Longarm his voice sounded like it was muffled by half a dozen blankets.

"The Empress!" Longarm gestured toward the destroyed plantation house. "Bound to be her doin'!"

Ki nodded. "Her hired killers may come to check the place, once the bombardment is over!"

That was exactly what Longarm was thinking. Katerina had sent Dumond and the other men to ambush them earlier, but since that attempt had failed, she would be worried that they might track her here. What better way to get them off her trail permanently than to level the place with artillery fire? If not for the Gilfeathers, Longarm and his friends would have been asleep in there when the shelling started, and might not have made it out alive.

Longarm motioned for the other two to follow him, and stumbled away from the house. There was no telling where their horses had gone, but San Antonio was only a couple of miles away and there were more horses to be had there. They could reach the city on foot. As they circled wide around the buildings of the old plantation, Longarm saw the lights of San Antonio in the distance.

They hadn't gone more than a quarter of a mile in that direction, though, before Longarm realized that most of his hearing had returned. He knew that because he heard quite distinctly the thundering hoofbeats of a large group of riders that was practically on top of them.

Chapter 32

The three of them had managed to hang on to their rifles. The weapons came up as the riders surrounded them. Longarm knew they were outnumbered, but if he was about to cross the divide, he was determined to take at least a few of the bastards with him.

But then he heard someone shout, "Halt! Hold your fire!"

That didn't sound like the voice of an outlaw. It sure as hell didn't belong to Andre Dumond. Longarm, Ki, and O'Malley crouched, back to back to back, as the riders surrounded them.

Whoever had called out the orders before said, "Lay down your arms, gentlemen. You're surrounded."

"Army?" Longarm guessed roughly.

"Yes, sir. Cavalry detail from Fort Sam Houston, investigating those explosions. Did you have anything to do with them?"

"Yeah," Longarm said. "We had nice big bull's-eyes painted on our backs." He lowered his rifle and motioned for Ki and O'Malley to do likewise, then said to what he guessed was a shavetail lieutenant, "I'm a deputy U.S. marshal name of Custis Long."

"No offense, sir, but how do I know that?"

"Tell your boys not to get antsy, Lieutenant ... It *is* Lieutenant, ain't it?"

"Yes, sir. Lieutenant Evan Darwin."

"Well, as I was sayin', Lieutenant Darwin, tell your boys not to get antsy, and I'll dig out my badge and bona fides. You'll have to strike a light to look at 'em, though."

Within minutes, Longarm had satisfied the young cavalry officer as to his identity, and had vouched for Ki and O'Malley as well. "What can you tell us about those explosions, Marshal?" Darwin asked. "They sounded like an artillery bombardment."

"There's a good reason for that. That's exactly what it was. But it's a long story, Lieutenant, and your commanding officer is gonna want to hear it, so why don't we save some time and you take us to see him, so I just have to tell it once."

Darwin hesitated for a moment, then nodded. "All right. You'll have to ride double with some of us."

"We've got horses around here somewhere, if you want to take the time to look."

"I think the colonel would rather know who's firing unauthorized artillery rounds as soon as possible."

Longarm figured that was probably right. He and his companions climbed up behind three of the cavalrymen, and they headed for Fort Sam Houston.

The fort, which had been founded less than ten years earlier, was just northeast of the main section of San Antonio. The eastern sky was gray with the approach of dawn, so that meant the fort was coming awake for a new day. Lights burned in many of the buildings, including the headquarters building next to the vast supply depot known as the Quadrangle.

Lieutenant Darwin took Longarm, Ki, and O'Malley into the office of Colonel Thaddeus Lancaster. Longarm had never met the colonel before, but he recognized the type—an old-timer, career army, a stickler for regulations and discipline.

"I'm the acting commander of this post until the next general arrives," Lancaster said when a clearly nervous Darwin had performed the introductions. "Now, what's all this about artillery fire on the edge of San Antonio?"

"That's what it was, Colonel," Longarm said, "and I've got a pretty good idea that the person responsible for it was a woman named Katerina von Blöde."

Lancaster's rather bushy gray eyebrows rose in surprise. "A woman? That's incredible! What woman has a cannon at her disposal?"

"I wouldn't put much of anything past this particular gal, Colonel."

Lancaster gestured curtly toward the chairs in front of his desk. "Sit down and tell me about it. But it had better be good," he warned. "I don't like disruptions in this post's routine."

Longarm spent the next ten minutes giving Lancaster a highly condensed version of the events of the past few days. The colonel's face grew darker as he listened, and when Longarm finished, Lancaster finally blurted out, "That's the most preposterous thing I ever heard!"

"Every word of it's the truth," Longarm insisted.

"And how do I know that?"

"We both work for Uncle Sam. I reckon that ought to count for something."

Lancaster shook his head. "For all I know, you took that

badge and those identification papers off the body of the real Custis Long. You look like an outlaw to me." He was just getting worked up, and his voice rose as he went on. "You come in here with a Chinaman and some shanty Irishman and the most ridiculous story I've ever heard, and you expect me to believe it!"

"I don't much cotton to bein' called a liar," Longarm said, his voice dangerously mild.

"And I am half-Japanese, not Chinese," Ki added. "Doesn't the name Starbuck mean anything to you, Colonel?"

"I've heard of the Starbuck ranch, but I'm not impressed by it. I'm a soldier, not a cattleman." Lancaster's eyes snapped over to Darwin, who still stood there nervously. "Lieutenant, take your patrol and go back out there and find out what *really* happened this time, instead of bringing me some lowlifes with a cock-and-bull story."

Darwin came to attention and snapped a salute. "Yes, sir!" He hesitated. "But if I may ask, sir . . . what are you going to do with these men?"

"What do you think I'm going to do with them, Lieutenant?" Lancaster rose to his feet, leaned forward, rested his hands on his desk, and roared, "I'm going to throw them into the stockade until we get to the bottom of this!"

"I thought ye said the army would help us," O'Malley said a short time later as they sat in a large, uncomfortable, sparsely furnished cell in the fort's stockade.

Longarm's jaw was tightly clenched in anger. He said through his teeth, "I didn't know they had put a total lunatic in command here."

"Some parts of the story *are* rather far-fetched, despite their truth," Ki pointed out. "Many people lack the imagination to even believe in a large criminal conspiracy such as the Cartel. Nor are they willing to believe that a woman could ever be in charge of such a thing."

"That's because they don't know Katerina von Blöde," Longarm said.

They had been disarmed and escorted to the stockade even though they were civilians. Longarm had protested that that wasn't legal, but Colonel Lancaster had ignored him. The hombre was a little tin-plated dictator, and he wasn't going to listen to reason.

One ray of hope remained. Longarm had asked the colonel to send a wire to Billy Vail in Denver, and Lancaster had responded, "I certainly will send a telegram to the chief marshal. I want him to know that some disreputable bandit is impersonating one of his men."

"Tell him to say hello to Henry for me," Longarm urged.

Lancaster had frowned at that. Longarm hoped the colonel did as he asked and included that message in the telegram. If he did, then Billy Vail would know that the man claiming to be Longarm was telling the truth. Anybody impersonating Longarm likely wouldn't know the name of Billy's secretary.

Now all they could do was wait. The fear that Jessie was still the Empress's prisoner—and that they were getting farther away with every passing minute—gnawed at Longarm's guts, and he knew from the worried expressions on the faces of Ki and O'Malley that they felt the same way.

The hours dragged by. It was hot in the cell. Longarm stood up and paced, but that didn't help any.

Around midday, footsteps echoing from the thick stone walls as they approached drew the three men off the bunks in the cell. As they went to the bars, Lieutenant Darwin walked up and nodded to them.

"Gentlemen," the young officer said. "I thought you'd

like to know that all the buildings on that old plantation were completely destroyed. It was definitely an artillery bombardment, and I've reported as much to Colonel Lancaster."

"What the hell is wrong with that scalawag anyway?" O'Malley demanded. "Has he got no sense at all?"

Darwin ignored those questions and said, "For what it's worth, I believe your story. Again for what it's worth, I hope the new post commander does, too."

"When is he supposed to get here?" Longarm asked.

"Any day now."

"Can't be too soon to suit me," Longarm muttered. "Do you know if Lancaster's gotten a response to that wire he sent to Denver?"

"I don't believe so. When that terrible storm came through several days ago, it tore down all the telegraph wires in the area. They haven't all been repaired yet, so Colonel Lancaster may not have even been able to send the wire by now."

Longarm's spirits sank at hearing that. He wasn't the sort to give up, though, so he would continue clinging to hope.

Guards brought food to them an hour later, and then the afternoon stretched seemingly endlessly in front of them. Longarm took out the cavalry insignia he had found in the plantation house and turned it over idly in his fingers.

"What's that?" Ki asked.

Longarm tossed it to him and explained where he had found it. "Turn it over," he said.

"CSA," Ki said, reading the letters aloud. He glanced up. "Confederate States Army?"

"Or Confederate States of America, however you want to look at it," Longarm said.

"It looks new."

"Just well taken care of, I'd say."

"So there was a Confederate cavalry officer there along with the Empress?"

Longarm nodded. "I reckon that's a good guess. Interesting, ain't it? What's the connection between Katerina and a bunch of unreconstructed Rebels?"

"The Confederates wanted to form their own nation," Ki murmured. "What if the Cartel has decided to do the same thing? She could have enlisted the aid of a large group of former Confederate soldiers and promised to provide a new homeland for them as well."

Longarm sat up straighter on the bunk. Ki's theory was intriguing, and it sounded like just the sort of grandiose plan someone who called herself the Empress might come up with—except for one thing. Katerina was no fool. The entire Confederacy hadn't been able to defeat the Union. She couldn't hope to accomplish that with only a few hundred men. Such a force might represent the largest outlaw gang in the history of the West, but it wouldn't amount to a hill of beans against the whole country.

No, Ki was on the right track, but there was something else going on here, Longarm decided.

By late afternoon, he hadn't figured it out, but he was seething at all the wasted time they had spent here. If it hadn't been a waste of breath, he would have cursed the bad luck that had sent the three of them blundering right into that cavalry patrol.

Then, as the light was fading, more footsteps sounded, briskly approaching the cell. A short, slender figure in uniform appeared out of the thickening shadows, and a raspy, familiar voice said, "Custis Long, by God!"

"Colonel Stilwell?" Longarm asked as he gripped the bars on the cell door.

"It's Major General Stilwell now," the bearded officer said with a grin as he came to a stop in front of the cell. Longarm had run into him several times in the past, although it had been a while since they'd seen each other. "I'm the new commander of Fort Sam Houston. Just arrived a little while ago, and one of the first things I hear is that I've got three civilians locked up in my stockade, and somebody's been shelling San Antonio! I should have known you'd be mixed up in this somehow, Marshal."

"I sure am glad to see you, General," Longarm said. "You're gonna let us out of here, aren't you?"

"Yes, as soon as I read you this telegram I found waiting for me on my new desk." Stilwell lifted a piece of paper and read from it. "Disreputable bandit my deputy. Stop. Request you render all possible aid. Stop. Vail, Chief Marshal. Stop." The general grinned. "Let's get you boys out of that cell. I want to have a serious talk with whoever started lobbing around artillery shells, and I've got a hunch you can lead me right to him."

"Her," Longarm corrected. "She may not have fired the cannon, but you can damn sure bet she gave the orders."

Chapter 33

General Tennyson kept the wagon train moving at a steady pace all night. It was impossible to hurry the oxen pulling the big, canvas-covered vehicles. The general didn't allow much time for rest, however, before pressing on the next morning. Nor did he allow many stops as the day went on.

Rugged hills broke up the terrain west of San Antonio. A geologist had once told Jessie that that line of hills, which stretched across Texas in a big curve hundreds of miles long, was known as the Balcones Escarpment. It was pretty country, but not that easy to travel in wagons.

That meant it probably wouldn't take Longarm, Ki, and O'Malley very long to catch up to the wagon train, Jessie told herself.

She was worried about what that cannon had been used for, though. Longarm and Ki would have been looking out for another ambush, but they couldn't have been expecting a barrage of artillery shells.

By nightfall, Tennyson had pushed the livestock as far and as hard as they would be pushed. The oxen would have to rest now. The drivers pulled the wagons into a circle, and Jessie was struck once again by how much like a typical immigrant train this was. She wondered about their destination. As far as she could tell, after circling to the south of San Antonio, the wagons had headed due west. If they kept going in that direction, in a few days they would reach Del Rio and the Mexican border.

Were they going to cross the Rio Grande into Mexico? Jessie had heard that a number of former Confederates had fled south of the border after the war. Maybe Tennyson had the same thing in mind. She couldn't see how that could possibly benefit the Cartel, though, and she was sure that Katerina wasn't helping Tennyson out of the goodness of her heart.

That evening, Sergeant Brackett kept an eye on her until Dumond came to get her. "The Empress requested that I escort you to her tent, *cherie*," the Frenchman said.

Jessie had seen some of the men setting up the large tent after they unpacked it from a wagon. Just because Katerina was accompanying a wagon train across the Texas frontier was no reason for her to give up all of her creature comforts, Jessie supposed. The men had carried a roll of carpet, a table, a folding bed, and several chairs into the tent once they had it set up.

Dumond took Jessie there now. Around them were the sights and sounds and smells of a typical wagon train camp—children playing after being cooped up in the wagons all day, men tending to the livestock, women cooking supper. These people didn't seem evil, Jessie thought. So why had they allied themselves with a criminal like Katerina von Blöde?

Maybe, like Brackett had said, they just wanted to live

their lives as they saw fit, without the government telling them what to do. But even if that was the case, throwing in with the Empress was the wrong way to go about it.

The soft yellow glow of lamplight came from Katerina's tent. Dumond held the canvas entrance flap aside so that Jessie could precede him. As she went in, she saw Katerina and General Tennyson standing beside the table, which was set for four. Did Katerina expect her to join them for dinner?

Evidently, she did. She smiled at Jessie and said, "Welcome. Would you like a drink?" She and Tennyson each had a glass.

Jessie shrugged. "Why not?"

"Andre, will you do the honors?"

"But of course," Dumond murmured. He moved over to the table to pick up an opened bottle of wine that sat there.

Once Jessie and Dumond had drinks as well, Katerina lifted her glass and said, "To the new world that's coming."

"With you in charge?" Jessie asked coldly. "Forgive me, but I don't think I'll be drinking to that."

Katerina's smile remained in place. "You may decide to change your mind once you hear the news. Your friends will not be coming to save you."

Jessie felt her heart sink. She said, "What do you mean?"

"I mean, I sent some of General Tennyson's men back to the plantation with a cannon to wipe it off the face of the earth. They succeeded in doing so . . . along with Marshal Long, Ki, and Captain O'Malley."

"You're lying," Jessie said through clenched teeth.

Katerina shook her head. "Tell her, Andre."

Dumond said, "I beg your forgiveness for the pain this causes you, *cherie*, but I talked to the men who checked the plantation after the bombardment. They found the bodies of several men. It was, ah, difficult to identify them because of . . . well, those explosive shells created quite a holocaust . . ."

"You don't know it was them," Jessie insisted. She felt dizzy now, and it wasn't because of the wine. She hadn't drunk any of it.

"Who else would it have been?" Katerina said. "We know they escaped from the ambush earlier last night. I'm confident that they would have trailed you to the plantation."

So was Jessie. She knew that once Longarm and Ki were on her trail, nothing would make them give up. Without thinking about what she was doing, she flung the contents of her glass in Katerina's face and cried, "You bitch!"

Katerina staggered back a step as the wine dripped off her cheeks, while Dumond and Tennyson stood by looking shocked. For a second, as Katerina's face contorted with rage, Jessie thought she was going to lunge at her. But Katerina controlled herself and lifted a hand to wipe away the remaining wine. She smiled again, but in her eyes only hatred burned.

"I can see that you're upset," she said, "but you might as well resign yourself to the inevitable, Jessie. My plan is well on its way to success, and there's nothing you or anyone else can do to stop it now."

"We'll see about that," Jessie grated.

"Indeed we shall, in several more days. It's going to take that long for us to reach our destination."

Jessie tamped down her own anger. Katerina seemed to be in a talkative mood, and Jessie thought she might as well try to take advantage of that. "And where is that?" she asked.

Katerina turned to Tennyson. "General, why don't you explain it to her?"

"I'd be glad to," Tennyson said. He smiled at Jessie. "You see, Miss Starbuck, we're bound for a land we're going to call the New Dominion, as a tribute to our friends from Virginia."

Jessie knew that part of Virginia was referred to as the Old Dominion. Many of the leaders of the Confederacy had come from there.

"You say that you're going to call it that," Jessie said. "What's it called now?"

"I believe it's the Blanco Verde Ranch."

With an effort, Jessie kept her jaw from sagging in surprise. Blanco Verde was one of the largest spreads in West Texas, maybe the largest with the exception of her own Circle Star. Several of the ranches in Texas were as big as some Eastern states, and Blanco Verde was one of them. If there was a place that might actually serve as a new Confederate homeland, the giant ranch fit the bill.

And there was something else special about the ranch, something made the whole plan fall together in Jessie's mind. She stared at Katerina and said, "Oh, my God. You're going after the railroad barons."

Katerina smiled again. "Not going after," she said. "I've already got them."

With a sinking feeling, Jessie realized that the Empress was right. She had lost track of the days because of the hurricane and the ordeal that had followed it. When she added them up in her head, though, she knew that today was the day the meeting was supposed to take place.

"The heads of every major railroad in the entire country," Katerina went on, "and they're in my power. They arrived at Blanco Verde today without having any idea that it had been taken over by my men. Now the men on whose shoulders rest the fate of the American economy are my prisoners. You could have simplified things for me by accepting their invitation, Jessie. Your refusal meant that I had to deal with you separately. But it all worked out. I have them, I have you, and soon the country will be brought to its knees . . . unless everyone does as I say."

Jessie still held the empty glass. She thrust it out toward Dumond. He started to pour some wine in it, then stopped and cocked an eyebrow at Katerina.

"Go ahead," the Empress said. "As long as she doesn't throw it in my face again."

Jessie had no intention of doing that. She needed a drink, if her brain was going to be able to cope with the sheer magnitude of Katerina's plan.

Months earlier, the men who controlled the railroads—the railroad barons, as Jessie thought of them—had begun making plans to meet in secret at the Blanco Verde Ranch, which was owned by an Eastern syndicate that included several of the railroad barons. The goal was to carve up among them the rest of the areas west of the Mississippi that the steel rails hadn't reached yet. In the past, disputes over new lines had erupted into bloody wars between various railroads. To these men to whom profit was everything, such wars were annoying—and expensive. They wanted to avoid them in the future. They planned to do this by setting up a "Railroad Ring," modeled after the old Indian Ring that had spread its graft and corruption across the frontier.

Jessie had been the only woman invited to this secret meeting, because the Starbuck business holdings included interests in several of the railroads involved. In the long run, Jessie couldn't stop the railroad barons from doing whatever they wanted to, but she could make it more difficult for them to implement their plan. That was why they wanted her in on it with them.

Jessie had told them in no uncertain terms to go to hell. She didn't want to be part of their shady scheme. On the other hand, what they were doing wasn't actually against the law, so she had told them that she wouldn't interfere—as long as they didn't start trying to run roughshod over anybody who got in their way. They could go ahead with their meeting, and she would tend to her own business, which just then had involved sailing off to Cuba to take care of some problems on the Starbuck sugar plantations there. Since returning to the States, Jessie hadn't even thought about the railroad barons until now.

But if Katerina had taken those men prisoner, she really could dictate to the government. If they were to all die at once, their railroads might well collapse, and without the railroads, the country couldn't function. Business would grind to a halt. Riots might break out, especially in the large Eastern cities once the food supply dried up, and things would generally go to hell. The government might consider ceding Blanco Verde to General Tennyson and his men a reasonable price to pay to avoid that crisis.

Only, General Tennyson wouldn't really be in charge, no matter what he believed, Jessie thought. The Cartel would rule Blanco Verde—or the New Dominion, as Tennyson called it—and that meant Katerina von Blöde really would be an Empress.

Dumond had filled Jessie's glass half full of wine. She lifted the glass and drank, swallowing every drop. After the stunning news she had just heard, she needed to be fortified.

"You see, Jessie, there's nothing you can do," Katerina

went on. "As soon as we reach Blanco Verde, I'll present our demands to the government."

"And those demands will be?" Jessie asked, although she thought she already knew the answer.

But as it turned out, she hadn't quite grasped the scope of Katerina's plan. The Empress smiled at her and said, "Recognition of the New Dominion, a formal treaty ceding ownership of Blanco Verde . . . and one million dollars in gold."

One million dollars. It was a stunning amount. With the railroad barons as hostages, though, the government might have to pay it.

"Otherwise . . ." Jessie said.

"Otherwise, I'll kill every one of them—and you—and the country can go straight to hell," Katerina said.

Jessie set the empty glass on the table and turned to Dumond. "Take me back to Sergeant Brackett's wagon."

Dumond hesitated. Katerina said, "I thought you were going to dine with us."

"We'd be pleased to have you join us, Miss Starbuck," Tennyson put in.

"I'm sorry, General," Jessie said as she looked at Katerina. "I'm afraid I've lost my appetite."

Chapter 34

The next couple of days settled down into a peaceful routine on the wagon train as its route curved northwest, away from the Mexican border and deeper into West Texas. Jessie rode rocking along on the wagon seat next to Sergeant Brackett, who was a pleasant, friendly companion. It was hard to remember that he was part of a plot that might endanger the entire country. As far as Brackett was concerned, he was just trying to help his old comrades get what they deserved—a home they could call their own.

Jessie knew that many injustices had occurred in the South following the war. The Northern carpetbaggers Brackett had spoken off, in collusion with corrupt judges, military officials, and politicians, had stolen hundreds of thousands of acres from the defeated Confederates who just wanted to return to their homes after four years of brutal fighting.

But that ugly period in the nation's history hadn't lasted forever. Eventually, the Southerners had been able to regain some control over their own lives. Jessie couldn't blame Tennyson and the men who followed him for the resentment they felt, but it was time to move beyond that, instead of using the sins of the past to justify their participation in Katerina's grandiose schemes.

Jessie planned to do what she could to stop the Cartel from taking over Blanco Verde. She wasn't sure what that might be, but she wasn't going to give up—although a part of her wanted to because she had come to accept the bitter fact that Longarm and Ki were dead. If they were alive, they would have caught up to the wagon train by now.

The wagons had left the hills and bluffs of the Balcones Escarpment behind, and now rolled over the vast plains of southwestern Texas. Jessie saw several cowboys riding the range, but the buckaroos just waved their hats over their heads and went on about their chores. Immigrant wagons were rare enough nowadays to be something of a novelty, but nobody really thought twice about them, Jessie suspected.

Those carefree cowboys had no way of knowing that in addition to supplies and household goods, the wagons carried weapons of war.

By the third day, Jessie figured they must be on Blanco Verde range. She had been to the ranch before, to finalize the sale of some bulls, and had met the man who ran it for the syndicate, Chet Spaulding. She hoped that when the Cartel gunmen had moved in and taken over, Spaulding and the rest of the ranch hands hadn't been killed. She knew it was unlikely that all of them had survived, though. They would have put up a fight, no doubt about that.

A few limestone bluffs jutted up here and there from the mostly flat landscape, and it was at the base of one of them that the ranch headquarters was located. A stream meandered along through there, and the trees lining it were a vivid splash of green against the white of the limestone behind them. That contrast had given the ranch its name, Blanco Verde, meaning white and green in Spanish.

The large, sprawling, hacienda-style ranch house was a dazzling white in the sun, too, with a red tile roof. Scattered along the banks of the creek were the other buildings, including a couple of large barns and a long bunkhouse. Jessie liked the Blanco Verde. It was a nice spread. Not as nice as the Circle Star, of course, but Jessie didn't believe she would ever see a ranch as good as the one her father had established.

The wagon train approached the ranch in the early afternoon. The sun blazed down, and Jessie was glad for the shade of the shapeless old hat she had found behind the seat of Sergeant Brackett's wagon. It had been his when he still had a farm, he'd explained, but she was welcome to it. He wore a Confederate campaign cap now.

General Tennyson turned and rode back to Brackett's wagon. This was the first time Jessie had seen him wearing his hat since the night he had captured her as she was trying to escape from the plantation. She noticed that the insignia on it was gone. She could see the slightly darker place where it had kept the gray felt from fading in the sun, in the shape of two crossed sabers.

Tennyson turned his horse to ride alongside the wagon. He nodded to Jessie and tugged politely on the brim of his hat. "Miss Starbuck, I just wanted to thank you for your cooperation on this journey," he said. "You could have made things unpleasant for all of us."

"I didn't see any point in that, General."

"I hope that y'all will continue to feel that way now that we've reached our destination. If everything goes as planned, this will soon be over, and you and the railroad gentlemen can all go home."

"You don't really believe that, do you?" Jessie asked. "The government isn't going to let you get away with this. As soon as the railroad barons are free, the troops will move in and—" She stopped. She had been about to say "slaughter all of you," but she couldn't bring herself to do it. She liked Sergeant Brackett, and she felt some grudging respect for Tennyson. He clung too stubbornly to the past, but a lot of people made that mistake.

Tennyson smiled. "I think you're wrong, Miss Starbuck. By that time, the territory of the New Dominion will have a treaty with the United States recognizin' our sovereignty. They won't be able to invade us without it bein' an act of war, and we'll give them no cause for that."

"What about kidnapping a handful of the most important men in the whole country?"

"Miss von Blöde did that, not us," Tennyson pointed out.

"And how about that million-dollar ransom?"

"Again, that's Miss von Blöde's business. We don't intend to take any of that money. We won't need it as long as we have our new home."

Jessie nodded slowly. She understood more now about Katerina's plans. She suspected that once the ransom had been paid, Katerina would kill the railroad barons anyway to plunge the country into chaos, then disappear with the loot in the ensuing confusion. With a million dollars in her war chest and the country in a panic, the Cartel could do a great deal to consolidate its power. Katerina might even be able to work behind the scenes and insinuate herself and the Cartel into the railroads and other legitimate businesses.

As unthinkable as it was, if Katerina's plan succeeded, she might wind up as the most powerful person in the country.

"I think you're making a terrible mistake, General,"

Jessie told him. "Katerina will betray you, and all that you've done will wind up accomplishing nothing. You'll even put the lives of all your followers in danger."

The lines of Tennyson's face tightened. Anger glittered in his eyes, but his voice was unfailingly polite as he said, "I believe that y'all are wrong, Miss Starbuck, but I suppose that only time will tell." He turned his horse and rode back to rejoin the group leading the wagon train. Jessie assumed that most of the men were former members of the general's staff during the war who had come back to resume their old duties in what Jessie regarded as an even more dubious cause.

A dozen men rode out from the ranch headquarters to meet them. Hard-faced Cartel gun-wolves, every one, Jessie noted. If she had harbored any hope that this part of Katerina's scheme had failed, it was gone now. Blanco Verde was firmly in the hands of the Cartel.

The wagons lurched to a halt. Sergeant Brackett turned to Jessie and said, "I surely have enjoyed your company, Miss Starbuck. I wish you the best o' luck from here on out."

"The same to you, Sergeant," Jessie said, and meant it. She added, "I don't suppose you could talk some sense to General Tennyson . . ."

"Sergeants don't tell generals what to do, ma'am. Not now, not ever."

Jessie sighed. "No, I suppose not."

Andre Dumond rode up and dismounted. "Let me help you, Jessie," he said.

"I don't need any help," she snapped. To prove that, she climbed down agilely from the wagon seat and landed on the ground beside Dumond.

"I'm supposed to take you into the house," he said. "The others are waiting in the courtyard."

"Lead the way," she told him. She wanted to see the railroad barons with her own eyes. She wasn't going to believe that such an audacious plan could actually succeed until she did.

As Dumond led her toward the house, she heard a lot of laughter and happy chatter from the wagons. These people were glad to be here. They regarded this place as their new home. Jessie felt a pang of sympathy for the women and children who had been dragged into this by their menfolks. She was sure it wasn't going to end well for most of them.

The thick adobe walls of the ranch house meant that it was considerably cooler inside than out. Jessie was grateful for that. She and Dumond didn't stay inside, though. He took her along a corridor and out through an arching doorway into the enclosed courtyard around which the wings of the house were built. It was a large area with a garden and fountains, surrounded by the two stories of the house and overhung by a balcony with wrought-iron railings. Jessie remembered it well from her previous visit. They might have almost been in Spain, in an old Moorish castle.

Half a dozen men sat around a table near one of the fountains. They had food and drink in front of them, but they were just picking at their meals. Their faces would have been known to anyone who read the illustrated weeklies on a regular basis. They were some of the richest, most powerful men in the country—but right now they looked dejected and despairing. Guards armed with Winchesters stood around the courtyard, reinforcing the status of these men as prisoners.

One of them caught sight of Jessie and came to his feet

in surprise. "Good Lord!" he exclaimed. "Jessica Star-buck!"

"Hello," Jessie said to him. The other men stood up and crowded around her. She greeted all of them. She didn't particularly like most of these men—their business tactics, while maybe not illegal, were a mite too high-handed for her taste—but she was going to be polite and friendly to them anyway, because after all, they all faced the same problem. They were prisoners of the Empress.

"Do you know what's going on here, Miss Starbuck?" one of the magnates asked. "No one will tell us anything, blast it! All we know is that when we arrived, we were at-tacked, and our guards were either killed or taken prisoner."

"Yes, I know what's going on," Jessie said, "but you're not going to like it."

"Sit down and join us," another of the men said. "There's plenty of food."

Andre Dumond put a hand on her shoulder and mur-mured, "I will see you later, *cherie*." She ignored him, and after a moment he shrugged and left.

"Who was that?" one of the railroad barons asked.

"Nobody," Jessie said, and meant that, too. She felt noth-ing for Dumond now except disdain. Their brief romance on board the *Harry Fulton* seemed an eternity ago.

Several men, more roughly dressed than the barons, were sitting on the low stone wall around another fountain across the courtyard. From the corner of her eye, Jessie saw one of them stand up and start toward her. For an instant, her breath caught in her throat, because at first glance the man looked a little like Longarm. He was tall and muscular, with a deeply tanned face and a dark mustache. His hair was a little darker than Longarm's, though, Jessie realized, and the mustache didn't curl up on the tips. A white bandage with a small bloodstain on it was tied around his head, giving him a rakish, piratical look. As he came closer, he raised a hand and said, "Miss Starbuck?"

"Who's that?" Jessie asked the railroad men.

"One of my bodyguards," one of them answered. "He has a detective agency, and I've used his services before, so I engaged him to come with me on this trip. He wasn't able to stop those gunmen from capturing us, though."

"One man couldn't," Jessie said. She faced the big, dark-haired man and asked, "Have we met?"

"No, ma'am, I don't reckon we have," he said. "But I heard about you from an hombre I ran into a while back when we got mixed up in the same ruckus. Fella name of Custis Long."

Jessie felt her heart thud heavily. "You know Longarm?"

"Yes, ma'am, I sure do." A dazzling grin split his dark face. "They call me Raider."

Chapter 35

No doubt about it, Jessie Starbuck was as pretty as Raider had heard she was. Smart as a whip, too, and nice enough so she didn't act like there was a lick of difference between them just because she owned some damn big ranch and had a ton of money and he was just a rough-as-a-cob gunhand and range detective. When she took his hand and grinned at him, it was like they were two of a kind.

Mainly because neither of them had a damned bit of use for that blasted Cartel and the gal who ran it, Raider suspected.

He looked past Jessie and saw those railroad tycoons watching the two of them with frowns of disapproval. They didn't like it that Jessie was talking to him instead of them, Raider supposed.

"If you're a friend of Longarm's, then I have bad news, Raider," Jessie said.

"Aw, no. Don't tell me."

She nodded. "I'm afraid so. He and a friend of mine named Ki were killed a few days ago, along with the man who was the captain of one of my ships."

Raider shook his head and said, "No offense, ma'am, but I ain't gonna believe ol' Longarm's dead until I see his body myself. Did *you* see it?"

"Well . . . no," Jessie admitted. "But there was an artillery barrage that leveled the plantation where I'd been held prisoner, and I know Longarm and Ki and Captain O'Malley were looking for me, and the bodies of several men were found there . . ."

"Had to be somebody else," Raider said. He knew he was being stubborn, but he couldn't help it. He didn't know Longarm all that well, but he figured the big federal lawman would be mighty hard to kill.

Jessie summoned up a smile, but she looked like it didn't come easy to her. "I hope you're right," she said. "In the meantime, why don't you tell me what happened here?"

"I reckon you know some of it already. The fella I work for and the rest of those railroad gents showed up here for their meetin', and when we all got here, everything seemed normal. But the ranch manager was nowhere around, and the hands seemed more like hard cases than regular cowboys."

"That's because they are," Jessie put in.

Raider nodded. "Yes, ma'am, the other bodyguards and I figured that out, but not in time to stop those varmints from jumpin' us. I slapped leather and so did the other fellas, but we were outnumbered and outgunned. About half of us got ventilated, and the other half had to surrender." He gestured toward the bloodstained bandage on his head. "I got creased by a slug pretty early in the ruckus, and it knocked me out. When I came to, it was too late to do anything. We were all prisoners, the ones of us who are still alive, that is."

"And since then?"

"Since then, I reckon we've been waitin' for you to get here," Raider said with a shrug. "Along with that Empress gal. I never met her, but Longarm told me all about her and how you first ran into her up in Nevada. Something about a whole town full of owlhoots."

"That's right," Jessie said. "But what she's up to now is even worse."

Raider looked over at the railroad men, who had gone back to their meals. "I'll bet it has something to do with demandin' ransom for those fellas. You won't find a richer bunch of hombres in the country."

"That's part of it." Jessie nodded toward a flagstone-paved path that twisted through the courtyard's garden. "Let's walk around, and I'll tell you about it."

For the next few minutes, that's what she did, telling him about the hurricane and the way she was kidnapped in Indianola, the time she had spent at the plantation, and the revelation of Katerina von Blöde's plan to extort a million dollars from the U.S. government, as well as set up a new Confederate homeland here at Blanco Verde.

"The government won't never allow that," Raider said with a frown when Jessie was finished.

"Of course not," she agreed. "Katerina is just using General Tennyson and his people. She'll abandon them once she's got what she wants."

"There has to be some way we can stop her."

"Between her own hired guns and Tennyson's followers, she's got a couple of hundred men," Jessie pointed out. "Plus cannons and Gatling guns. It really is a small army. It goes against the grain for me to give up, but . . . I don't know what we can do."

Raider rubbed his jaw as he frowned in thought. "The whole plan falls apart if the Empress don't have those hostages," he said. "If we could get 'em loose somehow and get them out of here . . ."

"Where could we go that they couldn't follow us and recapture us without any trouble?" Jessie asked.

"Yeah, that's the problem," Raider said. "Those fellas may be rich as hell, but they ain't had much experience at dodgin' owlhoots."

"You and I have, though," Jessie pointed out. "If you and I could get out, maybe we could find some help and bring it back. There's a Texas Ranger post at Del Rio."

"I reckon even a troop of Rangers would have their hands full with this bunch." Raider shrugged again. "But that sounds like our best bet. A smaller group might be able to get in and free those hostages, where a head-on attack by a larger force would have a harder time of it."

"My thinking exactly," Jessie said. She looked around. "Now all we have to do is figure out a way to get out of here . . ."

Even though she still grieved over the loss of Longarm and Ki, it felt good to have an ally again, Jessie thought as she and Raider began to formulate their plans. Longarm had told her about meeting the former Pinkerton agent during an earlier case that had also involved the Cartel. She knew he was a tough, competent man and that Longarm had respected and trusted him—although she recalled that initially there had been some friction between the two men.

Raider filled her in on the way the guards were posted and scheduled around the big ranch house. He had been taking note of such things ever since he'd been captured along with the others, just in case the opportunity ever came to make a break for freedom.

Before they could discuss such things for very long,

though, Katerina von Blöde walked regally into the courtyard, accompanied by Andre Dumond and General Tennyson. Her beauty instantly caught the attention of the
railroad barons, who didn't know who she was.

She introduced herself to them, adding, "I'm your host-
ess here at Blanco Verde."

"You mean you're the one behind this outrage, madam?"
one of the barons demanded.

"That's right," Katerina told him with a smile.

"Then you can tell us what this is about," another man
said.

"Indeed I can."

She proceeded to do so, and as the audacious nature of
her plan became apparent, jaws sagged in surprise and the
men seated around the table stared at her. Katerina introduced Dumond and Tennyson as well, then said, "If you
gentlemen will simply cooperate with us, you'll all be free
to go about your business soon enough. I don't wish to inconvenience you any more than I have to."

"This is madness!" one of the men exclaimed. "You
can't mean to take on the government of the United
States!"

"That's exactly what I intend to do," Katerina said with a
smile. "Now, if you'll excuse me, I have to get to work on
the letter that my ambassador will be delivering to Washington via telegraph from San Antonio."

From the way Andre Dumond smiled and preened when
Katerina said "my ambassador," Jessie had a pretty good
idea that the Frenchman would be filling that role. The letter Katerina had mentioned would contain the demands she
had outlined earlier.

When Katerina, Dumond, and Tennyson were gone, the
railroad barons erupted into loud, angry voices. Jessie let

them blow off steam for a few moments, then raised her voice and said, "Gentlemen!"

Surprised, they turned to look at her.

"What are the odds that the government will concede to the Empress's demands?" she asked.

"The whole idea is preposterous!" one man said.

"I'm not so sure," another put in with a frown on his face. "There's no such thing as an indispensable man, but I think the American economy could scarcely stand to lose us, especially all at the same time. Our deaths would cause widespread panic and financial collapse."

Jessie nodded. "I agree. That's why I think the government *will* pay. That's also why I believe that Katerina plans to murder all of us anyway, as soon as she's got what she wants. The Cartel can take advantage of such chaos."

Fear and consternation appeared on the faces of the men gathered around the table. They saw that Jessie had a point. Up until now, they had probably figured that sooner or later they would be able to buy their way out of this. Now they were beginning to see that that might not be possible.

"We have to get away," one of them sputtered. "There must be some way we can escape."

Another man said, "If we all rushed the guards at the same time—"

"They would just kill you and Katerina would claim you were still alive when she threatened the government," Jessie said. "I'm a little surprised she hasn't just gone ahead and done that anyway. I suppose she's kept us all alive just in case she needs us for something later on."

"What are we going to do?" one of the barons asked. His voice was a plaintive, frightened moan.

"It's going to take a few days of negotiation before anything is settled. If one or two of us can get away, we'll try to get help." Jessie repeated what she and Raider had discussed a short time earlier. "Without the hostages, Katerina's plan falls apart. We need to get back in here with a small force so that you men can be rescued. Then the army can move in and clean up the rest of the trouble."

"You said 'we.' Who are you talking about, Miss Starbuck?"

Jessie nodded toward the big, dark-haired man at her side. "Raider and me."

"But . . . but he's just a hillbilly gunman!"

Raider growled. Jessie put out a hand toward him and said, "Take it easy." To the railroad man who had made that comment, she said, "Raider is exactly the sort of man I want with me on a job like this."

"So we're to be saved by a roughneck and a woman?" drawled one of the other men.

"This ain't just any woman, mister," Raider snapped. "This is Jessie Starbuck. She's handled more trouble than all you gents put together, and so have I." He shrugged. "But if you want to go up against the Empress's gunnies, be my guest."

All the railroad men shook their heads. "No, that's all right," one of them said. "I believe that you're the right man for the job, Mister, ah, Raider."

"And you're the right woman, Miss Starbuck," another added.

Jessie gave a curt nod. "I hope you're right," she said. "I reckon we'll find out."

Chapter 36

The sooner she and Raider made their break, the better, Jessie thought. But they would have to wait for nightfall. The chances of getting away in the darkness would be higher. Then they would head for the Texas Ranger post at Del Rio. Several years earlier, Jessie had met one of the Rangers stationed there—Sam Colby, or something like that—and she recalled that he was the same sort of savvy, determined lawman as Longarm had been. She hoped that he was still there.

But if not, she knew that any of the Rangers could be trusted to help her. They were the West's toughest outlaw hunters, the sort of men who would charge Hell with a bucket of water.

As they walked around the garden, talking in low voices, Raider nodded toward the balcony and said, "I reckon the best way out would be up and over."

Jessie thought about her excursion onto the roof of the plantation house near San Antonio. She wasn't that fond of the idea of climbing around on another roof, but she thought Raider was probably right.

"What happens at night?" she asked him. "Do they lock you in your rooms?"

"Yeah, but not right away after supper. Those fellas like to come out here in the evenin' and smoke cigars and drink brandy, and the guards been lettin' 'em do that. To tell you the truth, the guards ain't all that worried about those railroad barons, as you call 'em, gettin' away. Out here in the middle of nowhere like this, where would a bunch of gents like that go, especially on foot? They keep a closer eye on me and the other bodyguards who lived through the fight when they jumped us. They post sentries out at the corral, too, to keep an eye on the horses. We'll have to get us a couple of mounts if we're gonna make it to Del Rio."

Jessie nodded. She had already thought the same thing.

"We need a distraction," she mused. "If we could get the guards busy with something else, we could climb up that iron scrollwork from the balcony to the roof." She tried to remember what the front of the house was like. "There's a stone-and-adobe wall about six feet tall. We could drop from the roof to that, and then to the ground."

Raider nodded. "Sounds like it'd work. Might have to take out a guard or two along the way."

"That's fine with me," Jessie said. She looked toward the railroad barons. "You think we can persuade them to cooperate with us?"

"I reckon they'll do anything they can if it'll help 'em get out of this mess."

Jessie strolled over to join the men at the table. What was left from lunch had been cleared away. An uncomfortable silence fell as Jessie sat down with them. She looked around and said quietly, "I hope I can trust all of you gentlemen. Raider and I have been working on a plan to get all of us out of here, but we'll need your help."

"Whatever you say, Miss Starbuck, we'll do," one of them assured her. He looked around at the others, who all nodded.

"All right, then," Jessie said. She leaned forward. "Here's what I have in mind . . ."

Jessie halfway expected Katerina to join them for supper so that she could gloat over them again, but the Empress didn't put in an appearance. Afterward, as Raider had said, the railroad barons went back out into the courtyard, lit cigars, and sipped brandy from snifters they brought with them from inside the house. The evening was beautiful, with millions of stars floating in the patch of ebony visible from the courtyard and a warm breeze that carried with it the scent of the flowers growing in the garden.

It was so peaceful, in fact, that it was difficult to realize they were all in such deadly danger—that the country itself, in fact, was imperiled.

Jessie and Raider drifted toward the open staircase that led up to the balcony. As they did so, the ugly sound of an argument broke out among the railroad barons. A couple of them shouted at each other, and then the others joined in the fracas, lifting their voices in angry curses. Two of them started throwing punches at each other, and in seconds the scuffle had turned into a full-fledged brawl among the millionaires—quite likely the first time any of them had been in an actual fight in years.

The guards came running to break it up, as Jessie had known they would. For now, those men were mighty valuable to the Empress, and she would have given orders that no harm should come to them, even at the hands of each other.

With that distraction going on at the other end of the courtyard, Jessie and Raider sprinted up the stairs toward the balcony. A guard with a Winchester stepped out of the shadows at the top of the stairs and started to say, "What the hell's goin' on down—"

Raider's fist crunched into the man's mouth, silencing him at the same time as it knocked him out. Jessie grabbed the rifle and wrenched it out of his hands. Raider walloped the hombre again for good measure, and dragged his unconscious form into a patch of deeper shadow. He and Jessie hurried over to an ironwork trellis on which vines climbed toward the roof.

"Who's goin' first?" Raider asked.

"I will," Jessie said. She handed the rifle to Raider, hiked her skirts up with no pretense of false modesty, and climbed up onto the railing that ran around the balcony. Raider reached up with his free hand and grasped her arm to steady her as she leaned over to get a handhold on the trellis.

He admired her—and not just physically—as she started scaling the ironwork. Jessie Starbuck was every bit as brave and icy-nerved as Longarm had described her. Raider still had a hard time believing that Longarm was dead, but if that turned out to be true, at least he had Jessie as an ally. The odds were against them, but they had a fighting chance, by God, and no man could ask for more.

Jessie's bare legs disappeared over the edge of the tile roof. Down below in the courtyard, the railroad barons were still yelling and fighting as the guards tried to separate them. They were carrying off their part just fine, Raider thought. Every eye in the courtyard was on them, not on the balcony.

Jessie's arm appeared as she lay at the edge of the roof and reached over it. "Hand me the rifle!" she said in a half whisper.

Raider took hold of the barrel and leaned out to extend the stock toward her. She grabbed it and hauled the weapon up.

Then he stretched out an arm and took hold of the iron trellis. He had to swing out from the railing, and for a second all his weight was on that lone hand. Then he got hold of the trellis with his other hand and started pulling himself up.

Climbing like a monkey wasn't something he was particularly good at, but he managed to get to the top, where Jessie was waiting to catch hold of his wrist and help him up onto the roof. He wound up lying on the tiles next to her, and felt the warmth of her hip pressing against his. He was very aware at that moment of what a lovely woman she was, and despite the danger they were in, he felt himself reacting to her.

Time for that later, if they got out of here alive, he thought. One of these days. Right now, he said roughly, "Let's go."

They crawled up the gentle slope of the roof, being as quiet about it as possible. Pausing at the top, Jessie whispered, "I'm glad you didn't break out of here before now, Raider. I'm not sure I could have done this by myself."

"None of us knew what they had in mind for us," he said, "so I was just waitin', tryin' to get the lay of the land. Once the Empress got here, though, and explained her plan, I knew our time was runnin' out mighty quick. If we don't get away now, we might not get another chance."

Jessie started to move toward the front of the house, but Raider stopped her with a hand on her shoulder.

"I'll go first this time," he said. "Might be droppin' down right on top of a guard."

He slid down to the edge of the roof, still moving quietly, and looked down at the stone-and-adobe wall that extended some fifteen feet out from the front of the house, enclosing a small area where defenders could stand and fire through rifle ports in case of attack. The wall was a foot thick, which meant that dropping onto it from the roof was going to be tricky. Raider's eyes searched the rest of the ranch headquarters. He saw lights in the bunkhouse, but no one seemed to be moving around outside. Sliding his legs off the edge of the roof, he sat there for a second, then pushed off and fell the few feet onto the top of the wall.

Both booted feet landed cleanly on the wall. He had to windmill his free arm for a second to maintain his balance. When he was steady again, he sat down on the wall. Just like Humpty Dumpty in that old storybook rhyme his ma had read to him as a kid. He grinned for a second, then dropped to the ground.

He had barely landed when footsteps sounded close by, and a voice said, "Hey! Don't move, whoever you—"

Raider didn't hesitate. He crouched and spun and lashed out with the Winchester. The barrel slammed into the head of the guard who had rushed up behind him. The man went down like a poleaxed steer.

"Raider?" Jessie called softly.

"It's all right," he told her. "Climb on down."

While she was doing that, he picked up the hat that had fallen from the guard's head. Raider put the Stetson on his own head. When Jessie dropped lightly to the ground beside him, he said, "Stay here. I'll go get a couple of horses."

He thought for a second she was going to argue with him. Jessie Starbuck probably wasn't used to somebody else giving the orders. But then she just nodded and whispered, "Be careful."

Carrying the rifle at a slant across his chest, Raider marched toward the corral. He knew there would be at least one guard out there, and he was going to walk up to the fella like he was supposed to be there. It was a general rule that folks weren't as quick to challenge you if you acted like you knew what you were doing. The fact that he was wearing the unconscious guard's hat might help, too.

Sure enough, as Raider approached the corral, a rifle-toting gent walked up to him and said, "Is that you, Ben? What the hell's all the ruckus up at the house?"

Making his voice as rough and guttural as he could, Raider said, "Those rich bastards got in a fight with each other."

"No shit?" The guard laughed. "You'd think they'd have better things to— Hey! You ain't—"

He had come to that realization too late. Raider drove the butt of the Winchester into the middle of the man's face. He felt bone give under the swift stroke, and the guard's knees unhinged, dumping him forward. Raider kicked him aside and leaped for the corral gate. A few harnesses hung there. He grabbed two of them, slipped inside the fence, and got the harnesses on the first two horses that would cooperate with him.

He was just leading them out of the corral when the front door of the ranch house crashed open and men boiled out through it. Following close behind the gunmen, Katerina von Blöde cried, "Stop them! Don't let them get away!"

Raider bellowed, "Jessie! Run for it!" then brought the rifle to his shoulder and started firing. He sprayed bullets toward the Empress's men, hoping to drive them back into the house.

They returned his fire. As slugs sizzled around him, he leaped onto the back of one of the horses. A glance toward the spot where Jessie had waited for him made his heart sink. A couple of men had reached her, and although she was struggling against them, she was unarmed and out-numbered.

"Raider!" she screamed. "Go on! Get out of here! Go!"

He bit back a curse as he snapped off three more shots
as fast as he could work the Winchester's lever. More men
were between him and Jessie now. He couldn't reach her
now, not without getting shot full of holes. And that wouldn't
help anything.

Hating what he had to do, he wheeled his mount and
jammed his heels into the horse's flanks. The horse leaped
into a gallop. Raider leaned forward as more bullets
whined past his ears.

He knew the Empress would send men after him, but it
would take a few minutes for any pursuit to get organized.
He intended to put as much distance between him and them
as he could in the time he had. And since the moon hadn't
risen yet, the night was pretty dark. He had at least a chance
of giving them the slip.

The horse ran easily underneath him, racing over gently
rolling plains dotted with boulders and slashed by ravines.
The hat Raider had taken from the cold-cocked guard flew
off and vanished behind him. He didn't care. Steering by
the stars, he headed southwest toward Del Rio. The border
town was a good ten or fifteen miles away, but he thought
he could stay in front of the Empress's killers for that distance.

He hadn't counted on someone flying out of the shadows as he rode past a large boulder, slamming into him, and
knocking him off the horse's back. Raider didn't even have
time to yell in surprise before he crashed into the ground
and the impact knocked all the air out of his lungs. He
rolled over several times before finally coming to a stop. As
he did so, the cold ring of a gun barrel pressed against his
head, and a voice he had feared he would never hear again
ordered, "Don't move, old son, or I'll blow your brains
out."

Chapter 37

"Ease off on that trigger, you blasted lawdog!" growled the man Ki had just tackled and knocked off his horse. "It's me—Raider."

"Raider!" The exclamation was shocked out of Longarm. "The hombre who used to be a Pinkerton?"

"One and the same. How about lettin' me up from here? I got a bunch of gun-wolves on my tail who'd be glad to ventilate us both, Custis."

Longarm took the gun away from Raider's head, reached down and grasped the man's arm, and hauled him to his feet. Ki said, "I hear a large number of horses approaching, Marshal. Perhaps we should take cover."

"Now you're talkin'," Longarm said. He hustled Raider toward the ravine where he and Ki had been hidden a few minutes earlier, keeping an eye on Blanco Verde. They had heard the shooting, then the hoofbeats of a running horse, and figured that somebody was making a getaway. They needed to find out as much as they could about what was going on at the ranch, and grabbing the hombre who was on that galloping horse seemed like their best bet to do so.

Knocking him off his horse was risky—he could have broken his neck in the fall—but Longarm and Ki had figured the gamble was worth it, so Ki had scrambled up on top of that boulder and made a flying tackle as the rider thundered past.

Now that Longarm knew who the rider was, the gamble seemed more worthwhile than ever. He had no idea what Raider was doing here, but he knew the former Pinkerton agent would make one hell of an ally.

Raider's horse had kept running after Ki knocked Raider off its back, so the pursuers galloped right past the ravine without pausing, still on the trail of the runaway horse. Longarm, Ki, and Raider crouched below the level of the surrounding prairie, with only the tops of their heads high enough so they could watch the men who had been chasing Raider.

Once those hombres had raced on by and disappeared in the night, Raider said, "I thought you two fellas were supposed to be dead. How about tellin' me what in tarnation is goin' on here?"

"In a minute," Longarm said. "We better get back to the others. And you got some explaining to do, too, Raider. I never expected to run into *you* here."

"Others?" Raider repeated. "What others?" He grasped the big lawman's arm as a thought occurred to him. "You ain't got Doc with you, do you?"

"What? Oh, you mean Doc Weatherbee." Longarm recalled Raider's former partner in the Pinkertons from that Golden Eagle dustup a while back. "No, he's back in Boston as far as I know. You'd know better than I would, more'n likely, since he was your partner, not mine."

"What are you talkin' about then?"

"You'll see," Longarm told him.

The ravine zigzagged across the rocky, semiarid landscape. The three men followed it about half a mile before it opened out into a large canyon. Raider stopped short and stared as he saw the men, horses, and artillery pieces gathered in that canyon.

"What the hell!" he exclaimed. "You brought the army!"

"Well, if you're gonna fight an army, you sorta need an army of your own," Longarm said with a grin.

Raider turned to look at him. "How'd you know?"

"How'd I know what?"

"That the Empress has got a couple of hundred ex-Confederates over there who plan on making the Blanco Verde Ranch their own new country."

"It was a theory we formulated when Marshal Long found evidence of a Confederate presence at a plantation near San Antonio where Jessie was held prisoner," Ki explained. "We knew that a wagon train had formed there as well, so we thought perhaps the immigrants were former Confederates."

Raider nodded. "Their leader is an old Rebel general named Tennyson."

Longarm held up a hand to stop him. "Hold on. Let's find General Stilwell, the officer in command of this bunch, and you'll only have to tell it once."

That didn't take long, because Stilwell was already striding out to meet them. "Who's this?" the bearded officer asked as he came up to the three men.

"An old pard of mine called Raider," Longarm said. "Rade, this is General Stilwell."

"I'm pleased to meet you, General," Raider said, "and *mighty* pleased to see that you brung some help with you."

"Were you inside the ranch house at Blanco Verde, Mr. Raider?" Stilwell asked.

"Just Raider. No need for the mister. And yeah, I was in there for several days, ever since the Empress's men grabbed my boss and the other fellas he was meetin' there."

"Who're you working for, Raider?" Longarm asked.

Raider told him. The burly ex-Pinkerton mentioned the names of the other prisoners, too. Longarm, Ki, and Stilwell exchanged surprised glances when they learned the identities of those men. Raider explained how Katerina planned to hold the men hostage and how Jessie believed the Empress would kill all the prisoners in the long run, no matter whether or not the government gave in to her demands.

"I probably shouldn't be tellin' you who they are," Raider said, "because they wanted the whole thing kept quiet, about them gettin' together and all. But I figure since they're all gonna be killed if we don't get in there and rescue 'em, they'll forgive me."

"What about Jessie?" Ki asked. "Is she all right?"

"The last I saw, she was," Raider answered. "We were tryin' to get out of there together, but we got separated and the Empress's gunnies grabbed her again. I got away by the skin of my teeth."

"What's that?" asked Seamus O'Malley, who had come up while Raider was talking. "Miss Starbuck is all right? Saints be praised!"

"You still ain't explained how you fellas came to be here," Raider said to Longarm.

"We've been followin' that wagon train for the past few days," Longarm said. "We stayed far enough back so nobody with the wagons would notice us. That many wagons leave a trail that's pretty easy to follow."

"Why didn't you just stop them before they got to Blanco Verde?"

Ki said, "We wanted to find out what their destination was and what sort of plan Katerina von Blöde was trying to carry out. Also, there are numerous women and children with the wagon train, and an attack on it would have endangered them."

Raider nodded. "That's true, I reckon. Now that you know, what're you gonna do?"

Longarm looked over at Stilwell and asked, "What do you think, General?"

"Our forces are evenly matched with the Confederates," Stilwell said with a frown. "Still, I'm confident that we would prevail in an actual battle. However, that would endanger the hostages, as well as the families of those Rebels."

Raider said, "Jessie and I planned to try to get the hostages out of there, if we could find some help." He grunted. "I'd say the help found me."

"Yeah," Longarm agreed. "If we can rescue the hostages, Katerina won't have any cards left to play. You can surround the ranch headquarters, General, and wait 'em out if you have to."

Stilwell nodded. "That sounds like a plan that might work. But who's going to free the hostages?"

"There are three of us right here," Longarm pointed out, nodding to Ki and Raider and including himself in the count.

"Make that four," O'Malley insisted.

Longarm considered, then nodded. "I reckon you've earned the right to be in on it, O'Malley."

"I can give you a couple of other good men," Stilwell offered. "That will make six. A larger force might have trouble getting in there without being discovered."

"Yeah, that's what I was thinking," Longarm said. "And the sooner we get in there, the better."

Jessie wasn't the type to give in to despair. She could always find a shred of hope to cling to. In this case, it was the hope that Raider had gotten away and would bring help.

It needed to be soon, though, because things weren't looking too good at the moment.

More than an hour had passed since she and Raider had tried to escape. Jessie had spent that hour locked up in a storage room, sitting alone in the darkness wondering what was going to happen.

When the door of the room finally opened, several men came in, grabbed her, and jerked her to her feet. Katerina appeared in the doorway and ordered, "Take her out to the courtyard."

The men hustled Jessie into the courtyard, handling her roughly. Several lanterns had been lit and hung from hooks on the pillars that supported the balcony. In the lantern light, she saw that all the railroad barons were gathered in the courtyard as well, under the guns of several guards. They looked pale and frightened.

Evidently, the men holding Jessie had been given their orders in advance. They took her over to one of the pillars and forced her to stand against it with her face pressed to the adobe, then lifted her arms above her head. One of them tied her wrists together with a length of rope that passed around the pillar.

No, this wasn't looking good at all.

Katerina snapped, "Bare her back."

One of the men took hold of the collar of Jessie's dress and ripped the garment down the back. It sagged open almost to her waist. He tore the shift she wore underneath the dress, too, and pushed it aside so that Jessie felt the warm night air against her back. She heard a hissing sound, almost like a snake.

Tied to the pillar as she was, it was difficult for her to turn her head and look back over her shoulder, but she managed to do so. Katerina stood there, a long black whip in her hand. As the blonde moved her wrist, the whip coiled and writhed at her feet.

"You've interfered with my plans for the last time, Jessie," Katerina said. "When I'm finished with you, you'll be begging for mercy and you'll never dare cross me again."

Jessie looked over at the hard cases who had tied her to the pillar. "You're going to let her get away with this?" she demanded. "What sort of men are you?"

"The sort who knows who's payin' us," one of the men answered with a shrug. "We don't have to like what the Empress is doin'."

Katerina laughed. "No one is going to help you, if that's what you're hoping, Jessie. My men are loyal, and these others—" She waved her free hand contemptuously toward the railroad barons. "They're nothing more than worms. Quick to crush others when all it takes is the stroke of a pen, but craven cowards when they're faced with any real danger."

The men on whom Katerina was heaping her scorn looked ashamed, but none of them made a move to stop her. They kept their eyes downcast as Katerina stepped closer to Jessie and raised the whip.

"Now," she breathed, "now you'll see what a mistake it was to cross the Empress!"

Her arm flashed forward.

Chapter 38

"No!"

Jessie heard the familiar voice, and twisted her head around again in time to see Andre Dumond leap forward from behind Katerina. The Frenchman grabbed her wrist just before the whip could leap out and slash across Jessie's back.

Katerina gave an incoherent cry of rage and slapped Dumond with her other hand. "How dare you!" she screamed. "Let go of me!"

"This is not necessary," Dumond insisted. "Jessie Starbuck cannot harm you."

"I'll decide what's necessary. My word is law here!"

Dumond shook his head stubbornly. "I will not allow you to harm her."

"You'd throw away everything for that . . . that slut?" Katerina demanded.

"I'm just trying to make you see that there is no need for such brutality."

"I'll decide that, not you," Katerina snapped. "And you know the penalty for defying the Empress."

Dumond still had hold of her wrist, but her other hand

was free. It came up from the folds of her dress, and Jessie saw lantern light wink on cold steel as Katerina lifted a dagger and plunged it with blinding speed into Dumond's chest. The Frenchman gasped in shock and pain and staggered back a step, releasing Katerina's hand as she did so.

"Empress . . ." he said. "How . . . how could—"

Katerina screamed as she jerked the blade out of his body and drove it in again. And again and again as Dumond stumbled backward with her following him. She stabbed him half a dozen times or more; Jessie couldn't keep count of the blows. Dumond fell to his knees, the front of his shirt darkening as blood welled from the wounds. Katerina dropped the dagger, doubled the whip, and slashed it across Dumond's face. The impact drove him to the ground, where he managed to crawl a foot or so before he gasped again and then lay still.

Jessie felt horror coursing through her at the sheer madness she had just witnessed in Katerina.

She also felt something tug at the rope around her wrists. It suddenly had slack in it, and Jessie knew that even though it made no sense, someone on the other side of the pillar had just cut her bonds and freed her.

Breasts heaving from the emotions that gripped her, Katerina turned away from Dumond's body and back toward Jessie. "Now you'll get what's coming to you, you bitch!" she cried as she lifted the whip again.

Jessie felt her mysterious benefactor press something into her hand. She realized it was the handle of the knife that had just cut her bonds. She whirled, saying, "So will you!" and flung the knife at Katerina as hard as she could.

After that, hell pretty much broke loose.

Katerina moved with more speed than Jessie would have expected, leaping aside as the blade spun through the air toward her. She couldn't avoid the knife entirely. Its keen edge sliced across her upper arm and made her cry out in pain as she dropped the whip.

Jessie was right behind the knife. She tackled Katerina. Both women sprawled on the flagstone paving of the courtyard.

Shots blasted in the night, echoing back from the wings of the ranch house that surrounded the courtyard. Jessie had her hands full with Katerina, so she couldn't look around to see what was going on. She would have been willing to bet that Raider had something to do with it, though. He had gotten back sooner than she'd expected.

Not a moment too soon, though.

Jessie had landed on top of Katerina, and was trying to get her hands around the Empress's throat, but Katerina twisted and threw a punch that connected solidly with Jessie's jaw. The blow drove Jessie to the side. Katerina heaved her body up and twisted again, throwing Jessie completely off her. She clubbed her hands together, smashed them down on the back of Jessie's neck.

Jessie grunted in pain as Katerina's knee drove into her back, pinning her to the flagstones. Katerina grabbed her hair with one hand and jerked her head back. With her other hand, Katerina reached for something, and Jessie realized it was the knife Katerina had dropped a few moments earlier. As Katerina's hand closed around the knife's handle, Jessie knew she had only a split second before the Empress slashed her throat wide open.

Getting into Blanco Verde hadn't been much of a problem. But, getting out again, thought Longarm, might be a different story.

With the stealth of an Apache, Ki had gone out ahead of

the other five men and disposed of a few guards in utter silence. That got them into the ranch house. The sound of voices had drawn them to the courtyard in the center of the big house. As soon as they saw what was going on, Ki had used the thick shadows under the balcony to conceal himself as he made his way around the courtyard to cut Jessie loose from the pillar. Longarm, Raider, O'Malley, and the two troopers Stilwell had sent with them waited just inside the courtyard while Katerina von Blöde went loco and stabbed Andre Dumond.

It was good riddance to the Frenchman as far as Longarm was concerned. The fella's own greed in throwing in with the Empress had finally been the death of him.

Now, as Jessie's desperate struggle with Katerina played out on the flagstones next to one of the fountains, Longarm and his companions opened fire on the guards. The possibility of freeing the hostages and getting out quietly was gone, so now the rescue party had to strike as hard and fast as it could. Their revolvers roared, cutting down the Empress's gun-wolves. Ki flashed out of the shadows, fists and feet flying as he didn't even seem to touch the ground between blows. The guards who didn't fall to the guns of Longarm and the others crumpled under the crunching impact of Ki's kicks and punches.

Longarm holstered his gun and charged across the courtyard as he saw that the Empress had the upper hand on Jessie. Katerina knelt on Jessie's back, and she had gotten hold of that knife she'd used on Dumond. She was about to sweep it toward Jessie's neck when Longarm reached her, grabbed her from behind, and jerked her off of Jessie.

"Hold on, Empress," Longarm said. "It's over."

Katerina screamed and slashed at him instead. Longarm tried to hold her, but being loco gave her strength. She

wriggled out of his grip. He had to jump backward to keep
her from slicing his throat open as she hacked at him with
the knife.

Then she turned and ran.

Longarm could have drawn his gun and shot her in
the back, but he couldn't bring himself to do that. Instead,
he charged after her, first pausing for a moment to make
sure that Jessie was all right. She was just out of breath and
waved him on.

Katerina headed for the stairs that led up to the balcony.
Longarm followed her, his big strides allowing him to take
the stairs two and three at a time. Katerina wasn't very far
ahead of him when she reached the top. She threw a frightened glance over her shoulder and sprinted along the balcony, regaining a little of the lead she had lost on the stairs.

There was another staircase at the far end of this wing. If
she reached it and made it down the stairs before Longarm
could catch her, she might be able to slip away in the confusion. Longarm wasn't going to let that happen if he could
help it. If only he had managed to corral her back in Zamora, the first time he'd run into her, none of this would
have happened. The new Cartel probably would have collapsed without the Empress to lead it. He couldn't take a
chance on Katerina escaping to cause new and deadlier
mischief in the future.

If she reached the stairs before he could catch her, he
would shoot her, he decided. Like it or not, this had to end
here.

And it looked like she was going to make it, because
fear had given her wings. She was almost at the stairs. Longarm reached for his gun.

Katerina came to a sudden halt at the top of the stairs.
Raider's voice called out, "End of the line, Empress!"

Longarm drew his gun and closed in. He could see Raider coming up the stairs toward Katerina, Colt in hand. The ex-Pinkerton must have seen Longarm chasing her and moved to cut off her escape route.

"Nowhere to run, Empress," Longarm said. They had her trapped between them.

But then another figure suddenly appeared at the bottom of the stairs, behind Raider. Covered with blood from the half-dozen stab wounds, Andre Dumond wasn't dead after all. He had regained consciousness and somehow dragged himself to his feet. Now he shakily raised a gun.

"Look out, Rade!" Longarm called.

"For the Empress!" Dumond cried in a hoarse voice, demonstrating that he was still loyal to Katerina despite what she had done to him in her madness.

Raider tried to twist out of the way as Dumond fired, but he staggered and went down, obviously hit. Longarm leveled his Colt and triggered twice, sending a pair of bullets sizzling down the stairs past Katerina. The slugs punched into Dumond's already-ruined chest and drove him backward. He went down, and this time he wouldn't be getting back up.

Katerina turned and charged at Longarm, yelling out her insane hatred. Instinct made him pull the trigger again, but this time the hammer snapped on an empty chamber. The Colt was empty.

Katerina had taken him by surprise. His feet weren't set. Otherwise, she never would have been able to budge him. As it was, she rammed a shoulder into his chest and knocked him backward a couple of steps. Normally, he would have caught himself then, and everything would have been all right.

But the balcony was narrow here at the landing, and the

railing at its edge caught Longarm in the lower back. Still screaming, Katerina rammed him again. Longarm felt his weight shifting. His feet came up off the balcony.

Well, this was a hell of a note, he thought as he toppled over the railing and started to plummet toward the unforgiving flagstones below.

He dropped the empty gun, reached out, and grabbed the railing as he fell past it. His hands caught hold and stopped his fall, although pain shot through his arms and shoulders as his weight hit them. He looked up and didn't see Katerina, but then she appeared again, looming over him with a gun in her hand. Raider must have dropped it on the stairs when Dumond shot him. That was the only place Katerina could have gotten the weapon.

Longarm expected her to try to shoot him, but instead she slashed at his fingers with the gun barrel as he hung on to the railing. "Die, you bastard!" she shouted. "Die!"

The drop was only a few feet. As long as he didn't land on his head, the fall wasn't going to kill him. Katerina didn't appear to be thinking too straight at the moment, though. Longarm was about to let go and drop, but before he could, Jessie appeared behind Katerina, looping an arm around the Empress's neck and spinning her away from Longarm.

"Watch it, Jessie!" Longarm called. "She's got a gun!"

He started climbing back up onto the railing as Katerina fired. Jessie dived forward, under the bullet, and crashed into Katerina. Both of them toppled onto the stairs. A thud cut short Katerina's scream as they fell and kept falling toward the bottom of the staircase.

Jessie only went head over heels once before Raider pushed himself up on an elbow and lunged out with his other hand to grab her and stop her fall. Katerina kept going, crashing into the stone stairs with bone-crushing force again and again on her way to the bottom. When she finally stopped, she lay there in a limp sprawl.

Longarm hurried down to join Jessie and Raider. "You all right, Jessie?" he asked her.

She lifted a hand and pushed a thick wing of reddish gold hair out of her face. "I think so," she said. "Just some bumps and bruises."

"How about you, Raider? How bad are you hit?"

"Bad enough so that it hurts like the dickens where that slug plowed a furrow in my side," Raider answered, "but I reckon I'll live."

"Can't say the same about Katerina," Longarm said.

Jessie gasped and looked down the stairs at Katerina's body. The Empress's head was twisted at an impossible angle on her neck, and a worm of blood trickled from her mouth. Her blue eyes were open wide, staring sightlessly back up the stairs at Longarm, Jessie, and Raider.

"It's over," Jessie whispered.

"Not yet," Ki said from the top of the stairs, where he had just appeared. "Apparently, we're surrounded."

General Tennyson stepped up next to Katerina's body, saber in hand, and looked grimly up the stairs at them.

"General, listen to me," Jessie said. "There's an entire regiment of cavalry waiting nearby, and they have more cannons and Gatling guns than you do. Plus they don't have their wives and children with them. You know that if there's a full-scale battle, innocent people will be hurt. That's not why you came here. Enough innocents have died already, going all the way back to the war. Let it end. For God's sake, let it end."

Tennyson took a deep breath. "We still have the hostages," he said. "The army won't dare attack."

"Funny thing," Longarm said, "from what I know of Jeb Stuart and Nathan Forrest, they never struck me as the sort of fellas who'd take hostages. They'd fight you all day and all night long, but they wouldn't hide behind prisoners. And they sure wouldn't get women and kids mixed up in their battles."

Tennyson frowned. "You know about Stuart and Forrest?"

"Yes, sir, I do." Longarm pointed to Katerina. "And I know that one, too. She took advantage of you, General. She never cared about you and the folks with you. She just wanted the money. Then, she would have gone back on her word, killed the hostages anyway, and left you to face the army on your own. You don't need to dishonor yourself and your people by fightin' her battles for her, especially now that she's gone."

Tennyson appeared to be wavering. "How do I know you're telling the truth?" he asked.

"Listen," Ki said.

They all listened, and Longarm heard the sound of a bugle coming through the warm night air. The shooting at Blanco Verde had stopped now, but there had been enough of it to prompt General Stilwell to order an advance. That had been the arrangement he'd made with Longarm: He would hold off as long as he didn't hear any shots, giving Longarm and the others time to free the hostages and escape, but once the shooting started, he was coming in. That was the way it had worked out, and now the cavalry was charging toward the ranch, backed up by artillery and Gatling guns.

"Better call it off pretty quick, General," Longarm said, "or else it's gonna be too late. Then the killin' will start, and it won't stop until too many have died."

Tennyson took a deep breath. "You're right," he said. He lifted his saber and threw it down beside Katerina's body, the blade rattling against the flagstones. "God help us, you're right." Then he turned and stumbled away, holding his hands over his face for a second before he lowered them and began to shout, "Hold your fire! Hold your fire! No shooting! We're going to surrender!"

Ki came down a few steps to join Longarm, Jessie, and Raider. "How did you know the army was coming?" he asked Jessie.

"I didn't," she said with a smile. "It was a bluff. But as far as I was concerned, the cavalry had already arrived, in the form of you three."

"And O'Malley," Longarm added. "He did his share of the fightin'."

"Seamus? He's here, too? Thank God. Katerina told me that all of you were dead."

"Not hardly," Longarm said.

Jessie leaned her head against his shoulder. "I didn't want to believe it," she whispered. "Every fiber of my being told me that you were still alive, Custis."

Raider chuckled. "Ol' Longarm's hard to kill."

"So are you, you big, ugly hillbilly," said the lawman.

"At least I don't carry a badge and have to abide by all sorts o' rules and regulations and account for every bullet I fire."

"Yeah, well, at least I'm the real law and not some fella who just calls himself a *dee*-tective," said Longarm.

Jessie laughed. "You two can squabble to your heart's content later. Right now, we've got to see about calling off that attack, free those hostages, and get that bullet hole in Raider's side patched up."

She stood up and went down the stairs, holding up her

torn dress so that it didn't fall around her waist, while Long-arm and Ki helped Raider descend behind her.

At the bottom, they all stepped past Katerina von Blöde's body and didn't look back.

Epilogue

In the end, it was fairly simple. Longarm rode out to talk to General Stilwell, who had halted his advance when no shots came from the ranch headquarters. Longarm explained the situation. As dawn began to break over West Texas, the two commanding officers met in the courtyard. The bodies that had littered the place earlier had all been hauled off.

"Your surrender is an unconditional one, General Tennyson?" Stilwell asked.

Tennyson stood stiff and straight. "No, sir. I ask that my men be allowed to keep their arms and possessions, and that they be allowed to leave this place unharmed, without hindrance from your men."

Stilwell shot a quick glare at Longarm, who stood nearby with Jessie, Ki, Raider, and Seamus O'Malley. Longarm and Jessie had worked out the deal with Stilwell beforehand, pointing out that while Tennyson and his followers had known what Katerina was doing, at least to a certain extent, they hadn't committed any actual crimes themselves. Katerina's hired gunmen had carried out all the kidnapping and killing. Even the bombardment of the plantation could be overlooked, Longarm argued, because the Gilfeathers were dead before the artillery shells ever began to fall.

Stilwell didn't like it. He considered Tennyson's intended actions treasonous. But since the attempt to extort Blanco Verde from the United States never had quite come off, he had to admit that it was certainly simpler to just let the former Confederates go.

Their only real crime, Jessie had said, was in hanging on to a dream that had long since passed its time.

"Very well," Stilwell growled in response to Tennyson's conditions, "as long as I have your parole, General, and your word that never again will you or your men take up arms against the United States of America."

Tennyson nodded solemnly. "You have it, sir, freely given."

"All right then." Stilwell held out his hand. "You and your people go home, General. You're Americans now, plain and simple, with as much chance as anybody else to make good lives for yourselves."

Tennyson gripped Stilwell's hand. "I hope you're right about that, General. Only time will tell."

A short time later, as the wagon train began to roll eastward again, Stilwell stood with Longarm and the others in front of the big ranch house and said, "I'll escort the, uh, gentlemen who were meeting here back to San Antonio, and from there they can return to their homes, too." He grunted. "I have a suspicion that the official version of this story won't mention that they were ever here. They wanted their meeting to be a secret, and they have enough influence, even in Washington, to get what they want."

"I reckon you're right," Longarm said. "So long, General."

Stilwell shook hands all around, then went off to rejoin his men.

Jessie turned to O'Malley. "What will you do now, Seamus?"

"I got a ship waitin' for me back at Indianola," the Irishman replied. "It's seein' to makin' the *Harry Fulton* fit for the high seas again that I'll be doin'."

"Why don't you come back to the Circle Star with Ki and me for a while first?" Jessie suggested. "Then we'll go to Indianola with you and give you all the help we can."

"Why, that sounds mighty fine," O'Malley said.

Jessie turned to Raider. "What about you?"

"I'm at loose ends," he replied with a shrug. "The fella I was workin' for fired me."

"What?" Jessie exclaimed.

"Yep. Said I didn't do a good job of bein' his bodyguard."

"Then you can come with us, too. You know, the way times are changing so fast, I think it might be a good idea for the Starbuck holdings to have a range detective on retainer."

Raider shook his head. "You don't have to do that, ma'am."

"I'm not doing anything except trying to protect my interests," Jessie insisted. "This way, whenever trouble crops up, Ki and I won't always have to go handle it ourselves."

Ki spoke up, saying, "I think it is an excellent idea, Raider."

"Well, I'll consider it, I reckon."

They all turned to go back in the house for the time being, until they were ready to leave. All except Longarm, who lingered in front of the house to watch several expensive carriages roll off to join the forces under General Stilwell.

Jessie came back and stood by his side. "There they go," she said quietly. "The richest men in the country. Some of the richest men in the world. And not a damned one of them said thank you for saving their lives."

"Nope," Longarm agreed. "That don't surprise me none. Since they ain't in danger anymore, all they're thinking about is how their meeting got ruined. Now they're gonna have to get together all over again to hatch their plans."

"You think they will?"

Longarm nodded. "If what you told me about them is true, I know they will. They ain't the sort of hombres who give up when they want something bad enough."

He slipped his arm around Jessie's shoulders, and as they stood there, Longarm hoped he was wrong . . .

But he was pretty sure he hadn't heard the last of the Railroad Ring.